Mary Lide was born in Cornwall and educated at Oxford University, where she read history. Her earlier novel, *Ann of Cambray*, won the New Historical Writer Award.

Mary Lide divides her time between homes in Cornwall and the USA.

By the same author

Ann of Cambray
Gifts of the Queen
Hawks of Sedgemont
The Diary of Isobelle

MARY LIDE

Tregaran

This edition published 1993 by
Diamond Books
77-85 Fulham Palace Road
Hammersmith, London W6 8JB

Copyright © Mary Lide 1989

Set in Sabon
Printed and bound in Great Britain by
BPCC Paperbacks Ltd
Member of BPCC Ltd

For my mother and father

Acknowledgements

I should like to take this opportunity to thank my many friends, both in Cornwall and America, for their support and encouragement. My special thanks to my daughter, Vanessa, for her help with typing, and to James and my other children for their patient listening; to Major John Bowers for his military expertise; to my Cornish neighbours, Carmella and Peter Harris, for information about the clay industry, and to my cousins, Jeanne and Henry Hutchings.

I should also like to thank my editor, Patricia Parkin, whose advice and continuing kindness I value; likewise, my gratitude to my American agents and friends, Elise and Arnold Goodman. And to Dieter Klein, my English agent, my special appreciation.

Introduction

Sometimes I wonder what has happened to the Cornwall I knew as a child, with its quiet villages tucked into the curve of the cliffs and its unspoiled beaches, and its moors. They are all gone now, along with the fishermen and miners who once lived there and wrested a livelihood from this harsh peninsula at the end of western England. And the big houses with their green clipped lawns and rhododendron-lined drives, like my own home at Tregaran, the long-established 'Cornish gentry' families, they have disappeared as well, the houses abandoned or 'sold up', the rightful owners gone abroad – how short a time it took to destroy the land I knew, gentry and workers alike, blown away like dust.

But in the 1920s, when I was a girl, we were a solid sort of folk, disliking change, rural people, upon whom the quick-moving outside world had not made much impression. We knew what we liked: things in their place and a place for everything. We were not easily roused; believed in God – for the most part a Methodist one, as dour as the land we lived on – and knew our ways would last for ever. Yet change was all about us, a change with which some of us have never made our peace, filled with modern conveniences as ugly as they were practical. Summer visitors poured in on us, with their fast cars and motor boats and their fast thoughts. And when war came our men went off to fight in places they had never even heard of, although before they might never have gone more than fifteen miles from home.

I still remember Sundays when the parks were closed, when swings were locked with chains and the seesaws taken down so that children should not amuse themselves. I remember when the only Sunday books were Methodist tracts that Em brought from Chapel, or the family Bible with its gory pictures. I remember the horsehair sofa we sat upon in front of the kitchen grate; the black kettle simmering on the hob while Em sang to herself; the plates of yeast and saffron buns, the elderberry wine, the clotted cream. That was a time when we felt safe in our little backward land, when Tregaran seemed as large as the moon, before the great outside world discovered us and buried our past as if it were as far away as Babylon.

Chapter 1

The first time I met Phil Tregarn, I nearly broke his skull and mine. It was the summer of 1927 when I was ten. It was my birthday. And I was as angry as a swarm of bees. It had been first light when I had awoken but I had not jumped up as I always did. I remember how outside I could hear the doves moaning in the Tregaran woods, echoing, further off, the rush of waves upon the beach. I could almost smell the sun coming up over the slate roof and feel its heat. But Em had to bang on the door three times before I stirred.

It was because of my birthday. And the parties my grandmother had planned. All week preparations had been under way for them, turning the house into an uproar. I suppose Tregaran must have entertained before; once we had been famous for our hospitality, but not within my remembering. And, like any child, I had resented that my grandmother had made her entertainment conflict with mine. In the end, at Em's insistence, she had arranged two affairs, one for her, later in the evening, one for me, tucked in at noon, in a recess of the hall, a concession, a nuisance.

She herself would not even have remembered what day it was. 'You are too old for such childishness,' she would have said. But having once agreed to celebrate, she had made things much worse by turning this children's party into an extension of her own, issuing invitations in her name, choosing the guests, making it as little to do with me as the greater one. And I hated the thought of both.

So began the day. But when I had started to dress, walking on tiptoe over the bare floorboards to avoid splinters and washing in the cold water from the ewer (for

9

we had no bathrooms then in Tregaran House and only one inside wc), I had struggled defiantly into my best dress, hours too soon (although 'wriggled' would have been an apter term, having grown since it was last worn, and it fastened down the back with buttons that were impossible to reach). Then, wearing my best lace-up boots, I had clattered down the backstairs to the kitchen to confront this birthday I did not want.

I must introduce Em. She was our housekeeper, who had come to Tregaran with my grandmother, had looked after my father and his brother when they were boys, and now looked after me. But as well as being children's nurse, she was also cook and lady's maid, the general manager who ran the house whenever grandmother said she was too tired. Tall and lank like a coil of rope, Em's gaunt face and bony frame were more familiar to me than any relative's, and, for want of anyone else, she acted as father and mother to me. But even she had changed this past week.

That day she sat on the edge of her chair, braiding her hair and twisting it in two large buns, too preoccupied to notice anyone. The grey coils stood out like muffs over each ear but she had no time to let me admire them. 'Must get on with it,' was all she had said. 'No time to waste.' She even failed to notice my party dress.

The table in front of her was piled with panniers of fruit and vegetables, with baskets of crabs and shrimps. Pots and pans were already steaming on the open fire. I had never seen so much food before, and at any other time I would already have been wheedling her to let me have a taste. But I knew that day she had not been in the mood. She did not even wish me happy returns.

Her hair arranged to her liking, she had pushed me aside, beginning to mix and peel and chop as if her life depended on it, her lips moving continually as she worked, almost as if she were saying her prayers. I was used to her prayers, good Methodist ones, and she often talked to herself. But these mutterings were different, fretful, full of complaint. Not about the work, although that of itself might have daunted anyone, but about my grandmother's foolishness. And she never blamed my grandmother for anything!

''Tis a crime,' I heard her say, in her broad Cornish way, ''tis a sin. Nobody can eat so much, who can afford to? Money don't grow on trees. Whom be she trying to impress? If 'ee calls the tune 'ee pays the price, and that's God's truth. And leave them figs be, Miss Joycelyn, not enough as 'tis, to have 'ee fingering 'em.' And she had slapped my hand away.

Down the hall I could hear the gardener, Jim Pondhue, dragging the dining-room table away from the wall so he could fit in extra leaves, making place for thirty guests. Not my guests, my grandmother's, the parents of the children I had to entertain first. And while my grandmother slept upstairs, in the great four-poster bed where generations of Tregarans had been born, Em and the other village women would set the table in all its magnificence; rows of knives and forks and candlesticks, tipped like Aladdin's jewels across the glossy wood, all the Tregaran silver on show at once, as if it were part of some county fair. As if it, and we, were on display; as if it, and we, had a reputation to uphold. And that was the feeling I disliked most.

Outside the sun was full up and the mist had burnt away. I remember going through the hall door and leaning over the terrace that ran along the house, staring down the slope of grass towards the trees. Between them, in a dip of the hill, the sea showed dark against the paler sky, almost as if it had been pasted on, and the trees themselves were a haze of green, like gauze. It was an irony of fate, I think, that the first time I ever noticed how beautiful Tregaran was, or had the words to know what that beauty meant, was when I also became aware of its impoverishment. Everywhere I looked I suddenly noticed things split and worn: the paving stones; the wall I leaned upon, so tumbled down that between the crevices on the steps wisps of grass and small flowers had found root; the façade of the house behind my back, whose stains and cracks had been caused by a leaking roof. Suddenly I did not see the shutters, but the rusty bolts they hung by; not the white window frames, only the peeling strips of paint. I had no way then to express my thoughts; I simply hung over the terrace wall, pretending to kick out at the air, as if I had not a care in the world. And it was then that I first noticed the figure in the trees.

I would never have seen him had he not moved so that the light glinted off some metal object, a button perhaps, or a buckle. Or perhaps the barrel of a gun. I squinted into the sun trying to locate the flash of light. In front of me, lower down the slope, the trees straggled across the grass, framing what had been a formal lawn (although we used it now for cow pasture). To my left, the eastern side, were the Tregaran woods, long run wild; to the right, a copse of ancient beech trees edged a fence which bordered the property. The figure was perched in one of these beech trees.

It would have been an easy climb. On the outside of the fence a deep path led from the main road down to the headland, ending a mile or so further on, in the fishing village beyond. The path was public, although we almost thought of it as ours, and anyone could have got over the fence. But no one had the right to sit there, I thought, staring at us. And what was the man looking at, or for? Suddenly I felt all my hairs standing upright like a dog's when it is aroused, and a rage began to burn. I cannot now explain how, or even why, I felt the way I did, but something made me want to run and scream at him, as if I could vent on him all my pent-up anxiety. And so, ducking quickly out of sight, I began to scuttle sideways like a crab towards the western end of the terrace. A quick dash took me down the side steps, towards the fence where there was plenty of cover.

I cannot explain either why I felt I should move so secretly, or why I did not run indoors and shout for help. Nor was my progress as easy as it sounds. The fence was covered with bushes and brambles that snagged my clothes. Soon I was hot and tired and covered with mud from an open stream that wound in and out among the tree roots. Several times I almost turned back. But when I came suddenly upon the thick-trunked tree where the man was perched and saw him there, stretched out full length, upon a branch, I felt a rush of satisfaction, quite out of proportion to the achievement.

Most of the intruder was hidden by leaves, just one black trouser leg dangling down, with a black misshapen boot at the end. I remember sinking back on my haunches and looking up at it. True, it did not seem so threatening of itself, but by then I did not care.

'Who do you think you are?' I cried up at the man. 'You're trespassing on our land!' And without allowing him a chance to explain, I reached up on tiptoes and tugged at his heel.

The consequence was disastrous. The branch itself was not much above my head but the man was balanced on it precariously, using his hands to look through some old-fashioned brass telescope. He had obviously not heard my approach, and my shout took him by surprise. With a cry he overtipped, crashing to the ground in a shower of twigs, landing on his side with a thud and pinning me beneath. And he was not a man at all, despite his man's serge suit, and his man's too big boots, but a boy, not much older than I was, with long thin legs and long thin arms, and a shock of black hair from which the blood began to puddle alarmingly.

Pushing his weight off me took all my strength for he was tall and seemed all bones. I scrambled to my feet and stood staring at him, horrified. Even when I recovered presence of mind to shake him hard, he did not move, and for the first time it dawned on me that he might be dead. And if he were dead then it would be my fault. Leaving him, I ran back to the ditch to wet my handkerchief, with some idea I suppose of trying to stem that gush of blood. But when I rolled him over on his back, I stopped again, forgetting what I had meant to do. I might have been looking at myself in a looking-glass, a masculine version of myself that is, he had the same dark hair that grows out from a peak, and curls when it is wet; the same long sallow face with high cheek bones, the same shaped lips, tilted up at the ends, all characteristics that Em had often explained had come from some long-forgotten Spanish ancestor. Except in him the nose was almost aquiline, and the curved lips and pronounced chin (covered with what in time would be the makings of a beard) seemed more finely cut than any Spanish grandee. And the eyes, when at last he opened them, were not dark like mine, but were a startling blue, as blue as that strip of sea between the trees.

He pushed me away and tried to sit up, holding his hand to his head. His face had gone pale, almost translucent, and the skin was white and smooth where, beneath his torn jacket, the too-large shirt had come unfastened. I was surprised how clean he seemed compared with the dirty clothes he wore. He blinked rapidly several times as if trying to focus and probed with his muddy fingers across his forehead. I had no idea who he was. I was certain I had never seen him before, but when he spoke his voice was rough, like the villagers, the distinct Cornish accent that cannot be disguised. Yet under it, even then, ran that lovely assonance which takes away the harshness, and gives a lilt to the most offensive words. It was a boy's voice too, just breaking into a man's, and he was in a flaring rage. If the roughness showed first I had only myself to blame.

'Bloody fuck,' he said, belligerence in every line of him, 'don't say 'twere a shit of a girl that tipped me off.' Then, striving for sense, 'Give over then,' he grunted up at me, 'God damn, be 'ee for drowning me after breaking my neck?' And he glared at me, with all his white teeth, like a wolf baring its fangs, while I stood there foolishly, letting the water drip on him.

'And who be 'ee anyway?' he went on, trying to sleeve the blood away with a flapping cuff. 'All dressed up like a tinker's moll. What gives 'ee the right to murder innocent folk?' If he could have stood up he would have hit me. 'Christ, what gives 'ee the right to shake me loose, as if I be some kind of plum? Back off. Were 'ee not a girl I'd make 'ee to know the difference.'

Shaken and bruised myself, my ribs on fire where he had jarred them against the ground, I snapped back, using harsher words than I normally would.

'Don't speak like that. What gives you the right to be here in the first place, on my tree, on my land? Why are you spying on us?' And I glared as angrily at him.

My reply must have startled him. He took a moment or so to recover, still sleeving away the blood. He must have struck his head on some stone or root, for the cut was still oozing along the hair line. But he was lucky; I might have knocked his brains out. 'Well now,' he began, shifting himself so that he could lean back against the trunk. ' "Your tree", you say. 'Twere rooted fast on public land when I last looked. At least it were when I climbed up it from the path not more than an hour agone. And the path were public too. Unless your ladyship's just bought it.' He glinted his blue eyes at me dangerously. 'As fer spying, there's only one here of the two who came creeping up in secret, to do harm. And by God, 'tweren't me.'

I had never met anyone who spoke out as he did. I was not used to village children. Those I met casually on Tregaran land were there to work for us, and treated me with exaggerated respect (which, snob that I was, I had come to expect), smiling as they saluted, or bobbing their heads in agreement with everything I said, as if I were some kind of little god whom they were surprised could talk at all. It was the first time I think that I had ever had the chance to speak to someone of my own age, both of us saying exactly what we felt.

'You were looking for something, all the same,' I told him frostily. And when he did not reply, 'Something, that's for sure. Something perhaps that wasn't yours, something to steal?'

My logic pleased me. It had the opposite effect on him. His black eyebrows drew together; his lips curled haughtily, and a flush stained the sallow skin. 'No,' he said in a voice like a piece of ice. 'No.' And then, as if recovering himself, with a sketch of a sneer, 'Not steal. Poach.'

Again I was struck dumb. I had often heard my grandmother protest about the way the villagers made free with game in the woods (although she herself never made any attempt to prevent them, and in fact had ignored the woods for years). 'When my husband was alive we had the best shooting in the county,' she was fond of saying. 'Had your Uncle Nigel lived, it would still be kept up. After his death the villagers took advantage of us. No loyalty left, although once there was. Had Nigel lived to be the heir, they'd have paid attention to him.' Always Nigel, the elder son, never John, my father, the younger, who had died with him.

'Poaching is stealing,' I said at last, just as she might have done. 'It's worse. It's wanton killing of poor dumb animals who can't defend themselves.' And was chagrined to hear him laugh. The laughter changed him, softened the angles of his face and made him seem less harsh.

'There's some argument,' he mocked. 'Isn't hunting "poor dumb beasts" your favourite sport? Fox-hunting be wanton killing, Miss Prim. Did you ever try to eat a fox? Whereas poaching bain't a crime, not by my reckoning, if you be starving otherwise. Then 'tis sustenance. Manna from Heaven, as the Good Book tells.' He held out his grimy fingers and shook the cuffs of his shirt at me, in a parody of religious zeal. 'And don't the Good Book say 'tis God's will to gather it.' He laughed again, at my expression perhaps. What he had said came close to blasphemy. 'There be a herd of deer in yon woods,' he went on, as coolly as before. 'You bain't be after eating all of them, and there'd be plenty left, even if I helped myself. If I could've got close to look at them some other way I'd not have needed to climb up in "your" tree. But you put the fence up to keep us out.' Again that dangerous flash. 'And the deer be there all the same, lazy and fat, just like their owners, waiting to be "gathered up", if anyone has the gumption to try. As I might.'

I must have gaped at him. There he propped himself against the tree trunk (whose roots indeed were growing on the outside of the fence), as nonchalant as if he were leaning against a mantelpiece indoors, like a welcome guest. I drew myself as upright as I could, and went up to him, anger welling in me like a tide, anger and some other thing that I could not name, except perhaps now I might call it a sense of justice, that what he said was right, although it irked me to have to admit it.

Beside him I came barely to his chin and he stared down at me even more haughtily than before as if defying me to argue with him. I made myself outface those dark blue eyes. 'If there are deer,' I told him without flinching, 'then they belong to my grandmother, or to me. So whether you take one or all, you are stealing what is mine. But if you are hungry,' for he certainly looked thin, 'you could

17

always ask for food. Em would give you something to eat if you went to the kitchen.'

'Hat in hand?' The scorn ran hot. ' "Thank'ee mam," and "Yes mam, no mam," like some Goddamn gypsy thief. That bain't my way. Nor anyone else's that I know of. We may be poor, we bain't beggars.' He frowned then as another thought struck him. 'Grandmother,' he repeated. 'Be that Ma Tregaran perhaps? Not much chance of getting naught from she, not even if we was to lick her boots. She wants what's hers and more besides. Just as you do. Alms to the deserving poor but they'd better be deserving.' He was imitating me now, making a mock of the way I spoke. 'When I Goddamn want something from your house I'll come in the front door like anyone else.' He cocked his head at me. 'But if she be your grandma then you must be the Little Miss Stuck-Up from the Big House, the Miss High Shithead that they talk about. Fancy that. Fancy Miss Stuck-Up speaking to the likes of me.' And he gave another grin in which there was nothing of mirth at all, and certainly nothing of liking.

For the last time I was struck speechless. Not so much by what he said (although afterwards it was to cut deep) but by the bitterness and hurt that ran underneath. I held my ground. There are moments in one's life, I suppose, when one reaches a turning point; whatever one does or says afterwards, a lifetime may depend on it. Such a time was that day when I was ten. Perhaps I was older than my years; perhaps loneliness had already given me extra insight, although never the chance before to show it. I could have turned and marched away in high dudgeon, as part of me wanted to, and there would have been an end, and my life would have taken another route. Instead I heard myself say, in a tone that surprised myself, almost conciliatory, 'I never meant to make you fall. It was your telescope I saw.'

His expression changed. 'Christ!' he cried, pushing

himself away from the tree. 'That bloody eyeglass. He'll have my hide if 'un's lost. Where did 'un go to then?' He tried to kneel to push the underbrush aside, although the effort made him rock with dizziness. The sudden anxiety in his voice overrode my dignity. I dropped on all fours and while he held the brambles out of my way, crawled into the thicket. It was dusty under the bushes, and the litter of last year's leaves made me sneeze, but eventually the same gleam of brass that I had seen from the terrace caught my eye and I wrested the telescope out from where he had let it fall. He seized it and ran his fingers over it experimentally, as if afraid it might be broken. And when he found it was still intact, he gave such a sigh of relief that I almost joined in out of sympathy.

'There's luck,' he said. 'My Uncle Zack do set a store by 'un, and that's the truth. I'd not like him to know I took it like, without his say-so.' He thrust it into his pocket before turning his attention to me. 'That was kindly done, Miss Joycelyn Tregaran,' he said almost formally, 'especially since you've got your best duds on.'

And it was not until then that I remembered my party dress.

I looked down at myself in dismay, trying to peer over my shoulder at the hem. I heard myself say, almost in his own tone of voice, with the same anxiety, 'My grandmother'll kill me if it's torn. Is it, is it? Oh please God, don't let it be! It's the only one I have.' And that was the second time I ever let another person know what I truly thought.

He folded his arms over his chest and stood looking at me, as if trying to make up his mind. Then, delving into the other pocket he brought out a handful of rusty pins. 'Turn round,' he said in a deliberately flat voice, 'let's have a look.' And as I obediently spun on my heel, 'Well now,' he said, and there was a ripple, was it of laughter? almost immediately gone, 'nothing that a few of these won't take

19

care of, if 'ee stands still that is. Although I uses them more for fishing than clothes.'

I felt him busy along the frills, bending and jabbing in and out, with a deftness that surprised me. Finally, unfastening the row of buttons, he thrust his hand down my back. It was large and cool against my skin, and I could feel the calluses upon the palm as he cobbled up the material around the waist. 'There,' he said, standing back, as if satisfied. 'Good as new, if you don't lift your arm. You'm split along the side, big enough to put a head through. Just keep your wrists turned in like this.' He tried to show me how, standing stiffly in that man's suit which hung about his lanky frame in folds. I had the impression he knew exactly how I felt, and had felt the same way himself many times. 'And don't turn round if 'ee can avoid it,' he went on, 'them pins do poke out a bit. What possessed 'ee to come out in such a rig?'

And when I told him, birthday party, grandmother's dinner, all the day's plans coming out in a rush, 'I'll be damned,' he said, his eyes suddenly shrewd. 'They said there'd be high jinks up here today; all the village's yakking about it. Your birthday, hey? 'Twas your grandma's party they was gossiping on. They say ...' He hesitated and bit his lip, as if remembering something, as if stopping himself. 'They say a birthday's special,' he recovered himself, almost as if the pause had been unintentional, 'tho to tell truth I've not set much store by mine. Won't there be guests, and candles on a cake? And gifts, and all that sort of foolery?'

The off-hand manner did not deceive me a bit. 'No,' I said. 'Grandmother doesn't believe in gifts. And as for guests, well, these are children of her friends. She chose them, not me. I won't know one of them.'

I turned to him, suddenly bursting with the wish to confide in him. 'And Em says we can't afford to entertain anyone. So why should there be two parties on the same

20

day? I'd rather not have one at all unless I could pick whom I invite. And if you'd come I'd ask you first.' And that was the third time I said exactly what was in my heart.

He continued to look at me with those strange sea-blue eyes that made me feel as if he was looking out into a vast distance. 'To my mind,' he said slowly, 'if a birthday stands for having gifts, 'tis meanness not to give one. So here's mine. Never give in to no one, fight back; the world's for the taking for everyone.' And when again I stared at him, for his words made no sense, he suddenly laughed, a genuine laugh and tugged at his pocket and brought out the telescope. 'Give us your foot then,' he said. 'I'll hoist 'ee up in that there branch and show you what I were looking at.'

He bent down and made a stirrup with his hands, just like a groom. Almost scared I stretched out my leg, and he shoved me up over his head until I was straddling the same branch, with his precious telescope in my hand. 'Look through the end,' he ordered me. 'To the left. More, more. See that clump of oaks, close to the cliff. See that dead one in the midst.'

Earth, sea and sky swung in great arcs as I tried to steady the glass against my eye and he held my ankles with one hand, giving instructions in the same steady voice. I found the tree, white and stark against the horizon's blue, but not the deer he had spoken of. Instead there was a big untidy mass of twigs, set like a platform on the dead tree top, with a great hawked bird poised over it, whose eyes, even from a distance, seemed fixed on me. 'There,' he said, pleased. ''Tain't every day you see an osprey on her nest. Mum's the word now, so they don't try to take the eggs. Not that she'd let 'em, she's that fierce.' He took the telescope back and held out his arms. I slid down from the branch, my skirts riding up so that his hands were clasped around my bare legs, and on some impulse he lifted me

21

high in the air. His arms were like stalks I thought, yet tough. I felt his strength, beneath the skin, like something he was growing into. My face was just above his own so that I was looking down on to that unruly mop of hair, with its matted streaks of blood. On the same impulse he spun round and round, although the effort made him pant, twisting himself like a top and smiling up at me until I felt giddy myself, but with happiness. Then, as abruptly, he dropped me to the ground and took a deep breath. 'Birthday greetings, then, Miss Tregaran,' he said, 'a long life and a prosperous one. And may your wishes come true.' He had assumed a different voice, affected, stiff, imitating what he would have called 'gentry talk'. His grin told me that he knew exactly what he sounded like, a copy of the vicar, down to the stutter on the consonants; and that, with the rough accent gone, he resembled everyone else I had ever associated with – 'my class of folk', as he would have called them – polite, well bred, and dull. People with cold, flat eyes and cold, flat smiles, complacent people, who never had an original thought in their lives. Of course, these ideas came to me later. Then, I only remember that lovely lilt, which gave the lie to his parody, as if, even in pretence, he could never lose completely what he was.

He looked at me again and stopped laughing, cocking his head to one side. 'There,' he said, 'you'm quite different with a smile, almost alive. Perhaps there's still hope for you. And there be the church clock,' although I had not heard it. 'I'd best be moving on.'

He shook his head vigorously one last time as if to clear it, thrust the telescope away and crossed to the fence with the long, quick stride that I was to associate with him. As he climbed over, his shirt tails still flapping, I thought of all the questions I meant to ask. 'Who are you?' I cried. 'Who's Uncle Zack? Why do we look alike? And where were the deer?'

From the sunken path below, which hid him as deep as in a well, I heard him laughing to himself, and presently there came the sound of rusty wheels. Peering over the edge, I saw him wheeling an old bicycle between the ruts, in the direction of the headland. Before he disappeared out of sight he turned round once and shouted something to me in his original mocking voice. I did not understand at first until he repeated it, something about deer never showing themselves at midday, and besides he never ate meat. Then he was gone round the curve and even the squeaking of the wheels was lost. And that was how my birthday began. But not how it ended.

Chapter 2

I could hear the clock's booming myself now, coming in gusts across the tree tops. I had no idea it was so late, and in a panic I began to run, my shoes so plastered with mud that clods dropped off at each step. I was still trying to keep the pins in place when I came up to the terrace. And there, waiting for me, with Em, were the first of my unknown guests.

I stood in front of them and saw them staring down at me, a row of them, their fine lace and silk clothes immaculate, their white shoes and white socks in line, their white-gloved hands folded neatly over each arm. It would have been impossible to picture these little ladies torn or soiled, and they observed me just as their mothers might, as if I were something not 'quite nice'. Beside the main steps leading to the drive their servants, who had accompanied them, stood in a cluster of grooms, chauffeurs, maids, pretending not to be shocked. I heard a stifled laugh. I thought, suddenly fierce myself, I can never compete with them; I shall never be like these girls, who have come together, driving up in their motor cars or brought by family retainers in pony chaises. How they cling to each other for dear life, no doubt as reluctant to be guests as I to be hostess. Even when Em has stuffed me into another dress, and pronounced me clean, they will expect me to trail behind, as demure and mouselike as themselves. And, defiantly now, I thought: but I shan't.

Em was equally horrified. She was dressed in her grey sateen and had rebraided her hair for the occasion, all signs of its importance for her. It hadn't occurred to me how she would enjoy showing off, despite her previous misgivings, and my dishevelled appearance must have seemed a reflection upon herself, for she bustled forward, wringing her hands. Ignoring the other servants, as if she instinctively sensed they would enjoy her discomfiture, and abandoning her air of superiority, she dragged me inside and slammed the door.

'Just look at 'ee,' she hissed, shaking me hard. She felt about herself for something to wipe my face, using the edge of her lace handkerchief. 'What've 'ee been up to?' There was genuine concern under the scolding, and her voice had lost its false gentility. 'And after all your grandmother's done.'

She gestured with the handkerchief to the row of wooden chairs set around the small table in the corner of the hall, to which my modest party had been relegated. 'And not even the sense 'ee were born with. I've been that worrit.'

When I was silent, 'And what's this?' she cried, bending down to tug at the hem of my dress. 'How come you'm trussed like some basting fowl? You'm that careless, child, better off without clothes at all, nakit like a heathen.'

'Birthday parties are for fun,' I told her, jerking my dress away. 'Grandmother wants those girls here, not me. She wants this party to please herself. I'm just the excuse. She'd be just as happy if I never came back.'

Em put her hands over her mouth, her habit when someone said something she did not like, or swore in her presence, mainly I suppose because her ears were already covered. Now I had known her all my life; she had cared for me since babyhood; there were not many things we had not shared. This was different. Perhaps my voice put her on guard, a new voice, too shrewd for my years, for she suddenly reverted to her usual mildness, trying to regain my confidence, all the while struggling to repin my dress so that the tears were less obvious.

'Where've 'ee been to?' she began, hoping to trick me

into confession. And when, as cunning myself, I smiled and shook my head, for once not willing to tell her the truth, 'You've been with them village brats,' she accused, holding up a pin. 'Someone put this in. How many times have 'ee been warned to keep away from them, thieving rascals the lot, down to the last Zack.'

Her triumph at her shrewd guess made her more like the Em I knew. I wound my arms about her waist, still smiling to myself. Her way of pronouncing 'Jack' as the Cornish do, 'Zack', had given me my excuse. 'In the village,' I said, imitating her, 'there be Zacks a'plenty. Which Uncle Zack do 'ee mean?' squeezing her tight in an effort to make her laugh. 'What be his family name?'

She grew rigid beneath my clasp, as if her bones had frozen. Her expression changed, became hard as the boy's had been. 'What Zack be 'ee speaking of? We knows no Zacks.' Her eyes narrowed, the frown lines deepened. 'Unless . . .' She forced my hands loose. 'You never mean Zack Tregarn!' she said. Then, almost to herself, 'He wouldn't! Brazen that he is, even he'd not dare stick his snout in here. Not today, of all days.'

'Why not?' I said, brazen myself. 'Tregarn, that's an odd name, it sounds like ours.'

'Half of it,' she interrupted, almost absently. 'Half of it,' as if a name could be broken off like a piece of stone. Then – as if, having begun, she was obliged to go on – 'Once, they say, 'twas the same, part of the same family, until the quarrel. How do I know what the quarrel was about? It happened all so long ago. There've been Tregarns as long as you, and as proud of their name, and the pigsty where they live, as you Tregarans are. But Zack Tregarn'd never dare come here!'

And when I still continued to smile, pleased with myself at having conned her into saying so much, so that no doubt my expression gave me away, 'Not that nephew of

26

his,' she cried, and wrung her hands, 'not that young devil, Phil.'

And that was how I learned who he was.

'What's wrong with him?' I said, more cunning than I had ever been in my life. 'I don't say 'twas him you understand. But what if it were?'

'You'm just a girt silly child,' she said. She drew a breath. 'What do 'ee know! He'm trouble, written large, ever since he were born. Wild, like an unbridled horse no one can tame. And after he was orphaned, and went to live with those uncles of his, what devilments he weren't born with he learned off they. Not that he cares much for them. Why, when time came to go to work, as a boy ought, would he help them on their boat? Not Phil Tregarn, as if he were some gentleman, even tho' Zack Tregarn thrashed him into leaving school. And them with the right to expect some return seeing that they've no sons of their own, and been a fishing family all their lives. Up on the moors as fast as he could trot, down in the clay pits, stubborn as a mule. There's no liking 'twixt sea and clay neither, as well he knows, nothing but trouble there, mark my words. And all for pride, all for spite, too big for his boots, I says, as if the world were made for he.'

I had seldom heard her speak so long or passionately. And yet, despite her disapproval, there was an unusual emphasis to her voice, that made me think she knew more than she let on. She's lying too, I thought, or rather, like me, not telling the whole truth. I put that thought aside for a future time, and concentrated on two things she had let slip. He was an orphan then. And as unhappy as I was. *He'll have my hide.* I suddenly saw his ill-fitting suit, his proud, unbearded face, too young to be more than a schoolboy's; I remembered his proud, angry speech. And yes, even then, when I had felt the roughness of his hands, I sensed the gentleness underneath. She knows about him perhaps, I thought, but she doesn't know *him* at all. I do. I shall.

Em had pulled out one of the chairs and had sunk down, as if dazed. She kept running her hands across her face as if the room had become too warm. Then another thought struck her. 'Lord love us,' she cried, starting up again, 'if your grandma knew 'twould be her death. And mine. She'd not forgive me for letting you give me the slip. Promise me you'll never see he again, not even to nod to, and promise me you'll not tell her, to break her heart. There's nothing but grief 'twixt his family and yourn, so she'd take it hard that he came to mock at her. Especially at a time like this.'

I remember starting to argue but Em beat her breast as if she were out of breath. 'There,' she wheezed. 'You've made me tell what I swore to keep to myself. But why else would any Tregarn come here today, except to gloat? Why do 'ee think your grandma's made such a show, except to put a bold face on, so that the likes of they wouldn't know how much it hurt? Why child, tomorrow 'twill all be gone, furniture, silver, portraits, the lot, all sold up, only this table left perhaps, and chairs to sit on. And the house itself, if she can afford it. Tregaran be entertaining for the last time. That's why today is important.'

And that was my birthday surprise.

Had I known before that this was truly the last time the house would be open to company, the last time that the family treasures would be put on display before being auctioned to pay our debts, would I have felt differently? Would I have pitied my grandmother's pride for putting her own self on show, in her own way defying the pity of the world? I was too young then to understand all these subtleties. I just kept quiet while Em finished tidying me. The truth was all this talk had overwhelmed me. So I ignored it, concentrating on my own adventure, hugging it to myself as an even greater secret.

She gave my dress one last jerk, more stern than I had ever seen her. 'I've told 'ee often enough to keep away from them village boys,' she said. 'There bain't one to trust no matter what they say. I know. I used to live with 'em.'

She took another look at me and pinched me hard. 'And behave. I know your ways,' she said. 'You'm as stubborn as your father was. But you'm as much a lady as your grandma.' Her face was set in its familiar dour lines. 'God put 'ee on this earth for a purpose,' she told me, grimly Methodist, 'and 'ee can't turn back from the place God set 'ee in. And,' more practical, 'just think how them other young ladies will laugh at 'ee, if 'ee lets us down. Do 'ee want them to believe we all be done for? We bain't paupers yet I say, not till your grandma's finished, and she be sound for many years. So mind your manners and keep them amused, so they'll have no more cause for gossiping.'

But when I came again on to the terrace it was too late. Grandmother Tregaran had already taken my place and was amusing them in my stead. And I became the thing she used to make them laugh.

My grandmother's maiden name had been Evelyn Carmichael. The Carmichaels too had been a well-known Cornish family, but the Tregarans were higher up the social scale, and for many years she had embodied the spirit of Tregaran House, especially after her husband's death and the death of her two sons in the Great War. I did not realize then how wilful she had been when she was young, nor how beautiful. She had long ago removed all pictures of her early self, and had ordered Em never to speak about her younger years. But to me, as a child, she was formidable.

She was dressed in black that day, in long thin material that was so draped it hid her ever-increasing bulk. Rows of necklaces hung about her neck, jingling when she moved, enhancing my usual impression of her as some

29

large shadow that blocked the light, bedecked with a glittering cascade of pearls and stones that trapped the sun. In those days she always seemed much taller than I was, although in fact she was quite short, and I have a distinct memory of her small feet since I kept my eyes fixed on them. They were encased in patent leather shoes that had to be made especially for her and had been fashionable in her youth, and they were planted now at the top of the stairs, firmly in charge. Afterward, when I was grown up myself, people used to marvel how she had been the best dancer in the west country, the coolest rider, the steadiest shot, the most elegant hostess. Always the best of everything. I do not know when I had first sensed her disappointment in me, but I was always conscious of it, unspoken before perhaps, but at times almost tangible, making me more awkward and tongue-tied than I was. Today she made no attempt to hide what she felt.

'So here you are at last,' she said, 'all cleaned up, like something that the cat's brought in.' Her voice was clear and cold, so cold that I might have been that unfortunate object, not worth her contempt. It made the other girls titter nervously, and look at each other uncertainly as she turned back to them, her dark eyes flashing. She had outlined them with black so that they stood out even larger than they were from the folds of flesh about her nose and cheeks. I thought she looked like some kind of witch and her jet black hair, that I suppose she must have dyed, was coiled in a great loop down her back, with not a hair out of place. She moved gracefully despite her girth, and smiled as if she were a queen. All her charm now was in her voice, that charm she could exercise whenever she chose, causing tradesmen to extend credit, and bankers money, and men, perhaps, admiration and love. But never shown to me, her granddaughter and adopted heiress, her only living kin.

'While we wait for the other children to arrive,' she

said, as if these little girls were belles of the ball, of more importance to her than their parents (and perhaps they were, she could manipulate them; she could make them feel and see what she wanted them to), 'shall I show you Tregaran House?' And when they hesitated, 'With all its treasures,' she smiled again, 'and without its ghosts. Unless we count an apparition held together with safety pins.' And when they giggled as she had meant them to, she threw back her head and laughed, a laugh that suited the tinkling of her beads and the tossing of her black hair. And struck ice into my heart.

So that was how, after all, I came to trail behind my guests, as they in turn trailed behind my grandmother. She led us through the house, opening doors that had long been locked, throwing wide the shutters and letting in the light, permitting herself the indulgence of admiring the beauties of each room, as if all was new to her, as if there were not more pain than pleasure in doing so, as if it were not for the last time. She dwelt upon each artifact as if giving a history lesson; sometimes she even picked a piece up and caressed it with her long thin hands as if it had a life of its own. I saw only the embarrassment that her behaviour caused, as the children began to squirm, scuffing their shoes across the wooden floors. Who wants a history lesson out of school? I became aware only of the things that I had never noticed before: the faded wallpaper where some picture had hung, the empty shelves in the drawing room, the empty places on the library shelves. I could think only of those rows of crested silver that someone else would use. I could sense only the malice behind those pitying smiles.

'So there, my dears,' said Mrs Evelyn Tregaran, releasing us, letting us drop like spoons on to a plate she had no more use for. 'Now you will remember Tregaran House on a day when it wore its best. Not all old houses look so beautiful all dressed up. For nearly five hundred years we have done our part to keep Cornish hospitality alive. The rest is up to you.'

She was addressing the others I suppose, at least she looked at them, the same bright smile upon her painted lips. The warning of the last sentence was implicit there for me. I took it up like a challenge, revealing perhaps, for the first time in all my life, what my own courage was. Not the same as hers, perhaps, yet courage of its own kind. But I rush ahead. The rest of that day must still be told.

Imagine us now, gathered around that birthday table, a bevy of bright little girls, most of whom were dressed in the height of fashion, without a care, too full of their own importance to notice the great external world. Poverty and decay and death were far from their thoughts that day, yet they lurked in the background. But there was one thing that I could not put aside, those scornful titters, those pitying looks. I felt them with a resentment that I had never had before, and that I knew had to be appeased.

Perhaps even then the day would have ended as quietly as it had begun if one of the girls had not started to complain. She waited until we were left on our own, pretending to behave as long as Em hovered over us, although some of the remarks whispered sotto voce were loud enough to make the others collapse with mirth. As soon as Em had withdrawn to preside over the kitchen tea (a task more suiting her dignity), the teasing began. I wonder now that Em left us when she did. The excuse I suppose was her own pride. It would be the last time for her too; the last time to play her part and revel in her superiority. Pride goeth before a fall, as for us so for her.

The girl I have mentioned was tall and strong, slightly older than the rest of us, and self-assured, daughter of one of the other county families, and proud of her social status. Fresh home from a year at boarding school she was the natural leader of the group, and although I had claimed to know no one, I had met her before, and had been in awe of her. Now I began to hate her. I hated her clothes, new and expensive; I hated her looks, petulant and spoiled; I despised the way she talked exclusively to the other girls about people and places I did not know. I thought her manners rude and offensive, and resented her whispering. But most of all I hated the way she ignored me, as if I were not there at all.

First she threw her serviette aside and made a face. 'I've not eaten stuff like this since nursery days,' she said, pointing to the cakes and trifles that Em had prepared. 'After all that boasting, I'd have expected caviar on plates of gold.'

I did not know what caviar was but I did recognize scorn. 'We have gold plates,' I said, rashly jumping into falsehood, 'but only to use on important days.'

'And this isn't one?' She tipped her chair back and shook her head with its carefully arranged curls. 'Oh,' she smirked, 'I beg your pardon then, I thought it was. I thought that was why we were all here, to prop you up one last time before the fall. Aren't you bankrupt, like they say? I heard you're selling all your things to help defray the costs. I doubt if even this is paid for.' She made another scornful gesture, wrinkling her nose to make the others laugh.

I see her now, old enough to listen to adult talk and capable of turning it to her own ends, her eyes sharp and knowing like a cat's, pale green and chill. I see her pause for effect just as my grandmother did, and preen herself at the expected applause. I pushed my own chair back with a scrape. 'God damn,' I said, pausing for effect. 'If it's bloody treasure you bloody want, come with me. I know where the bloody best things are.'

Bold as brass myself, I led the way out on to the terrace into the bright sun, half expecting that no one would follow me. But they did.

Something about my voice may have surprised them, something that told them I was more than the nonentity that they had been laughing at. Or perhaps they wanted me to make a fool of myself. And perhaps too, I was hard on them. I was to live most of my life in company like theirs, and they were not all as insensitive as they seemed. But I was too angry then to think of that. My courage was up, my pride ran hot, nothing could have made me stop.

The terrace was deserted. All the servants, theirs I mean, had gone into the kitchen for their own meal, with Em lording it over them. There was no one about to see where we went. I have said that the terrace stretched the length of the house, added in the eighteenth century when some ancestor had remodelled the earlier building. Underneath the terrace was a flight of older steps, green with age, leading to the even older cellars.

The entrance was dark and festooned with cobwebs, and I heard the girls behind me gasp and fuss as the strands caught in their hair. 'If you bloody well want a thing,' I said in my most haughty fashion, embellishing Em's homilies with my new-learned vocabulary, 'there's always a price. Treasure doesn't come easily. Are you scared?'

I suspect it was my way of speech (for even without Phil Tregarn's additions I had a quaint turn of phrase) that put them on their mettle, not my moralizing. One by one they crowded after me, the oldest one close behind, all eager to see what I was supposed to be showing them. What did they really expect; hidden gold perhaps, or perhaps more prosaically, the chance to make fun of me? And what did I intend them to see?

Inside the door the blackness was all the more dense in contrast with the bright sunlight outside, but I knew where a stub of candle was left on a shelf. After I had lit it with the matches kept there, I moved forward, holding the candle steadily, with a confidence I was far from feeling.

The flame threw a little pool of light across a musty-smelling vastness. Casks and barrels loomed out of the edges of the darkness; a line of bottles marked the remnants of my grandfather's wine; odd heaps and piles of wood and debris flickered into our line of vision and sank down again, like crouching beasts. The cellars were enormous. Even I did not know their full extent, and although I had occasionally been allowed to accompany Em, I certainly had never been there on my own. Normally I would have been terrified. Now, as we wandered on, the others clinging together in a line, myself in the lead, 'If you are looking for ghosts,' I said importantly, in my grandmother's voice, 'this is the place for them. Did you know this was once a Norman fort? The first Tregarans used its stones to build a new house in King George's time, and kept this part as dungeons for their enemies.'

I let my voice drop dramatically. 'They chained them up here, side by side with the treasure they tried to steal.'

My guests were frightened too. I heard one stifle a sob, while the others grasped their neighbours' hands, shivering with anticipation of worse to come. Their absorption encouraged me.

I let my voice drop low again. 'There is a curse,' I whispered. 'Whoever mocks the Tregaran name is doomed, and left to starve here without a grave. To make it worse, it's said that the smells from the kitchen, just overhead, drive them mad before they die.' A long pause while my audience hugged itself in delicious fright. 'Those shitheads wouldn't have turned their noses up at birthday cake,' I added ingeniously. 'They'd have been glad to eat anything. Rats or mice or cats would've been delicacies for them, down here, alone in the dark.'

By this time I was enjoying myself hugely, with a captive audience and imagination running wild. I had opened my mouth to elaborate when a current of air from some unknown source flowed towards us, making the candle flame gutter alarmingly. Then its light went out, and we were left there in the dark ourselves.

It was of course no use to scream, as the others did, for the walls were too thick to let sound out, and even if the kitchen were overhead (which I doubt) no one could have heard us anyhow. Nor did I remember the way to the door, having little idea of direction and no recollection of how far we had come nor how far we had yet to go, nor what would be there at the end if we reached it. I did have sense enough to know that as long as we kept together and stayed where we were we could come to no harm, but my companions had had enough of listening to me. Some tried to run away and blundered into things; others, too scared to move, simply collapsed on the floor in a heap and moaned. The girl who had teased me reverted suddenly to childhood, clawing at my clothes, and crying with all her might that she was not an enemy to be left to die.

The noise she made was deafening and it took all my strength to shake her off. 'I told you so,' I said calmly, above her screams. 'I warned you there was a curse. And you've brought it on yourself.' With a sob she shrank away, dragging the others with her; I set about finding my own way out, alone. And when I found the door and opened it, I slammed it firmly shut and locked it behind me as I left.

Whether I meant from the start to lure them in and leave them; whether I simply used what happened without forethought, is idle conjecture at this point, especially since I myself did find the way out, and I did leave them behind. Sufficient to say that when we were missed, I had long escaped, and had made no attempt to tell anyone. And sufficient too, to add that the rest of the day was spent in search.

How anxious servants scoured the grounds, how frantic messages went back and forth (for Tregaran had no telephone), how parents who had been expecting to come to dine, arrived post haste to hunt for missing children, are things better left unsaid. The dinner congealed or burned while Em joined in; local workmen clumped up and down the cliffs, and warned each other about the tides; police, finally summoned, arrived importantly to take notes, moving uneasily among the wreck of the festivities. The long summer twilight was almost done, the trapped 'prisoners', worn out by tears, had fallen asleep, before someone thought of opening the cellar door.

So that was how Tregaran entertained on a grand scale, for the last time. And what I did to contribute.

And where was I? Amid the confusion of rescue, while mothers and daughters screamed and wept and fathers snarled and workmen drank the whisky supplied for their betters, where had I gone? They found me last, where I had hidden myself up in the vaulted corridor which joins the newer with the older part of the house. We still call it the Great Gallery although its portraits have long been gone. By then it was late at night, later than I had ever been up, and through the high windows the sky was as dark as the cellars had been, but lit with myriad stars, like silver dust. The sounds of departure were over, the back-firing of cars, the slamming of doors, the stamping of ponies, the splutter of policemen's motorbikes, men's deep voices. My grandmother had said her farewells to those who had been persuaded to linger on for one last drink, she dressed in her evening clothes, they in their everyday ones, no one in the mood to enjoy all that planned magnificence, no one left to eat that feast.

Nor was I really in hiding. I had merely gone there to try to understand what it was my grandmother had really wanted to show us. I remember how I squatted down on the floor and stared about me wonderingly. Most of the paintings then were still in place, those that tomorrow were to be taken away and sold. My grandmother had spoken of them this afternoon as if the people in them were alive, of this Tregaran who had founded the line, and another who had first rebuilt the house, all the men of our name who had lived and schemed and fought, centuries ago. In the starlight they stared back out of the heavy frames with the same veiled look that I have, their women folk haughty beside them. I remember thinking, but grandmother is not Tregaran born as I am; their looks, their deeds, are part of me as they cannot be part of her. They are my inheritance, not hers. And she is selling it away.

There was one portrait that had always been my favourite. It was of a young man dressed in Cavalier clothes, a blue band of silk hung over his shoulder. He had fought with the Cornish for a king in a civil war long ago, and had left his home to go off to the wars, perhaps never to return. He had been painted in profile, staring out into a distance, aquiline-nosed, stubborn-chinned, one slender hand resting on a dog, the other gripped firmly around the hilt of his sword. For the first time ever I took note of every detail of that painting, the rich brocade of the undercoat, the froth of lace at wrists and throat, the dull gleam of the breast plate. He stood in a shadowy room, almost as dim as the one I was in, and behind him an open window let in a slant of light that fell upon his high cheek bones and outlined him, as if drawing him away from the dark into a rich and splendid future. The window framed a stand of trees, clothed in their full summer foliage, deep and mysterious, stretching far away. Suddenly they took on a familiar look, and there, between their green leaves, was the same glimpse of blue sea I had noticed from the terrace today, repeating the blue of the broad ribbon. I was not hiding, I repeat. I simply stayed in front of that painting, never taking my eyes from it as if to impart it all to memory. And I remember the sudden insight, like a lightning flash, as I recognized who the man reminded me of. It was the boy I had met today, the same profile, the same curled smile, the same sense of determined pride.

And the same blue eyes. I remember thinking, in a way that was quite unchildlike, as if I had gone beyond time or its passing, whoever this man in the painting is, this unknown ancestor, he will be lost to me and to this home of his where he belongs. But the boy I shall see again. Whenever I want I have only to go and look for him and he will be there, waiting for me. And long after the day was done and they had brought me down at last, that thought was to comfort me, like a candle in the dark. And in all the years afterwards, it never went away.

Five years were to pass before I saw Phil Tregarn again, almost a lifetime. Yet not as long as it might have seemed, for, being a child, I lived from one day to the next, oblivious to time. And the years raced along, through the remainder of my childhood, until I came to be sixteen, half-woman, half-child, running wild amid the ruins of an old estate, ripe to be plucked by the first passer-by. Except, it wasn't like that at all. There was only one man ever for me.

I often thought of Phil Tregarn and of the day that we had met. I never went looking for him as I had promised myself I would. I think now it was because I was too young. Or too wise. Perhaps I knew instinctively that when the moment was right, that would be the right moment, not before. Country life thrives on gossip however and he soon eclipsed his uncles' place (there were two of them it seemed, fishermen both, poachers, the village reprobates). Talk of fights, of affairs with girls, of trouble in the claypits, none of these bothered me, innocence being its own reward. But why our families hated each other, what the feud had been about, what the nature of the relationship was, never a hint from anyone. Those facts, if facts they were, were buried too deep for even gossip to rake up. Yet underneath the passing years, they remained with me, the loadstone of my life.

Em never spoke of the quarrel again. She shut up like a

clam when I tried to pry information out of her. And sad to tell, after that day we never could regain our old affection, I wary of her, she suspicious of me, our one-time closeness a casualty too of that summer disaster. We continued to live on the edge of poverty, owning a house and land perhaps, but not much else, too late to restore them to their past glory, the house too large for three people, too big to sell, the land alone draining money off like a well. Isolated from the great events that already were beginning to reshape our world, I came to rely on story books for a view of life, disastrous for an imaginative child, in some ways wild as a cat, in others more reserved than those Victorian heroines I loved to read about. For, after that summer, my grandmother refused to give me lessons, wanting to have nothing more to do with me, seeming to dislike even being in the same room, a blessing in disguise as far as I was concerned. Since she refused also to let me attend the local school ('She'll grow up a ruffian, besides, the village children smell!') and lacked, or would not spare, the money to send me away, she farmed me out into the vicar's care, the one whose speech Phil had imitated. A quiet man, more used to tutoring boys and afraid of girls, unwilling to cross the lady whose patronage he enjoyed, he accepted me as pupil because she asked, and then let me do what I liked best, devour books, however unsuitable.

But I must have inherited something of Tregaran obstin-acy. My grandmother's hatred of me, and it was hatred, gave me an inner strength which one day I was to use. I came to understand the real meaning behind Phil Tregarn's birthday wish; I too learnt to bide my time in patience, waiting to grow up.

Two final memories to round out that day: I had been prepared for my grandmother's anger; I would have been furious myself in similar circumstances. Her punishment was to make me an outcast in my own home.

40

'Blood tells,' she said that night, when I was dragged, protesting, down to the hall. I shall never forget the way she looked, her eyes sunk into dark shadows, her lipstick smudged, her beaded gown crumpled as if she too had gone crawling in the dark. She held a glass of whisky but her hand shook so that the liquid splashed upon the floor. 'Your father was a fool,' she went on in that deliberate way she had. 'First to choose a tramp [whatever that meant] who died in bearing you, and then to get himself and his brother killed on the eve of the Armistice, leaving me to pick up the pieces of his life.'

Her black eyes bored into mine. 'But there's a limit to my patience,' she said. 'At my age I've had enough. It's the last time I'll be made a laughing stock. Next time out you go, back to the streets you came from, lock, stock and barrel, and be damned to you.'

Perhaps she was drunk, as now I realize she often was. Perhaps she did not mean to be so cruel. Em had once said that grandmother had adopted me out of guilt, after my parents had both died. And perhaps she did not hate me as much as she thought she did. But I can honestly say that fear of her and what she might do to me discoloured the rest of my childhood, so that even in my dreams I felt its cold, as bitter as winter in my room.

The second is rumour only. It was said that when the workmen who had been pressed into the search retreated afterwards to the local pub, they had drunk my health and laid bets on what they thought I would do next. Young Tregarn, too young to drink but not too young to stick his head in at the door, had shouted out above the din that he would wager me to match anyone, and to prove his bet slapped down a pound note, more than half of his week's wages. I did not like to be made fun of, least of all by him, and he lost his money I suppose. At least for five years it was lost. That sixth summer I gave it to him back, with double interest.

Chapter 3

So we are come to my sixteenth year at Tregaran, and I had grown to puberty. On the surface that summer seemed like all the preceding ones; underneath, it was full of yearning and promise. Even the weather added to the general restlessness, weeks of balmy days and cool nights that seemed to have drifted from the Mediterranean. Every morning unwrapped itself from mist as if hatching from a cocoon; every evening burned itself out in a golden haze; every night brought welcome coolness that rejuvenated the world.

And perhaps it was the same for me. Perhaps, at last, nature had remembered me, and removed the veils of childhood. I remember still how I would start awake, without memory of how I came to be out of bed, to find myself before the window in my room, gazing down upon the moon-striped grass as if waiting for someone. Where once I would have been content to lie on the beach, devouring books, no matter how unsuitable, filling my head with Victorian claptrap (and incidentally creating an old-fashioned romanticism both in my thoughts and writing style), now Tregaran seemed like a trap. I was out all day, scaling the cliffs for nests, delighting in the most difficult climbs, or swimming to the rocks that edged our cove, like a mermaid looking for a home. Sometimes I scrambled along the path beside the house, the one Phil Tregarn had used, until I came out on the headland. From there I could look down at the slate roofs of the village below, carved out from the backdrop of the hill. But I never went there. Nor did I go up on the moors where he worked, that expanse of barren plateau north of us, which coiled along the centre of the land like a backbone. But the white pyramids of sand, which marked the workings of the claymines, were clearly visible from Tregaran, and they too loomed into my dreams, like ghosts from an ancient world. The fret of the sea, the screams of the seagulls, echoed in my head, until I felt that like those birds I was ready to launch myself into the air; all that was lacking was the impetus. And when it came in a form that I did not recognize, that added only to the expectancy.

One morning then, when I was standing by the tree stumps where the ospreys had made their nest, gazing out over the cliff edge at the vague shimmer of sea, a small fishing boat edged out, crablike, around the point, as bright as a streak of red upon a pale distance. I watched for a while, disinterested. In those days there were always fishermen setting nets and lobster traps among the rocks, and the sea beneath me was dotted with small painted buoys, each colour denoting a different owner. But this boat seemed different. Its oars moved in and out with scarcely a splash, in a strange lopsided way. The water beneath it was so still that it seemed to float above a sea of glass, as if its reflection was painted on, and the old man who rowed was hunched intently over the oars as if hugging a secret to his chest.

His face was concealed by a shock of thick white hair, and his wide shoulders were bowed as if they lacked the strength they once had. As I watched he shipped the oars, and threw an anchor out with one hand, close to shore, and still bent over, began to pull up the floating buoys. Their ropes came writhing up, festooned with weed; the water fell in glistening drops; fish scales suddenly sparkled in the sun. He moved from buoy to buoy, laboriously, always keeping his face turned from land, pulling in each buoy in turn, emptying nets and lobster pots methodically before dropping them back over the side. I felt comprehension sweep over me like a wave. Those buoys could not be his, not all of them, and some of them I recognized. And I stood there, like an unwilling accomplice, watching while a thief went about robbing them.

And then, as unexpectedly, a shiver ran across my spine, as sharp as pain. I cannot explain all I felt, but it was as if having been blind, I could suddenly see again. Everything stood out in sharp detail, the rocks, the sea, the drift of waves along the shore. And I knew exactly who the man was, although I had never met him in real life. There could be only one fisherman who would have the gall to poach so openly for his neighbour's fish; or do it so blatantly off Tregaran land. And if I went down to where he was and called him by name, I knew exactly how he would turn, what he would look like, the older version of his nephew, and with what familiar speech he would answer all I asked him. I had learned enough of Jack Tregarn over the years to count on him to say exactly what he thought, without prevarication or lies. And so, with never a backward look myself, never a thought, that is exactly what I set out to do.

Once on the beach (which I reached in breakneck time) I kicked off my boots and ran towards the point, slipping and sliding on the wet shingle. I should explain that Tregaran beach was like a half moon, bounded by rocks which, when the tide was out, joined our cove to the next in a succession of little crescents, each isolated from the next when the sea was in. At low tide, as now, the rocks jutted far out to sea, and if I had gauged right, the boat was anchored just around the first point. I splashed through the pools left by the tide, the water cool against my bare feet, the wrack of seaweed smooth as satin. The rocks were dark and pointed, drying in the sun. Under them long strands of kelp swept to and fro in the currents, like drowned hair, and the sea curled over them in a froth of foam. As the tide came in the waves would rise and dash against the base of the cliff which rose up here in a sheet of slate. And there, just round the point, was the boat, not more than a few yards out, with the man still bent over the lobster pots.

He must have heard me of course. I had made no attempt to hide myself, but he did not look up, not even when I called to him. Finally I made myself shout his name. 'Jack Tregarn, Jack Tregarn, I want to talk to you.' And then, as leisurely, he finished winding in the rope before he turned to me, with his arms stretched out, in a strangely theatrical pose. 'I bain't Zack Tregarn' was all he said. 'I'm Tom.'

I knew there were two uncles, of course, but they had merged into my thoughts as one. But I never had time to think of that. I was looking at a face so divided of itself it might have belonged to two men. One side was seamed by a puckered scar that ran down from the empty eye socket to the jaw; the other was smooth, like a child's, with pale vacant eye and slack mouth, the reverse side of a coin whose distinguishing marks had all been beaten out, making the contrast the more dreadful. And of the hands which he had flapped at me, the right one was curled into a stub, as if most of its fingers had been torn off.

He must have noticed my shock, perhaps he was used to it, for he said, in the familiar, deceptively mild voice, but with a monotonous singsong that was equally shocking, 'Seed 'ee on the cliffs a while back. Didn't take 'ee long to get down, did it? Just like your dad. What's all the hurry for? The war's been over a long while, and he be dead.'

He smiled aimlessly, and reached over the side of the boat again for the anchor chain. Close to I could see how difficult it was for him to throw and pull with his maimed hand, and why his movements had seemed so odd. But it was the voice, the disjointed, mindless voice that kept me quiet. Useless to say to him as I had planned, 'I want to know what the secret is. I want you to tell me why we

45

can't be friends.' Useless to ask him anything. There could be no sense behind that twisted mask.

He did not speak again for a while, and I thought he never would, as now he went about tidying the coils of rope, stowing whatever catch he had taken to one side. There was no sound, even my panting had stopped. As he sat down to unship the oars I saw the glitter of a boat hook in his good hand, the gaff which he must have used to spear the fish or hold the rope tight. Suddenly I began to feel frightened. I had come upon this simpleton, for lack of a better term, while he was engaged in an illegal act. I was alone, no one could see me from the shore. It would have been easy for him to knock me off the rock with just one swing of those broad shoulders, with just one thrust from that gaff or oar. And I was perched on a slippery edge, beneath a blank wall of cliff, with an equally long drop under the water to the ocean bed. But it was the horror of him that made me feel faint, so that I had to lean back, grasping for the rock with trembling fingers. I still remember the feel of the wet slime of weed under my nails and the hard outlines of the mussel shells. I remember thinking, no wonder they keep to themselves, hiding him away. No wonder no one speaks of him.

Perhaps he sensed my thoughts, for he grunted, and slewed about so that his smooth, unblemished side was facing me. 'Got t'other in the war,' he said. He cocked his head in a gesture that I recognized. 'With your dad.' His stump sketched a vague circle in the air. 'Didn't matter naught then who was who. Big house or small. If your name were called, you got caught square.'

He pushed the handles of the oars into place and began to draw them against his chest. He said, 'But I'll tell 'ee what Zack said. "Never hounded a man, nor stole his land, nor destroyed for spite," that's what Zack said.' He began to paddle away from the rock. 'So now 'ee knows

46

my face and I knows yourn,' he said. 'What more do 'ee want?'

And without my meaning to, without my knowing that the words would come out, I cried, 'The truth.'

He squared his shoulders. And a change came over him like the stirring of some deep underwater current. It made me ashamed. He could not always have been like this, I thought. The explosive that had blown him apart must have blown away part of his brain as well, but left him enough to recognize what he missed. I shivered again. Pity washed over me. I watched him work away at thought, as laboriously as he had worked before with oar and rope. And when he spoke it was with a simplicity that hurt.

'Truth's some slippery,' he said, his face pale and strained, and yet with the mark of some old fierceness that was only half-forgotten. 'Like fish. Keep it too long it stinks. What do 'ee want to fool with it? Go on back where 'ee belong.'

For a heartstopping second I thought he might raise the boat hook again, for his fingers tightened around it convulsively. Then he turned his head away as if looking out to sea once more. In profile, his good side had the tautness of a former beauty, a family resemblance that I had missed before. The enormity of what I had asked him swept over me, the thoughtlessness on my part, the pain on his, as he struggled for coherence in his darkness. But I couldn't unsay what I had said.

He said, slowly, dragging the words out like that anchor chain. 'Your father and his brother used to come with me when they was lads. Many's the time. In this here boat. Never thought to outlive 'em both. Never meant to of.' He began to sniff, like a child. "Tweren't my fault,' he cried. 'It comed too fast, like a cricket ball, with a whoosh and a wham. Nothing more, all golden red.'

There were tears now running down from his good eye. 'Saw it, heard it,' he said. 'Tried to push 'em back. Your father got there first. Always were quick. Nothing left of 'un; he and his brother, both gone to glory, just like that.' He wiped his nose on the edge of his jacket. 'Didn't want naught from she,' he cried. 'Didn't expect naught that didn't belong to me. But there were no call for she to treat I like dirt because Major Tregaran packed it in. I was batman to your father, first, nothing to him.'

I understood what horror he was remembering; I understood who the 'she' was; I knew the 'Major' was my uncle, my father's older brother, the one my grandmother loved most. I remember thinking, but my grandmother can't have blamed Tom Tregarn for her favourite's death. But I knew she could. I had always known she blamed my father too. It made sense that she should have hated anything that lived, Tom Tregarn perhaps. And perhaps myself. But I had never known before how my father had met his death; no one before had ever spoken of him kindly, with such affection.

I made myself look at Tom Tregarn again, the man my father had tried to save, just as he had tried to save my father. He must have been in his fifties then but he appeared younger, as if all that pain and suffering had leached age out of him. How much his junior had my father been? And what had bound all four of them, two Tregarans, two Tregarns, in some special way? I thought, at least I was partly right, there was a link once. What broke it?

I think he guessed what I was thinking; sometimes the simple have that gift. 'There were two of 'em in the Big House,' he said in a kind of chant, 'birthed a year apart, dead the same day. We Tregarns was three. First Zack, then me, then Sister Alice. How she did laugh. Her hair went round and round and her skirts flared. Out all night till Zack took off his belt to her. But on she danced.' He spat, and spun his stump in the air like a top. 'There was fourteen years betwixt we boys,' he said, suddenly smiling as if the thought pleased him. 'And twelve again before Baby Alice. Not counting all the little 'uns that died between. And after Alice died there were only Zack and me.'

He suddenly straightened himself up, making the boat rock, and saluted me. 'Corporal Tom Tregarn,' he said, military precise. 'Born 1884, May 16th. Duke of Cornwall's Light Infantry. Fought with Major Nigel Tregaran; batman to his brother, John. All present and accounted for, halt, who goes there?' And he smiled again at me, triumphantly, as if to say 'Didn't I get that right?'

He sat there laughing to himself, his mouth working, the lip curled up on the unwounded side. His voice was like some gramophone record that has stuck in a groove, and then jumps the track. Or an electric light that switches on and off at random. Yet even as I smiled and nodded in turn, behind my back my fingers were doing frantic additions. If he were right his brother Zack was four years older than my grandmother, and she had been born in 1874, in the middle of Victoria's England. Zack would have been too old to go to war. But my grandmother's sons (for she had married at eighteen and had them almost at once), her boys had been twenty-one and -two when the Great War broke out, cannon fodder, wasn't that the name? Tom Tregarn, nine years older than my father, would have been thirty. I gave a shudder. How quickly all those years had passed for them, I thought, how quickly done, their lifespan snuffed out in an instant's flash of red and gold, nothing left of what they had been, except this poor imitation of a man.

Tom Tregarn coughed, the sort of cough a child makes when preparing to recite a lesson. I cannot tell you how sad that cough made me. And the voice that followed, with its lilt, was like the wind in a hollow reed. 'Once us Tregarns bred like rabbits,' he said. 'But blood do thin. Once half the country round was peopled by Tregarns. As was them foreign parts we sailed to.' He cocked his head again. 'We was sailors first, before we was fishermen,' he said, 'Sailed round the world, old to new. A queen gived we a medal in them times.' He frowned, the thread lost. 'Zack knows it all,' he said. 'Got it all writ down.'

He suddenly glared at me, his one eye hard. 'Owned all this land,' he said, making the now familiar sweeping gesture, 'more than you Tregarans. You was nothing then, poor stock, biding your time.' He leaned forward, as if bunching his body up to get the meaning right. 'Took it from us,' he said. 'There's some tale. A great king were selling off churches like gingerbread, and we was meant to get a share. Hired 'ee to make a bid for we, there were the first mistake. Off 'ee trotted to London town, bold as brass. Gived your name to the king's men as Tregaran; sounds like ourn, don't it, or close enough. Up 'til then 'ee'd been more common like, Smith or Brown or some such, but who in the king's court cared.' He drew a breath. 'So 'ee got what should've been ourn, and paid for it with our cash. And when 'ee had a toe in the door, didn't 'ee dig and mole to push all the way in? I'll say 'ee did. While we was off fighting for the king, married one of us to keep warm, and there, bam, true relatives at last, snoozing in our bed, in our house, on our land.'

Here then was another truth of sorts, not one especially nice either. *How do I know what the quarrel was about?* Em had said. I had always imagined that we had been here first. I had thought their name sounded like a left-over part of ours, not ours tagged on to theirs. But whether this story was true, or whether it was an invention of his addled mind, there was a ring of satisfaction in his voice, over and above the satisfaction of reciting it. Truth is slippery, alright. It would be hard to accept that perhaps all those legends about Tregaran House weren't really true, all those stories I had been so proud of, about the Norman fort and castle walls. Worse, perhaps many of those things my grandmother had sold had not really been ours, not if they had belonged to Tregarns first. That man in the painting for example. Was he the adventurer who had stolen Tregaran House away? Whose ancestor was he then, mine, or Phil's? Or were we both throwbacks to the same common source; was that why we looked like him?

Tom Tregarn saw nothing of this, nor would he have understood it if he had. He gave another of his choked coughs, to show that he was through. 'Fooled 'ee,' he said, full of glee, like a child who has played a joke. 'Never thought I'd get it right, tho' it did happen a while back. Leastways, Zack said it did. Zack'll be the one for telling it. 'Cept,' and now his voice hardened and his stubbed fist gestured at the sky. 'That'll be the difficulty with Zack; 'ee never knows what mood 'un's in. And I be that scared of 'un.'

He started to sniffle again. Then straightening his shoulders he began to pull at the oars. 'Wait,' I cried, scrambling along the rocks as close to the water as I could get. 'That was so long ago, surely it's been forgotten since.' (For I was almost certain he had got things in the wrong historical sequence, although perhaps the incidents themselves were right.) 'I want to hear more about my father. And his brother. Who was your sister Alice? Was she Phil's mother? And what about your brother Jack? You haven't said why he hates us Tregarans.'

This was too much. The tears were dry; the intelligence had flickered off. He swung the oars in his crabbed fashion. 'I don't know naught,' he said sulkily. 'God save the king. Salute the flag. Old soldiers never die, bain't that the truth? Ask Zack Tregarn, for all I care. But leave Phil be. He's trouble enough without 'ee. And if 'ee don't get a move on you'm in as deep as him.'

One more gesture from that stubbed claw made me aware of how fast the water had begun to rise. I made a quick turn round and almost cried out. Used to the sea all my life, I had forgotten to watch the tide. Already it was creeping up towards the cliffs, and lapping at their edge. I could hear the swish of the undertow as it curled back upon itself, and even as I looked the first white foam broke upon the rock where I was perched.

Tom Tregarn was eyeing me with a cunning look, the sort of cunning a child has when it plans a trick. 'If 'ee don't say naught about seeing me,' he said, 'I'll take 'ee back. No need to tell what I were doing when 'ee did. No call to tell 'em where I was at.'

'And if I do tell?'

'Then swim,' he said. And giggled.

He knew it was too far to swim and the current was too strong. I knew I'd tire before I got halfway although I was proud of my swimming ability. So I let him hold the boat steady with one hand until I had scrambled over its side and taken a seat in the stern. The tide was running fast and the swell had risen as it often does, making the turning round the point hard work even in a boat, nothing for a two-handed man but difficult for a cripple. I watched the way he swung out and returned, holding his bad hand against his chest, giving him that hunched-over effect. And on an impulse that also I could not explain, I slid onto the bench beside him, and put my hand on the oar close to his maimed one. I do not know if he noticed for he said nothing, but after a while he let me pull with him. So we rowed together towards the beach, bending and stretching in unison.

It was hot work for the sun burnt down and the distance seemed longer than it should have been. The swish of the water beneath the boat, the occasional flap of fish under the seats, the hollow boom of the waves among the rocks, all seemed old and familiar, and when I licked my lips I could taste the salt. It was pleasant sitting like that, companionably, hands side by side, working in harmony, stroke for stroke, so pleasant that I wished that it would never end. For the first time I began to imagine what my father had been like, and what he and Tom might have done when they were young, sharing the rowing like this perhaps, sharing all those other things I would never know about. If they had trusted each other well enough to go to war I thought, to be wounded and die for each other, friendship must have been possible for them. So what else had happened in between, something more than war and death, to put that hatred there? Tom Tregarn hasn't spoken of it all, I thought. There must be some parts he doesn't know, or has forgotten. Or has put aside because he doesn't want to know.

And so it was, even before he had eased the boat up through the foam and I had jumped out, knee-deep, to wade ashore, my mind was made up. I watched Tom back away without a nod of goodbye, and work his way leeward, hugging the west side of the bay, until he rounded the headland to the safety of the village. Then, I retrieved my shoes and went up the cliff, not hurrying especially, but determined, sure of what I should do next.

I had always known where to find Phil Tregarn. It was just a question of doing it; of putting one foot before the other and starting. Not in the village of course. But in the place that he had chosen as his own, that no-man's land of moor and mine, where outsiders are barely tolerated and strangers are seldom taken in.

The moors need explanation too. If one is not used to them, as I was not, they seem barren and inhospitable, running along the granite rocks which divide the county, north and south. From their crest one can glimpse the sea on three sides, stretching along the horizon in a thin blue line, marking the natural boundaries of the peninsula. Nothing much grows there, except gorse and grass of the coarsest kind; nothing much lives there except sheep and cattle, and wild ponies. And the clayworkers in their windswept villages.

Even at Tregaran we could not avoid evidence of clay. In summer the hedges were covered with its dust and in winter the roads were rutted from the weight of horse-drawn carts, lumbering down towards the coast with the dried clay in bags. Sometimes when I heard the jingling of the brass harnesses I used to run out to watch the horses straining past, their coats shiny with sweat, curdled like cream, while their drivers walked at their heads to ease the load. Now that trail of white dust acted as a guide, at first along the main road, then branching off north, going uphill all the way.

The rise from sea level is not great, the highest peak on the moors being only about a thousand feet, yet the gradient was steep enough to make me puff. Presently, when a smaller lane cut off to one side I followed it gratefully, partly to get out of the sun, partly to avoid the road where I might be seen. This lane was new to me, although I came to know it well. Shaded by gorse and bracken it wound along the side of the hill, only steepening at the end when it opened out on to the moor. It was hot under the bushes too and the flies bit and buzzed, but I was good at scrambling in those days. And when I hauled myself up the last slope of rock, worn slippery from winter rains, I found myself in a world so different from my own, it took my breath away.

I mean that literally. There is a wind upon the moors that is never still, no matter how calm it is elsewhere. In summer, as then, it eddies in gusts, like currents in the sea, bending the folds of moors into waves, stretching them into a purple distance, where those same white pyramids dominated the landscape. And as I stood and stared, turning myself round and round in the wind, like Tom Tregarn's sister, dancing with myself, I heard a hooter's blast. I did not know then it was a sound that controlled the clayworkers' lives, bringing them to the pits and sending them home again. I only knew it startled me, and startled the sheep that must have heard it a hundred times, for a small flock of them came at a run out of the gorse and disappeared down the way I'd come.

I ventured forward, still half-hidden by the thick bushes. I soon found there were no clear paths up on the moors, only a mesh of trails that appeared to run together and then fan out again. From time to time an outcrop of grey rock, surrounded by a mud patch, barred my progress, and after I had stepped knee-deep in bog, I learned to avoid the bright green grass that grew there in tufts.

Winding a way round such obstacles soon made me tired and I quickly lost all sense of direction. The sun swung huge and golden in a dark blue sky; the dry grass rustled underfoot; sometimes moor birds broke with flapping wings from the heather clumps. I might have been in a foreign land, walking forever, without purpose, had not I stumbled, by luck, upon a main path, just as the workers started home.

They came in groups like moorland birds themselves, walking stiffly in twos and threes, their corduroy-trousered legs stumping along as if the joints had stiffened. Everything about them was white, their faces, their hair, their caps, their waistcoats which they wore for decency over their shirts. They never spoke, as if the clay had hardened their mouths shut, just a brief nod goodbye as each came to a parting in the track. I had sunk down behind a gorse bush to wait for them to pass, and when the last straggler was gone, I still sat there, numb with disappointment. Nowhere among that silent group was anyone even vaguely resembling the Phil Tregarn I remembered; no one as tall or with as black hair, or with as vigorous a stride. Could five years have changed him that much, I thought, so that I can't even pick him out behind his clay mask? Or, like his uncle Tom, has he altered beyond recognition? I sat there blankly for a long while, waiting in the sun, a wait that seemed longer than those five years. And then I heard a strange creaking sound like wheels over grass.

Far off up the track a man was pushing or rather dragging a bike. It might have been the same one that he had had before, and he might have been wearing the same rusty black suit, or a larger version of it. But I knew him at once. He had his head bent in a book, oblivious to everything, so that when I stepped out of the bush in front of him his start of surprise sent bicycle and books flying, the second time I had caught him off guard.

'Hullo Phil Tregarn,' I said. 'You're late.' I smiled at him. 'I thought you'd gone home some other way.'

For a moment he stared at me, so hard that I had the sudden sinking feeling that he did not know who I was. But I knew him. He was taller than I remembered, and had filled out so that his shoulders were as broad as his uncle's. His wrists still stuck out of his sleeves, wiry thin, and his eyes were still that same fierce blue. His face was brown from the sun, but his neck and arms were white, not white from clay but from his natural fairness. I noticed at once that there was not a speck of clay on his clothes or skin, as if he had put himself under a pump. And when he came up close to me, leaving the bike and books scattered on the ground, I saw that his hair was still wet, so that it stood up in spikes, blue-black like a raven's wing.

He walked around me with an exaggerated frown as if he were surveying me. 'So 'tis you after all,' he said. 'All grown up and gussied down.' He looked pointedly from my stained skirts and mud-caked boots up to my wind-swept hair, so that I had to resist turning away to put myself to rights. Any moment now, I thought, he'll fish in his pocket for some pins. And for some reason that made me cross, as if I didn't want him to look at me as a child.

'Haven't changed much,' he went on, as if echoing my own thought. 'And who'm, who, are you spying on this time?' Just as if those five years had never been.

I don't remember thinking of what to say. I don't remember really thinking at all. I only known that all those questions I had meant to ask went out of my head and the first thing that came in was what I said. 'And you don't look much of a clayworker. Where's the clay?' I pointed to his hair. 'Have you been taking a bath somewhere? I thought you didn't like the sea.'

I expect my answer came out more crankily than I meant, for he stared at me again. After a while, 'I don't,' he said. 'Well, well, your tongue's not changed. What's wrong with clay-dust anyhow?'

His voice was just as I remembered it, deeper perhaps, but with the same lilt. I began to notice that he spoke correctly when he wanted to, although now he made his accent thick. 'Why, girl, I works all day long in clay, up to my knees in it, wet with it, dry with it, five years of it. It's a mark of what I do, see, no harm to wearing it.' He sounded suddenly as he had when I first had met him. 'It's just that, come night, I like to wash it off. No call to track it home with me.'

'Up here?' I tried to laugh. 'Where's the pond? Or is it a lake? There's no water on these moors.'

He had bent down to pick up his scattered belongings. I noticed the books seemed full of mathematics, not like the novels I was used to, and I was curious what he did with them. He saw my look. 'I read 'em,' he said. 'I can read, you know. Perhaps I make use of 'em.' He righted the bicycle. 'As for water,' he said. 'Don't 'ee know anything, shut up in that ruin of a house of yourn? We stand in water too, all day long, why do you think those men walk so stiff, rheumatism gets their joints before they'm thirty. And where would I find water to wash with at home? We've no "bathroom" [he mimicked the word] as you call it. But there be ponds up here, right enough, or lakes, as you'd prefer I suppose [again he mimicked me], tho' not like the ones you're used to. They'm the pits left when the clay has been dug out, hundreds of feet some of 'em, as deep below as the sand-burrows on top. Full of water like blue glass. And more deadly than that sea you'm so fond of.'

It was not the way I had meant to start, not with a quarrel. I stared past him almost in tears while he busied himself with dusting down the bicycle and straightening the bars. At last I said, 'I saw someone today, someone you know.' And as he looked up, 'He was fishing. He spoke of you.' I faltered on, 'Your Uncle Tom. He said . . .'

'I know what he says,' he broke in curtly. 'I know what he sounds like. So what is it to you?'

I stopped, thwarted a second time. Those blue eyes were glaring into mine almost as if looking for an insult. Any moment now he would ride off and there would be an end of it. I said suddenly, 'You'm some crabbed, Phil Tregarn. I never comed to cause harm, and well you know. I came here on purpose.'

He did not reply for a moment, bent over the handle bars again. 'What for?' His voice came muffled, bleak, not giving anything away. All I saw was his broad back and that thick hair. I thought, perhaps that was how Tom had looked, when he was young; when he walked or cycled, hunting for girls; perhaps that was what he and the Tregaran boys did at nights, they in their world I suppose, when we were rich, he in his, until the war destroyed them all. I said, 'Don't be stupid, Phil Tregarn. What should I have come here for?'

There was no reply. I heard the wind soughing a long way off. Sometimes they say you can smell the sea in it, sometimes the hay; that day it brought the honey taste of heather and gorse. I thought, if he does not say something soon I shall leave and never see him again. And then he smiled. That smile I remembered too; it softened his face, lit up his eyes. It made me see what those village girls had found in him. 'Then come along, Miss Joycelyn,' he said.

58

'You've been waiting long enough. 'Tis time we got a move on.' And it was only afterwards that I understood the real meaning behind his words.

He seized my arm, so tightly I couldn't have held back even if I had wanted to. I remembered the cool touch of his hand with its callouses running along the palm. I could feel the broken nails that dug into my skin. I didn't mind, they showed him for what he was. He pushed the bike into a bush so it was hidden and pulled me after him, off the track, plunging along with great strides, moving fast without looking back, as if he knew the way and expected me to follow him. I suppose I might have hesitated; I suppose I might have considered where he was taking me; young ladies in those days were supposed to think of such things, not the things themselves of course but their consequence. And Em had been a good teacher; her warnings about village boys had stayed with me. Yet I never thought of that. To accompany him seemed as natural as the air I breathed, the wind that blew, the flowers in the grass. It would have seemed more strange to have held back than go on, so go on I did.

Gorse and bracken grew even more thickly on this downhill side, closing behind us like a tunnel. No one could have guessed where we were, even if they had come looking for us. In the thickest part he let go my arm and began to beat his way in, holding the brambles aside as he had done that day long ago, when I had been searching for his uncle's telescope. And still I followed him. I cannot say I did so innocently; innocence and its opposite had no meaning in that place. All I knew was what was meant; all I felt was how right it was.

We broke suddenly out into an open space, far off the path, set in the middle of the thicket. It was ringed round with a small circle of stones, and again I had the impression he knew it well, for he made his way instinctively to the largest stone, threw off his jacket and sat down, leaning his back against it. And when more slowly now I came up to him, he took my arm again and gave a tug so that I dropped on my knees beside him. 'Here we be, Miss Joycelyn Tregaran,' he said. 'Alone at last. So what did you want to see me for?'

It was very quiet in that circle of stones. The bracken fronds met like a wall and, in between, patches of blue sky were spread like a canopy. There were many things then I could, perhaps should, have said, a string of Methodist homilies coming to my aid. There were many things I could have done, had I been a different sort of girl. I didn't think or do any of them. All I knew was that in all my life I had never felt so safe, so hidden from harm.

He looked at me again, his eyes bright. There was grass and gorse in his hair and a bramble had scored along his cheek, but he was smiling. 'Not a word,' he said, 'not a peep. Then let me guess instead. Was it this, or this, or this?' He reached out to touch my face, to hold it with both hands, to kiss it gently on the lips.

I felt myself cling to him like a limpet on a rock, the more you try to pry it off the tighter it holds. I felt my hands go round his neck, clasping his head against mine; I felt his mouth covering my mouth until his taste and smell were in me and mine in him. And when his hand slid down beneath my blouse, along the spine, it was as if it had never left me from those years ago.

Our bodies were touching length to length, foot to foot, knee, belly, thigh. My clothes felt on fire, and I wanted to throw them off as now his other hand pulled up my skirts, smoothing quickly along the skin, like a trail of fire itself, up to where pleasure begins. I felt him raise himself over me. 'Wait now,' I thought I heard him whisper, 'I'll make it right for 'ee.'

But it was already right. Right and true and meant to be. And when he had shucked his own clothes off, it was right for him as well.

Afterwards, 'Did I hurt 'ee then?' he asked, turning on his back to look at me. His eyes were that brilliant blue as I remembered them, his eyes, his face, his hair my own, part of me, as I was of him. 'Christ, girl, but you'm nice to hold. Never thought ...' He swallowed hard, began again. 'Is that what you comed for, is it, is it?' I felt his laugh, as he leaned on his elbow to tease me. 'Just look at you,' running a finger along my chin, my nose, making me laugh myself. 'Like a cat that's caught a mouse, some pleased.'

I let my hand do the same, feeling the contours of his face, tracing out the line of his eyes, tangling my fingers in that thick black hair, knowing how to please without being asked. 'Did 'ee miss me all these years, were 'ee waiting for me then?' I thought, it wasn't just missing you, that would be like losing an arm or leg; it was more than that, like losing myself. And what's been wrong all these years is not having what you've just given me. And having had it, I know without being told that it's what I have always been waiting for.

'Can't get over it,' he was saying again. 'But Christ, you'm beautiful. Like a gypsy running wild, with that hair, with them eyes. Never seen their like before, lit up like stars.

'Never meant to hurt 'ee,' he whispered. 'It do hurt a bit the first time. But not again.' He had bunched my clothes and his against the stone to make a kind of pillow, our bodies were naked on the grass, his white and long, boyish thin, with ribs that showed. I didn't like to stare at it, having never seen a man naked. But he stared at mine. It was browner than his, where I had been lying in the sun, rounder where his was flat, except in that one place where all the difference was. He traced a finger down towards that place, between my breasts, down to my waist, circling it, then down again to that centre cleft, dividing, separating me from my own flesh. 'I've thought of this,' he

61

whispered, 'I've thought of doing this a hundred times. Been waiting too, you see. When you was ready like. But Christ, I never thought 'twould be like this.'

And moving in unison with him, I cried, ''Tis time.'

I drew him in, the rest of him that completed me, into that part of me that completed him, nothing between us then, the dry grass warm against my back, the sun bright above his head, earth, sky and sun merging into one, until he steadied me and brought me back. We lay together like that for a long while, he sheathed in me, I holding him. And that was how we met again, that first summer when I was sixteen. And how our life together began.

Each afternoon then, for as long as that summer heat lasted, when the whistle blew I was waiting there in that circle of stone. Each afternoon when the other men had gone, I would tense to hear him breasting through the bushes at a run. Freshly washed and shaved (he always made a point of that), he would come bursting into the open, shedding coat and shirt. Sometimes I lay there naked and ready for him; sometimes I let him undress me as I undressed him, our fingers fumbling with buttons and loops, the very touch of them almost as exciting as the act of love itself. And when we had loved all through the long late day, we would lie together, bodies wrapped round each other like a cloak, as if this was what we had been waiting for, this happiness; as if there had been nothing else but this, the same dry wind and same warm grass, the same hot sun.

What did we talk about, in between the love-making, and afterwards, when we returned to the road, I riding sometimes on the handles of his bike, or walking side by side down the path I had first found, or lingering for as long as I dared before parting for the night? Nothing I remember now, only five years of silence to fill in. I know that all those questions I had meant to ask went out of my head as if I had never thought of them. I never considered the danger of being found out (although now I think it gave an added taste of adventure to our meeting). I ignored the differences between us, in our lives and backgrounds. Like someone in a dream I put reality aside, speaking only of what I thought and felt, as if that was sufficient unto itself. If I had never loved before, now I gave unstintingly, pouring love out like a stream. And if my willingness in one so young and inexperienced surprised him, he never said so openly. ''Tis some nice,' is what he said, 'to have 'ee be so generous. Makes me feel some proud, to have 'ee lavish yourself on me. Not many girls does, you know; most be stingy tight. Makes me love 'ee more, if 'twere possible. Never had such luck before, never expect to have again. So I mean to hold on to 'ee.' He suddenly put his arms about me, enfolding me. 'Never change,' he whispered. 'Passion in woman is a gift. Don't let them old Methody women tell 'ee different. Hard to say before 'ee start, if 'tis there or not, but if 'ee 'ave it, 'tis a crime not to appreciate it. As I do 'ee, as I dote on 'ee, my love.'

He seldom paid me such compliments, showing, rather than speaking, what he felt. Yet underneath his feelings were as complex as mine. He taught me more than how to enjoy sex; he showed me what loving meant. And if he was less exuberant about what lay ahead, perhaps it was because he was older, or knew the world better than I did; perhaps he guessed that the world would never leave us alone.

One day he asked me to come with him to the old claypit where he swam, and was surprised when at first I refused. I'd never refused him anything. ''Tain't that it's much,' he tried to explain, 'but I be used to going there. Of course you know best, you might not think it so pleasant.' He was too generous to insist, but when at last I gave way, he wasn't deceived. He knew his secrets troubled me. I wasn't sure what they were, you see; I wasn't certain how they fitted me. This was his way of revealing them, for better or worse, as they were, not as pretence. But I convinced myself that wouldn't matter. Hadn't he said once that if you want a thing you have to fight for it? I could hold on as tightly as he did. But when I agreed, I never thought how long and hard that holding on would have to be.

Chapter 4

From the start, the thought of that pit had frightened me. We waited until we were sure all the miners had left, for to reach it we had to come close to the one where he worked. I always remember how the noise of our feet sounded especially loud as we crunched over the quartz and mica path that glistened in the sun. And how, right in front of us, the thick triangular shape of the sand burrow blocked our view. On one side, a little trolley cart on a kind of cable whined up and down, emptying more waste upon the tip. The sand fell like waves down the side, scoring a great white scree, and the sound it made was like a wave rolling over shingle. But when we came up under the tip, its shadow felt wet and cold and its smell was raw, like fresh concrete.

'See that,' he said suddenly, standing still under the elevated track where the cart swung over the path. 'When I first comed, came, up here to work, they dared me to ride in 'un. Never thought I would of course. 'Twere at the end of the day and it were empty else I never could've got myself squeezed in, and even then my knees stuck out.'

I stood looking at the little cart, as it swayed overhead on its cobwebbed tracks, and shivered as it went by. I wanted to ask, wasn't it dangerous, but had the sense to keep quiet. I knew danger wasn't the point.

After a while, 'How the wind did blow,' he said. 'Thought 'twould swing me off mid-way. And then at the top, upside down, hanging heels over arse in the air, I thought I was a goner. But I tell 'ee, it were almost worth it, the whole of the county spread like a map under your head.' He began to laugh. 'Knocked some sense into mine,' he said. 'When I came back down they gived me the ten bob I'd won, and I gived the fellow that set me up a taste of his own medicine.' He grinned. 'Them moor lads are great big louts,' he said, 'and Joe Penhire is bigger than most. And a poor-spirited sort of bugger, to take advantage of a young 'un. Couldn't fight him on the straight. He's a wrestler, see, like many of them up here, and twice my size. Could've bust my ribs quicker than that tip if he'd got hold of me. But I floored him first with a trick.' At my look, 'Well, I'd no hope of pinning him to the ground, not unless I weighed a ton myself. But I'm as tall. So I let him square up to me, with all that arm-waving caper they wrestlers love, and when he were within range I just put up my fists and knocked him out.' He laughed again at the thought. 'Nearly broke my wrist!' he said. 'Broke his nose I heared. But 'twere a fair exchange by my book. And I don't bear he a grudge, tho' he do me. Hates my guts he does, for making a fool of 'un, threatens to get even. But taught me a lot. Showed me not to be a fool myself, leastways not unless you know why. And taught me what them moorlanders are like, a mean bunch, the whole crew of them. And mule stubborn. The riches of the earth under their feet and they turns their noses up; lets every Tom, Dick and Harry walk off with it, because they'm too stupid, or proud, to stand up for their rights. And don't like anyone else to try for them.'

We had gone right under the cold damp shadow and his voice echoed hollowly, as if all that mountain of sand had swallowed the sound. But on the other side, the moors spread out again, running westward. The sea was shrouded today and along the horizon faint smudges appeared, like wisps of vapour. He cocked his head knowingly, and afterwards I remembered them, the first clouds I had seen for days. But it was still hot as we began to slant downwards, towards what seemed like a fold in the moors which deepened as we approached almost into a ravine, edged with old overgrown sand heaps that hung over its lip like a hedge.

He stopped and ground the toe of his boot in, so that the silvery quartz flew up. 'An old shaft here,' he said, suddenly serious. 'Underneath us, the ground's honey-combed with mines.' He kicked at the sparse grass again, scraping it away to reveal the grit underneath. 'Mining's the Cornish birthright at that,' he said. 'Since olden times. They say the Romans used to come here for their tin. Well, there bain't many of them tin mines left. Oh, there's tin alright, tin and copper both, but they say the mines have gone too far underground to be worthwhile. Some even stretch under the sea.'

He grinned at me. 'Been down some,' he said, 'along our cliffs. Some strange, to hear the waves over your head. But you can still see the veins of ore.'

'Why don't they work them then?' I asked. 'Is it dangerous? Why don't the Cornish miners start them up again?'

He looked at me as he sometimes did, the smile gone, and burst out, 'That's the point. Don't you know anything, girl? Of course, 'tis dangerous. All mining is. But to work a mine takes more than know-how. It takes money. And where would a Cornish miner find the cash to start a mine even if he wanted to? Who would lend it to him if he did? He's been told so often that he'm just an ignorant pit worker, he believes it.'

I had not heard him speak like that since he was a boy and I watched how he bit his lip as if he had let too much escape. It was the first inkling I had of all that pent-up bitterness. I watched him begin to scramble up the side of the tip, the nails in his boots sending off puffs of sand like smoke. I called out after him, 'Hasn't there been a disaster, a Depression, isn't that the name, everyone's money lost? Em says it would've ruined Tregaran, if grandmother hadn't ruined it first. Is that why the mines have closed?'

He did not reply. A chill suddenly passed over me, as cold as the shadow of the claypit. 'But here's all right,' I said. 'Aren't these claymines safe?' And when again he said nothing, almost defiantly, 'They won't close.'

He had reached the top and was looking down inside. When he turned I saw that sudden glint that I remembered as a child. 'Safe,' he mimicked me. 'Safe for whom? Your grandma'd kick up some stink, wouldn't she, if she didn't get her dividend's worth each month.' Again he bit his lip. But he did not apologize. 'The big families always come off best,' he said. 'They get their share, and the devil take the workers who give it them. And when it's not worth their while, then close the mines, let the miners starve. There're ghost towns further west, everyone left who should be living there, wandering the world for work. And we'll be wandering too, if it pleases them bastards that owns us.'

He plunged down the other side, his boots catching on the ground with sharp clicks. I was struck dumb. The thought of his leaving suddenly obscured everything else. I scrambled after him but when I reached the top he had already disappeared. And I was looking down into a basin hemmed in by sand, a coarse gritty beach, fringed with bullrushes and reeds surrounding an oval pool, perhaps a hundred yards across, pale blue and deep, so deep that its waters had a lifeless stare, like a blind man's eye.

I don't know what I had expected but that blank blue repelled me. It seemed to take the colour of the sky and drown it. And for a frightening moment I thought it had already drowned Phil for I could not see him anywhere. I cannot explain how desolate I felt, as if I were left stranded on the edge of some wasteland, as remote as the Gobi Desert. Then I spotted a broken heap of timber at one side, the ruins of an engine house I suppose, and in a moment or so he came out of it and went down to the water's edge.

He was naked. He ran along some planks of wood that edged the pool, balanced for a moment, then dived in with a great splash, sending the water up in a shower. The ripples spread and rocked the reed beds; a covey of marsh birds squawked away; that opaque surface closed over him in a viscous mass. And I felt fear leap in me again.

When he came up for air I was sitting on the beach, near the planks, which I now saw were stretched across a kind of white clay bog, in which animal tracks were clearly visible. He trod water, laughing at me, shaking his head so that the drops spun out from his hair like a dog's. 'Take care,' he said, "tain't your everyday beach like. Step on the wood and when you jump, jump clear. The clay's soft around the edges there. Once in it you'm caught fast. But where I be is deep enough.'

He dived underneath again to show me. And again, and again. I sat where I was. Nothing could have persuaded me to go into that water, I felt sick even thinking about it. And yet I was a good swimmer too, more graceful than he was, for he swam like someone who lives inland, head down, arms thrashing. It seemed strange, his not minding swimming there, I mean, although he had such aversion to the sea, and it seemed stranger, my sitting there and watching him, as if it had been planned.

After a while he hauled himself out across the planks. Even so, the clay left long streaks across his chest and flanks, and his feet were caked with it. I turned my face away. Suddenly I could not bear to see that clay, nor look at his body, white against that dead blue, as if it were an indecency.

He guessed at once something was wrong. 'What is it?' he asked, crouching down beside me, towelling himself with a strip of ragged cloth that I suppose he kept there for that purpose. It was my turn not to reply. It felt wrong to see him like that, against that vast expanse of emptiness, as if nakedness was not a sin, to be hid from the light of day. For a moment I almost hated him.

'What is it?' he repeated, bending down to touch my hair. His hand was so cold too that I shivered. I wanted to cry out at him, 'Will you leave me as well? Will we become enemies like the others were?' but I was afraid to.

'Hush now, my love,' he said soothingly, 'hush now. 'Tis not that bad.' He was smoothing down my back, cupping my haunches with his hand. Long fine hands he had, strong wrists, not worker's hands. Their touch alone was my undoing, stifling questions, fears, as cloth gives warmth. He stooped over me, unfastening my clothes, long-sleeved blouse, mid-length dark skirt, all those garments with which country females at that time hid themselves. They rustled to the ground in folds until I too lay naked in the sun. 'Don't fret,' he whispered. ''Twill all come right in the end. Ain't nothing to harm us here.' He made me raise my head so I could see for myself, the empty pool, the empty shore, the empty sand hills. And yet, I swear, even with his body covering mine, I felt exposed, as if some old malevolent presence was watching us.

He stroked my spine, feeling out each bone; he touched my legs, parting them, spreading them wide so that he could reach between. 'No one else but me,' he said, his voice husky with desire. 'Lie still. I'll show 'ee what 'tis like.'

And then I could not think, or remember what thought was.

'Belong to each other, you and me,' he said, each word a kiss, each word an embrace, the words themselves like sparks, heady as wine. 'Always have done, since the first. Hold on to that. Nothing else.' And then he was entering me, first slow, like silk, then fast, like flame, my body ground into the sand, his heavy on mine. And at the end, 'Like this,' he said rearing up so that I could look at him where he entered me, pale flesh to flesh, caught between the dark mats of hair, 'Here we be, me here, you there, joined like one. We'm safe here, joined like this.'

And in that rush of joy I believed him.

I never did swim with him in that pit pool although he tried to tempt me to. 'Makes you wonder,' he told me, laughing, 'all that empty sky, no one but God. But a nice friendly God, none of your Methodist fire and brimstone.' He turned me round, brushing the sand off my back. 'Want to show 'ee to the sun,' he said, 'want to show 'ee off to everyone. Wanted to go swimming with 'ee. Used to watch 'ee on the cliffs sometimes.' He grinned at my look. 'Nought wrong with looking,' he said. 'Sleek as a seal, I thought, lady of leisure, lying on the beach. Wondered what 'ee did all day. Wanted to stroke 'ee, like this.

'Used to be men lived up here,' he said, 'long ago, prehistoric men they was, safe up here from the dangers in the valleys. Think I'll keep 'ee here like that, my woman, in my hut.' He tickled along my ribs. 'Some skinny woman tho' you'd be,' he said. 'I like mine with some meat on.' But when I began to protest 'Like those village girls, I suppose,' he put his finger to my lips. 'Only tried 'em on for size,' he whispered, 'told 'ee no one else but 'ee. No one else so nice to kiss, no one else so nice to fuck. Bain't no Methodist to 'ee. Made for fucking, girl, 'ee be. So why waste time.'

So he lulled me through that long afternoon. One other thing, which afterwards I was to remember. Before we left he took me into his shack, its wooden jumble surprisingly snug inside for it was covered with tar paper and the walls were sunk into the sand. There were a couple of planks for seats, a scrap of old blanket for warmth, and, underneath a tarpaulin, a locker full of books. He showed them to me almost shamefacedly, these books he spent his wages on, mining books, engineering, mathematics, a pitiful little collection I suppose and yet he was proud of them. He kept them here he told me 'out of harm's way'; he came here to read them whenever he had time. He meant of course that he couldn't study in his uncle's house; there'd be no welcome there for books, and I felt a surge of empathy.

I crouched beside him in that hut, listening to him with only part of my mind. I sympathized with his efforts to change the way he spoke (doubly difficult in these circumstances since the moorland folk were notoriously rough of speech); I understood his fetish about keeping clean; his insistence on that oversize suit and white shirt, for example, ridiculously at odds with his thick workman's boots. And I understood some of the difficulties he faced. The Cornish are a conservative sort. For someone like Em, a trip to the nearest market town could turn into an expedition fraught with peril. Any attempt then to change one's place in life was doomed from the start. Once a clayworker, always a clayworker; that was that, and God punishes those who rebel against their lot. I could appreciate what he was trying to achieve; what daunted me that day was the enormity of it. Those books are more than a symbol of the education he wants, I thought, they are his passport to escape, escape to that outside world, where he would have a chance to make something of himself. The outside world, far away from here, and me.

He was leafing through the pages, the criss-crossed pencil marks, the underlinings, showing how often they had been re-read. 'If the Cornish workers had any sense,' he was saying, 'if we had some spirit, we could put our mark on pits like this. T'other day a Welsh chap comed, came, to talk to us, told us what the miners there were aiming for, but here, he were shouted down. There's a crisis, girl, alright, all over the world, and it'll hit Cornwall hard, unless we do something about it.'

He said, "Tis the waste I mind. These clayworks are as big a waste as that old house of yours, like a sieve letting

72

water through. Clay be hosed out of the ground with great pipes. Think how much is lost. You've seen how the streams run white, like milk. And after a storm, don't Tregaran Cove turn grey? That's lost clay, washing out to sea. Them sand tips there, they should be used.' He jerked with his thumb. 'Could make something with them if we spent the time and money. Could be levelled off and seeded with grass, for sheep, not left to stand for hundreds of years afore nature does it to 'em. And the pits themselves, they're too small, the machinery's too old. Each one's owned by a little group of men who won't put money in to make things run right. They'm satisfied to sell the clay for the same old price to the same old manufacturers, who use it in the same old way. But there's a market bigger than that.' He pulled out another volume. 'Cornish clay's the finest in the world, the sort of clay they used for Chinese pottery. Kaolin's its real name, made from decaying granite. And there's more granite hereabouts than fish in the sea; the moors be riddled with it.' He hesitated. 'There's a fortune here,' he said. 'And we should take it for ourselves before some stranger comes in and takes it instead. And I say, if we let him, we'll be pitworkers all our lives. And serves us right.' Before I could reply he went on in the same intense way, 'Why should we work and dig and die and let outsiders wax fat? Yes, we do die, of cold and wet and pneumonia and pleurisy, like miners everywhere. And then when it pleases our masters, they'll turn us out. Or send us off to fight in a new war they'll make.'

His torrent of words overwhelmed me. At first I was not exactly sure what he meant. I had sympathized with his ambition, not his bitterness. And his politics were new to me. I fastened on the one thing I understood. 'You don't think there will be a war?' I cried. 'Why do you say that? My father and uncle died in the last one.'

He said bleakly, 'War's coming alright. Don't you read

the papers? Doesn't your grandma let you listen to the wireless? We'm in deep trouble everywhere, girl, over our heads. And I want to get on with my life while there's time.'

I repeat, I understood some of what he said and sensed the rest, so that understanding came later, in flashes. But like everything else about that day I came back to the thoughts that meant most – separation, leaving, loneliness. I suddenly clung to him with all my strength. I didn't have to cry out what I felt, it must have been there in every move, every line of me, as now I made love to him, feverishly, as if my yearning could never be satiated, as if my body knew what my spirit feared, as if the future was in that hut with us, threatening us. And he responded to me with equal abandon, as if he had seen the same threat.

It was late, later than we had ever been, when at last we came to the edge of the moors and took the path down to the road. Already the sun had gone under a bank of cloud and there were bats darting in the translucent sky. The twilights are long at this time of the year, the nights short. I felt how right it would have been not to have to part. We had never lain in a bed, slept together. All the familiar comforts that lovers expect we never knew. Truly like the wild animals we met and mated in the open, believing we were far from the rest of the world. But neither of us could have guessed what malice had been tracking us that day, although afterwards I felt I had.

When we reached the road, he rode on ahead, I waited for a while before slipping out. I remember feeling at ease with myself that evening, body and soul, as if I had grown into myself, had faced a crisis and come through. Perhaps I even hummed to myself, a tuneless tune, as I ran down the road, enjoying the feel of the dew, smelling the sweet hedgerow grass. I know I felt hungry, and began to imagine what I would say as Em put the food before me. 'I forgot the time,' I would lie. 'I was too engrossed in my book.' And she would grumble as she often did these days, and let me be. But when I came to the entrance of Tregaran I never went in.

I have described how Tregaran House lay close to the high road, with only a hedge separating the two. Successive centuries of remodelling had turned the main building away to face the sea and some great-grandfather had designed a new drive to sweep up with a flourish beside the great terrace. The kitchen remained in the front, where it had always been, before people had become particular about such things, opening out on to what had been an original courtyard, giving easy access to indoors, especially if one used a gap in the hedge which I knew about. But that evening some instinct made me stop. The courtyard was made of cobbled stones, roughly repaved in spots, and the hot weather had dried up all the mud, even around the drinking trough where water from the open ditch usually overflowed for the animals. Across this dry surface then, fresh clumps of white stood out like miniature pyramids, clods of clay in a line, knocked off someone's boots. Instinct made me stop. Instinct made me creep quietly to the small mullioned windows and peer in. Instinct made me guess who the man was who sat at the kitchen table talking to Em.

I could not be sure of course, but his size, his thick bull-like neck, his miner's cap shading his piggy small eyes, all helped me guess. He was sitting almost primly, knees together, brawny arms clasped across his chest, mouth shut up tight, and whatever he had just finished saying had made Em put her hands across her own mouth. Em was sitting opposite him in the lamplight so I could see her clearly. It occurred to me for the first time how old and grey she had become, although she had always been grey I suppose, and these past six years had not seemed to alter her. But whereas I had grown up, she had grown down, her back more hunched, her rheumatics more crippling. *He holds a grudge.* I thought, there can only be one miner I have heard of who holds that sort of grudge, or is mean-spirited enough to act on it. And then, in a final flash of understanding, if Joe Penhire has come ahead to tittle-tattle, why has he come so late to Tregaran, when it's the place he passes first? Unless, and that thought did make me cold, unless he went somewhere else before coming here.

I did not underestimate the danger to me. I knew, without her saying so, what Em would think, to her mind any loving a sin, and coupling out of wedlock a disgrace. And I knew where she would run first thing. There would be no point in trying to reason with her to make her change her mind. 'Duty, girl,' she would say, her mouth prim small, as if that explained it all, as if that gave her the right to ruin us. 'I brought you up for your grandma. I owes her that much.' And even if in these six years I had grown up myself, I still feared my grandmother, more perhaps because I had seen her so seldom. But I was more afraid for Phil. And so that is why I finally came to the fishing village to warn him, and how I met Jack Tregarn. And how I finally learned most of our family secrets.

I had never been to the fishing village alone, and even then it was not always safe after dark. The fishermen were up at dawn and went early to bed themselves, but their sons were not always so countrified at night, and the local pubs were often full. Even with a Depression there was money for a pint of beer, and when drunk the fisherlads were a rough bunch too. The village has changed now of course. The wharfs and canneries along the harbour are gone, or turned into souvenir shops; the cottages that were built into the cliffs are used for summer holidays, and almost all the fishing boats have disappeared. Then, I could hear the water lapping round them at their moorings, and if there had been any street lamps I could have seen them tied up along the quay, their nets and lobster pots all tidily arranged for the morning tide. The streets were slippery underfoot, narrow, smelling of fish. Sometimes when I had come visiting with Em (for she was village born), I used to watch the women carrying pans of food to the bakery to have their dinner cooked. On Christmas morning the whole village smelled of roasting fowl and goose. But now the bakery and the one general shop were shut up tight, and I had come to the centre where the Mission Hall and Methodist Chapel held pride of place, before deciding what to do next.

I knew the Tregarns lived somewhere on the other side of the village, away from us, but had no idea how far that was. The paved street stopped at the Mission Hall; beyond, there was only a dirt road with a few cottages on the landward side as the path climbed the cliff above the quay. Knowing no better I began to climb it too, steep at the best of times, doubly difficult in the dark. In places there were steps cut out, and a wooden railing had been jammed in the rock to give leverage. Soon the last of the village had been left behind and the freshening wind told me I had reached the headland, beyond which there was open cliff again. I stood straining my eyes into the dark, trying to guess where the path went. I could hear the sea on my left, the familiar deep booming of waves, and feel the wind soughing through the bushes that bent against it into umbrella shapes. I tried to remember what Em had said. When she was a child, she used to say, the boys would come up on this cliff and watch for fish. The herring came so thick that the sea would boil with them, no need to use a boat; the tides brought the shoals round the point in their thousands. From here, the boys would spend all day on guard, looking miles down channel, to the west. I thought, if he lives up here, this will be the place to find him. And, as if in answer to my thoughts, a tiny speck of light suddenly flared out through the dark, as if a lamp had been lit.

The darkness must have magnified distance, for soon the path sloped down again, and at the foot of the next incline, close to the water's edge, I came upon the place the Tregarns called home. I do not know what else to call it: house, shack, hodge-podge of outbuildings roofed with galvanize, surrounding the ruin of a main structure whose thick stone walls defied all attempts at description. A litter of machinery, nets, tar-coated timbers, broken lobster pots, made a barrier through which I tried to pick my way, and in front of the house a skeleton of an old boat upon its side served as a kind of guard-room, in which a dog stood guard.

As I approached it began to snarl, leaping up as far as its rope allowed and then falling back with a choking sound. Its ferocity forced me to stand still and the noise it made aroused more attention than I meant, although I am not sure now what I did mean. I suppose I should have considered that before. There was little I could have done, and certainly any warning I could give would come too late. When the door opened abruptly, and a yellow light from the lamp fell outside I suddenly became aware of just how late. Phil stood holding the lamp. It lit the step in front of him but when he raised it, it lit his face as well. I cried out. One eye was swollen shut, the other blackened, long bruises marked his cheeks and jaw and his mouth was cut. But before either of us could speak the man who had beaten him like that elbowed him aside.

I had wanted to meet Jack Tregarn ever since I first heard of him. I did not want to meet him now. Nor did he want to meet me. Whoever he might have thought I was, neither he nor his nephew had expected that. 'Bugger off,' he snarled. 'Get off my land. Or I'll set my dog on you.' And he strode out towards me with equal ferocity so that I thought he'd lunge at me himself.

Several things happened then all at once. Phil Tregarn dropped the lamp and leapt after him; limping perhaps would be a better word for he could not put his weight upon one leg. The dog, hearing itself mentioned, gave one last convulsive tug and snapped the cord. I dodged round the side of the boat away from its teeth and found myself trapped against the house. And in the doorway behind my back Uncle Tom stood peering out and rubbing his hands. 'I told 'ee she'd come back one day,' he mouthed into the darkness, in his unconnected way. 'I always told 'ee so. Come in, come in, Alice me dear. We'm been waiting for you.'

He seized my arm with his good hand, aiming a kick at the dog, and dragged me inside. And there I was, no way out, and Jack Tregarn blocking my escape.

He stood with hands on either side the door, a black mass, his thick fisherman's jersey adding to his bulk, legs apart, the buckle of his belt gleaming in the firelight. The rest of the room was dark and hot, for even on a summer night they kept the fire, and I thought that I would faint. Then Phil came in with a rush; Tom Tregarn cringed away and his brother picked up a brand from the open fire and relit a lamp. I was looking at Phil's older self, the whole of what Tom Tregarn should have been, and all three men were shouting at once.

I said as loudly and clearly as I could above their noise, 'Be quiet. How dare you? Leave us alone.' And to Phil, 'Are you hurt? What has happened to you? Don't let that old quarrel come between us.' While he, holding me and smoothing my hair, said almost the same thing. 'Don't matter a bit, I swear. Gossip never killed anyone, and I told the old fool so. But what about you and your grandma?'

'Never mind about she,' Jack Tregarn set the lamp down and seated himself before the fire, although every chair seemed littered with clothes. 'Tom, bring my tay.' He swiffled his head round at his brother. 'And don't be so daft. 'Tis only Miss Tregaran from the Big House, and you knows she. You and she have met before, don't 'ee remember where? As for hurt,' he turned back to me, ''ee've done the harm. And if I give him what fer, that's my bloody right, not yours.' He suddenly let out a laugh, a harsh grim laugh, and in the firelight now I could see where his face too was bruised and his gnarled cheeks cut. 'Gived it to me back,' he said. 'Well, he's grown. Let him dig his own grave. But he'll have naught more to do with 'ee, mind that; 'tis done with. No point in raking up the past to be a grief to everyone. But the past is there, can't be forgot.'

He took a pull from his mug. And when we remained stubbornly silent, 'What's all this claptrap then?' he shot out, his voice dangerously quiet, 'You've had your fun.' He looked at me. 'Don't tell me 'tis all for love,' he sneered, never taking his eyes from me. 'Don't tell me that 'twill last. Tell him that if you like. But I've heard that story twice. And when you'm through, throw him away like a toy that's broke.'

Phil kept his arm about my shoulders and began to walk me to the door, leaning on me heavily. 'Come on,' he said, ''tis over here. I'll take you home.'

'But it bain't.' Tom Tregarn piped up from the shadows where he had withdrawn. 'First Jack and she; then Alice and him. Now Phil and this one all over again. Ain't that right Zack? Ain't that the truth? Tell'un how it were when Alice'd come back late of nights, and how 'tweren't no good beating her, not when she'd made her mind up. That's what you used to say, those years ago. And weren't we all friends once before that time?'

He began to sing in a quavery voice, some Cornish song, until his brother pounded the wall with his fist, so that the tea hissed upon the coals. Tom cringed away and began to sob. 'Don't mean no harm,' he sniffed. 'Don't mean no wrong. But they be cousins like, bain't that so Zack? Bain't they be some relative?'

'Shut up,' Jack shouted. 'Hold your bloody tongue.' But it was too late. I guessed who the 'she' was, but not the 'him'.

'Your Uncle Tom told me about our taking your name and house,' I said to Phil. 'And about his friendship with the Tregaran boys. But not why they quarrelled. Better that we get it straight. Cousins he said. Are we? And how?'

Before he could answer Jack Tregarn stood up. He was as tall as his nephew and much thicker, like a tree trunk to a sapling, and his voice had the same undertone of bitterness. 'Cousins,' he said, sneering the word, 'perhaps, if the wrong side of the blanket makes it so. He be your uncle's bastard, miss, and now you know a part of it. Major Nigel Tregaran, didn't he do a favour to us, didn't he condescend? Took our sister's heart to break, just as his mother once broke mine. Why should your grandma grieve; what's she lost that we didn't first? Took us up and throwed us away, because we was only fisherfolk. Let her son do the same when he were growed. And now I suppose your turn is come.'

He looked at me with the same bleak stare. 'No love lost between your house and mine,' he said. 'Never was, nor can be. And that's the truth.'

The words were a drum beat, the echo of what Em once had said. Isn't it a truth that truth hurts? Oh God, I thought, looking from Zack to Phil as if I hadn't seen them before, is hatred all there's left when love's gone? Did my grandmother kill hope in Zack? Did she and her son spoil it for Phil and me before we were even born? And I thought, bitter myself, they left a cruel legacy. And I am heir to it.

The idea was frightening. I'm not like her, I wanted to cry. The burden of my family's deceit kept me quiet. I couldn't plead in self-defence when I was party to the evidence. And a wave of something primitive, a fierceness, possessed me to make her pay for the evil she and my uncle had caused, that by my actions I might atone for theirs.

Chapter 5

There was nothing else to say; no further reason to remain in a place where old sadness lay coiled like stale smoke. Somehow we found ourselves walking away, robot-like, without clear memory of how we came to be outside. Phil's face was masked behind its cuts and bruises; I could not tell what he thought, but I know my own thoughts surged round and round as the consequence of these former events now began to loom over us, imposing themselves anew on our lives.

By mutual consent we turned away from the cliff path towards the sea, as if we needed to be alone. I remember noticing how awkwardly Phil walked (although he never mentioned it, ignoring it just as he ignored the marks on his face caused by his uncle's fists). That gait seemed the outward expression of his inner turmoil, and I felt my heart lurch in sympathy. But I knew we would never feel right again until we spoke of it. And I knew he must speak first.

Beyond the scatter of debris around the house, an area of coarse grass and shingle opened on to a little bay, its typical half-moon shape fringed by a distant line of white where breakers came creaming over the sands. Once on the beach, with the house dwindled again to a mere pinpoint of light, Phil came to an abrupt halt, staring out to sea. And, putting my own difficulties aside, I began to concentrate on his. If I had already guessed there was some tie between our two families, more recent than historic ones I mean, had Phil? Zack's unhappy affair would not be new to him. Who else knows of his parentage? I thought. Does Em? Does my grandmother? What does 'being cousins' mean for him? I had not consciously considered marriage before, but now I did. Could cousins marry? I thought. Would he want to? Could anyone stop us if we tried? No wonder my thoughts went round and round. I can truthfully say that if in some ways I had still been a child before that night, lost in my dreams, now I had to grow up hurriedly.

When Phil spoke it was with a bleakness that made his words all the more poignant. 'Always known what I were,' he said. 'See'd it on my birth certificate. They leaves a space for the father's name, and if there bain't one, then they stamps you illegitimate, for all the world to look at. Methodists can't abide sloppiness; they want everything written down and clear, even sin. And children be worse than their parents. I had a rough growing up in the village school, until I learned to fight back. For years now, no one has called me bastard to my face. But I swear that until now no one, not even Zack, told me who my father was.' He suddenly shot a look at me. 'Zack's right,' he said. 'The past can't be changed. Sooner than you know, it's caught up with you.'

He turned back to his study of that white line of foam. 'Sorry for Alice most,' he said slowly. 'And sorry for you. Things be bad enough as they are, without dragging you down with me as well.'

I suddenly took his hand and held it tight. 'Don't,' I said, for the misery tore at me. 'It's you I want, not who you are. It's you I love, not father, uncle, family.' And for a while neither of us said anything.

'I remember Alice,' he said at last. 'Always called her that, Alice. I were four, perhaps five years old, when she died. In the great influenza epidemic. Don't remember any man about, except a sort of impression like, of someone tall who stood in front of a fireplace, and let me play with his soldier's belt. But that may be things she told me afterwards. I do remember when she stopped laughing

84

tho', and put aside them pretty frocks she wore.' He scraped in the sand with the toe of his boot. 'Never liked to see her cry; never liked her dressed in black.'

He frowned. 'In the beginning what I remember seems bright, like a sunny day. But afterwards, everything was dark.' He said, 'We lived in some big city, dunno where. Remember coming here tho', with Zack. Screamed when I saw 'un. Wouldn't go with him for all he tried. Clung to the bed post, wrapped arms and legs about it, had to pry me loose. Suppose it started us off on the wrong tack. When we crossed the Tamar in a train, over a bridge, "Open your eyes up sharp, lad," he said. "We'm home."

''Twere raining,' he said, 'and out of the windows all I could see was mist and a great dirty river and a heaving tide. Made me sick to look at it.' He began to laugh, his shoulders shaking, as if with sobs. 'Sicked all over his shoes,' he said. 'And never did feel like home. All them empty fields and lonely cottages; all that expanse of sea. Never liked the ocean after that. Always were trying to run away.'

He said, 'She were young, Alice, my mother.' He hesitated, savouring the word. 'Realize now how young, not much older than you, with laughing eyes. Deserved more out of life than be left disgraced, with a child to bring up and no money to do it with. Don't seem right to be abandoned, far from them that loved her, left to die alone.

'I remember how she used to cry sometimes,' he said softly. 'Even Zack can't know that. If your grandma did, 'twere shameful, to a poor soul who did no harm to anyone. But if your uncle was the favourite, like you say, your grandma'll not admit wrong of him. Perhaps she never knew that Alice had a child by him. Sometimes when I were a youngster I used to egg Tom on, hoping he would talk; talking like, would have eased the loss. But he never let a word drop about my father neither. 'Twas all about past days, see; your father, Alice and Tom, as if 'twere as it used to be, and they were friends.'

He squinted at the line of waves. 'If Tom knew different,' he said, "tis something he's forgotten since. Or meant to forget. Or perhaps just pieced together, and by chance hit it right. Well, 'tis a habit of his. But Zack's different.'

He said simply, almost in the same words his Uncle Tom had used, 'That be the difficulty with Zack. He meant harm. Grief's eaten him so long that one more wrong is like a goad. He charges it, fighting back, never mind what more hurt it causes him, or others.'

He said softly, 'Never heard him speak of your grandma neither, except with hate. Can't forgive she for jilting him.' He shot another look at me, his eyes gleaming in the reflected light where the moon swung low behind a cloud. 'Can't blame him,' he said. 'I'd feel the same. If it was you and me that is.'

He eased himself down on the sand, stretching his long legs out gingerly. Not knowing how to reply I sat down beside him, and began to let the dry sand trickle through my fingers, gathering up the warmth of the day, as if trying to hold it fast. The night air was warm and moist, like a greenhouse, with a splatter of cold spray on the veering wind, bringing a taste of salt to my lips, and making me think of that boat ride with Tom, how many years away that seemed. I looked about me, almost in wonderment. We are like two survivors, I thought, two little specks, left stranded after some shipwreck. And there can be no turning back.

As if echoing me, he said aloud, 'If that's all there is to that family quarrel that the old ones harp about, it needn't matter much, unless we want it to. But it isn't only us; it touches others around us. My Uncle Zack. Your grandma.'

I said, 'My grandmother doesn't care for me anyhow.

86

Why should it bother her what we think? Why should she care who your father was? She hated mine.'

'But 'tain't only past scandal,' he insisted. ''Tis fresh. And we'm the cause. She can't let that pass. And no way now to hush it up. Joe Penhire'll blab it out. Unless,' he looked thoughtful, 'unless he were in a rush to get to your folks and mine and then drank too much afterwards. Which, with luck, he did. Depends who else he saw along the way, and who else he told his story to. Depends what it'll take to silence him.

'And how much he saw,' he went on after another pause. 'Must have followed us to the pit, filthy lout; must have been watching us.'

His words suddenly conjured up that spread of blank blue, those walls of sand, that frightening expanse of space that I had sensed. I turned impulsively to Phil, and again caught his arm. 'Never'll matter to me,' I heard myself cry, 'as long as it won't alter what we had. That was good wasn't it – that wasn't sin?' And I took his head between my hands and kissed his mouth, just as once he had kissed mine.

The sea rushed forward and withdrew, the sound of its waves part of a greater mystery. Like those two survivors we clung together on the rough sand, impervious to everything, except our bodies' need. He pushed my clothes up anyhow; I fumbled with the buttons of his trousers, the rough cloth rasping against my skin. Then he was entering me with short fierce thrusts, as if to stamp himself in me, and I was arching to meet with him, rocking him within myself, and then it was true that there was nothing else.

And so we spent the night together after all, using his jacket for covering, alternately loving and sleeping the short darkness away. And when dawn came, and there was light enough to see the bruises on his back, and the great weal running down one side as if he had been lashed with a stick, we got up before anyone else was about, and came back to Tregaran House, not by the cliff path this time but along an inland road where we would be less conspicuous.

He wanted to come in with me and face my grandmother together but I begged him to go on. 'This is something I have to do myself,' I told him. 'You dealt with your Uncle Zack, I'll deal with her.'

I tried to laugh. 'Perhaps it'll not come to fisticuffs for us,' I said. But he did not smile. 'She'm clever,' he said. 'Like Zack, she's got old wounds to heal. Be careful. She'll be stronger than you think.'

He bit his lip. I knew how helpless he felt. And when he had disappeared up the moorland track, left alone I felt my own vulnerability too. But I had set myself a task. Six years of waiting had come to a head and I owed myself something. And although the thought of my grandmother still terrified me, I had discovered that there were worse things to be terrified of.

Tregaran was very still that morning, encased in mist like a Sleeping Beauty's palace, where time had been put aside. I was not to know this was the last day of the drought nor that these mists were to herald the start of a month of rain and storm. Then, I felt only that I was returning to some place that was about to be startled into wakefulness, and I was destined to be the catalyst.

Em was already in her usual place in the kitchen, at the long deal table. For a while, unseen, I watched her through the windows as she sat and braided her hair into its two coils. I thought how long ago it was since that party day when I had watched her like this. And I thought also of the many times, too many to count, that I had sat there in that room with her as she went about our everyday life. I thought, suddenly sad, I shall never sit there with her like that again, helping her cook, listening to the wireless, toasting bread in front of the fire, joining in her hymns. The words of one rang in my ears:

> Lead kindly light, amid the encircling gloom
> Lead thou me on;
> The night is dark, and I am far from home

I thought, once when I was a little girl, I longed for her to comfort and reassure me. She betrayed me then, just as she betrayed me last night. But I no longer mind. And so, when I was done with watching, I turned and went up the stairs to my grandmother's room. Em's hymns would be of no use there.

I had seldom ventured into the wing where grandmother spent most of her time and she had seldom imposed herself on me in the kitchen, except perhaps once or twice a year at some occasion she could not prevent. Usually I would have tiptoed past to avoid making my presence known, but now I approached the passage boldly and walked along. This part of the house had been remodelled in the last century so that the rooms opening off the corridor had a view of the sea. They were unexpectedly bright and modern, unlike the older part where I slept, which still had a medieval feel. The rooms were better furnished too, more comfortable than I was used to, and there must have been some sort of heating system, since the air was hot, much too hot for summer. I thought, suddenly angry, but in winter Em and I would have been glad to have shared in it. At one side of the corridor was a line of bottles, covered discreetly with a cloth. I looked at them curiously. I knew who drank their contents. I knew how Em ordered them from Plymouth, by the crate, to avoid embarrassment from local merchants. Now I only hoped it was too early in the morning for my grandmother to have started on the first one of the day.

Her sitting room was large, holding all the good pieces of furniture that had not been sold. Its door stood ajar, and as I approached she must have heard my footsteps over the carpeting. 'Is that you, Em?' she cried. 'Has she returned? What else have you found out, eh?'

My grandmother's voice had not changed, was as sharp and petulant as I remembered. And when I did not reply, 'Answer me, you idiot. Is she back, or shall we send out a search party again?'

I heard a banging noise, as if she were thumping on the floor with a stick. 'And when she comes in, tell the slut I'll see her dead before I put up with such behaviour in my house. Tell her . . .'

I took a deep breath to steady myself. 'Tell her so yourself,' I said. And I pushed the door wide and went in.

She was up and dressed although I had never known her leave her bed so soon before. She was seated before a fire, in a high-backed chair, with a stool to support her legs (for she suffered from arthritic attacks that made walking painful). It struck me as strange that again it was her little feet I noticed first, for they were propped up, sticking out at me as if unattached to her. It was hard to sort out where the chair began and where she did, for its dull red blended with the colour of her clothes, and they were draped artistically to hide her shape with a variety of scarves and shawls. But nothing could hide the fullness of her face, nor the deep creases around her eyes. They looked out at me like some animal trapped by the light. Yet her glance was as alert and hard, her hair was as black, as six years before. And her dislike for me was as deep.

'Here I am,' I said unnecessarily, a slight tremor in my voice betraying my nervousness. 'No need to use Em as a messenger. I'll tell you where I've been, and gladly. If you'd ever bothered to ask, I'd have told you before. I've been with Phil Tregarn. Last night I was with him at his uncle's house. Jack Tregarn that is,' I said, as the silence stretched before us like a rug unrolling out its length. 'I think you remember him.'

She had been reading some paper, and now she crunched it up. It did not occur to me until later what a shock it must have been for her to see me there, and how perhaps my very presence must have appeared like a gust of cold air in that hothouse atmosphere. For a moment she seemed to sag under the effect, slumping under her wraps as if I had dealt her a body blow. And perhaps I had. My vitality must have seemed all the more striking in contrast to her age, and she must have felt and resented it. I felt a flash of pity for her. I had feared her all my life, and yet, had she ever given me the chance, I could have loved her with all the love a lonely child can give.

'I'm sorry, grandmother,' I began awkwardly, then stopped. That was a lie. I felt no sorrow for anything, only joy. And the word 'grandmother' made her shudder again. I'm not sure I had ever called her it before, and she obviously did not like to have me use it. With an effort that was plainly visible, she straightened herself and began to arrange her scarves, patting them into place with her ringed fingers. 'Phil Tregarn, eh,' was all she said. 'The nephew. Son of that sister Alice they all adored. Well, well, I am surprised. You could have aimed higher than that. You must have been hard up.'

Her casual, almost uninterested tone was so different from what I had expected that I was stunned. It was as if she did not really care what I had done, only with whom I had done it, and was more distressed at my lack of taste than any possible disgrace. In fact, the way she shook her head suggested surprise that I had let myself be caught red-handed, like a naughty child in some nursery crime. Her unexpected frankness shocked me more than anger would have done. Anger I could have handled.

'Your father was a fool,' she went on, 'that's something you must have inherited. Along with your mother's sluttish ways.' She began to smooth the paper, folding it neatly. 'But I told you once before I'll not have you making a spectacle of yourself. I'll not have you running wild at my expense.'

Again, there was nothing of morality or reproach in her

voice; all was clearly and coldly practical. I had no weapons to use against it, except one. I made myself look at her, challenging that coldness with like coldness. 'The Tregarns were good enough for you once,' I heard myself say, in a voice that matched hers. 'And for your son. So why not for me?'

It was another body blow and I saw its mark. But she knew how to parry it. And I was young. I made the mistake of putting all my cards out at one time. 'The Tregarns were once worth the twice of us,' I cried, 'and Phil is worth twice his Uncle Zack. I love him. And he loves me. Zack . . .'

'Don't talk to me about Jack Tregarn,' she interrupted me, so loudly that his name seemed to ring across the room. Her black eyes snapped. 'Don't ever mention him in this house. Fool.' She let her voice sink back to its normal tone, and tossed her head. But I saw the beads of sweat along the hairline. 'What do you know about him; what do you know about anything?'

She reached for her cane and began to lever herself up, a great mountain of flesh in which her will, her spirit, were imprisoned. 'And what do you know about the Tregarns, except things they've fed you? Oh yes, I know they were once lords of the manor and so forth, knights in armour and similar romantic twaddle. All that was lost centuries ago. We took over from them, and we mean to keep what we won.' She made a gesture of flicking away a speck of dust. 'The winner wins; the loser loses,' she said. 'That's the way it's always been since the world began. Tell that to Phil Tregarn.'

She thumped with her stick. 'Look around you, girl,' she cried. 'See this house, see these lands. I own them still, don't I? The Tregaran estate belongs to us, and when I die, it will be yours. Unless you throw it away.' She took up the paper she had been folding and shook it at me. 'That's my will,' she said. 'I've been reading it. My sons are dead. The only heir I have is you, a trick of fate I could have done without. But don't count on anything. I can write you out as easily as I wrote you in.'

She looked at me, her eyes dark and impenetrable. 'Go live with Phil Tregarn if you want,' she said. 'Try life in a hut as a clayworker's woman, see how long love lasts. Oh, I already know about him, all that I need to know.' She overrode what I was trying to explain. 'Phil Tregarn, the rebel, the misfit, who's appealed to your sense of adventure I suppose. The little upstart who thinks a few books will drag him out of the mud; who thinks a few smart phrases will make him a leader of men.' She gave a snort of disgust.

'I suppose he hopes to retrieve the family fortunes by seducing you,' she said. 'That's nothing new. We played that same game ourselves five hundred years ago. But these days, seduction leads to only one thing, and I'll not have any bastard brats in Tregaran.' And again her cynicism silenced me.

She followed up her advantage, her voice unexpectedly softening. 'But I'll tell you who was a man,' she said. 'Twice his Uncle Zack! Girl, you never saw Zack when he was young. You have no idea what he was like or how it was with him.'

She said, 'I could tell you what love was, and how I gave it up. Why, you ask? I'll tell you that too. For this.'

She gestured again about her, taking in the house, the woods, the land. 'Oh, your grandfather was a good man and Tregaran in those days was a show place. I thought I'd relinquish it all just to be with Zack. There, I'll admit that much. Do you think I was always like this?' She struck herself upon the breast, as fiercely contemptuous of herself as she had often been with me. 'Wasn't I inexperienced, eager, romantic, like you? Didn't I marry young, before I knew what loving was? But I also had common sense. I knew how to break things off before too late.

'You think that was easy for me, girl,' she went on, 'you think I didn't suffer? You're wrong. I know what I felt; I know what Jack felt. And when my husband found out, God help me, I know what he felt as well.

'Your father was the result,' she said blankly. 'My husband made sure that I knew what my duty was too. Child of love,' she spat out the word, 'or child of hate. Take your pick what your father was for me. But he was my husband's son; my husband took care of that, whether I wanted one or not, conceived in connubial bliss or connubial rape, who could say what it was. But connubial, no by-blow for him, or me, dropped in some hayrick.'

And for a second time I felt old passions surge around me like a wave.

She looked at me. 'But never tell me I don't know Zack Tregarn,' she said. 'Or the difference between duty and love. I learned the hard way. So will you.'

'*She'm clever*,' Phil had said. Now I was to learn how clever.

She stood there on her little feet, balancing upon her cane. 'Come here, girl,' she said into that cruel silence that engulfed us. And as I approached reluctantly, 'I won't bite. I need someone to lean on.' She put her hand upon my shoulder, the first time I ever remember her touching me, and pressing heavily with all her weight she began to shuffle towards the windows. The sun had not come out today, and the trees stood out like dark shapes against the mist. 'I underestimated you,' she said abruptly, into that greyness. 'You aren't as shallow as your mother after all. She was a flippety sort, not worthy of this place. And your father never cared for Tregaran. He used to say that it was a prison. Nigel was the only one who loved and wanted it. If he had lived we wouldn't be in the difficulties we are today.'

She burst out passionately, 'Nigel never should have died. Your father muffed that just as he muffed everything.

94

Nigel never would have married beneath him like your father did; Nigel would never have left me with an orphan girl to bring up. He'd have given me a real heir, had he lived.'

She looked at me belligerently as if defying me to contradict. It was the only time she ever hinted at my uncle's part in that old sadness, and the ambiguity was such I didn't have the heart to challenge her. And when it was clear that I would remain silent, 'We've had a long run here, girl,' she said, 'longer than the Tregarns had. I told you once the rest was up to you.'

Now she pivoted round on those ridiculously slender feet, and eyed me, as if coming to some decision. Her expression changed, became almost conspiratorial. 'I've been waiting for you to grow up,' she said, 'and I won't deny I've been caught short. I never thought you'd turn out with so much spirit, such a sullen, secretive little thing you were, without a speck of charm. Well, you've proved me wrong. There must be a few of the family genes tucked in somewhere, although God knows your father never inherited them.' She tapped the floor with her stick, not exactly impatiently but as if to emphasize some point in an argument. 'You remind me of myself,' she went on. 'Strange, isn't it, this thing called inheritance? I wouldn't say we shared anything, you and I; not looks, manners, mannerisms, not a thing I could put a finger on, and yet it's clear we do. There's a wildness there, a wantonness, that's cropped up. That's the thing we share; that's what we both have in common, the thing we have to live with. And down.'

And of all the things that were said that day, for me this was the worst.

'Well, you've had your little fling,' she said, after what seemed a hundred years, while I fought myself not to scream denial. 'It'll pass. Oh, don't be a goose. You can do better than furtive loving in a hedgerow; you're meant for greater things. Just because you've lived under Em's shadow all your life doesn't mean you have to take her preaching seriously. Tregaran House may be set down in a backwater, but we don't live in the Middle Ages. Besides, haven't you realized it yet? Tregarans are above the law. We set the pace here, not follow it; no Methodist hypocrisy for us, thank you. And when the fun's played out, then we adjust and survive. I don't deny that Tregaran is sinking fast; I know what people say, that since Nigel's death I've not managed the estate as I ought, that I've ruined everything and nothing's gone right. Perhaps. But it was only money that was missing. Marry money, girl, and we're saved.

'You've come of age in a rush,' she said. 'That's typical of all the Tregarans I've known, cold-blooded men and passionate women. Don't fret. We'll find you a husband soon to take care of you.' And she put her hand upon my cheek as if to stroke away the offence implicit in her words.

And 'No,' I said. But I did not know then, and do not know now, if it was denial of her marriage plan that I meant, or denial of our common heritage.

Nor can I explain how much effort it took to refuse her. Her softened voice, her appeal for help, had made her strangely likeable. She made me feel guilty, as if refusing her would be unkind, would make me as insensitive as I had always thought she was. 'Look how much I love this house,' she seemed to say. 'You feel the same. My loss, my disappointment, is repeated in you, your life has become the continuation of mine. That is something too we share.'

Taking a big breath, I pushed her aside. At the time it seemed one of the hardest things I had ever done. I remember how clinging her hands were, as if she needed support. 'I can't,' I repeated. And when she raised her eyebrows frowningly, I rushed rashly into untruth. 'We are promised,' I began.

'Promised?' She lunged at the word, as if she knew I exaggerated, for what were those promises but vague hopes and dreams? 'If he promised you anything, he's as big a fool as you.' She banged her stick, the mood broken. 'What can he give you, girl? What does he have to offer you?' She smiled her shrewd self-knowing smile. 'Children playing with fire.'

She said, in her original cold, cynical voice, 'I know what you were up to on the moors. Flame-hot. Well, village boys like that, it's all they know. But they soon tire of it, like other men. Give loving for free, girl, and you end up as his mother did, with no one but yourself to blame.

'It can be hushed up this time,' she said, after letting that thought sink in. 'It's easy to buy off the Joe Penhires of this world. Show a pound note or two, he'll hold his tongue, if he knows what's good for him. There's nothing in this world that can't be bought. Even love,' she said.

She gestured with her stick again. 'Tell Em I need her,' she said. 'You, you stay indoors until I give you permission to go out. Get yourself tidied up; get some new clothes. You look like a rag-bag.' And as I turned to leave, 'Remember, you are still under age,' she said softly, her voice a sliver of sound that echoed more loudly than her previous shout. 'You'd not want me to consult the law. And this is the only home you've had. You owe me something, for your father's sake if not your own. The Tregaran name is still worth more than any other in this part of the world. Remember it can protect as well as destroy. So don't throw it away.'

I remember every word she said that day; the bargain she offered, the threat she implied. I remember how she looked, less than her seventy years or so, and yet much more, as if she were set outside time, and we were part of some age-old feminine conspiracy. It was the first glimpse I ever had of what she must have been as a young woman herself, and how her mind worked, so much at odds with that simple Cornish world I knew that to her we must have appeared an anachronism. As for myself, brought up on sin and old-fashioned fire and brimstone, I had expected to be smothered with guilt. Her offhand approach took guilt away, reduced sin to a passing inconvenience, like a case of measles. Conversely, her cynicism made her seem more 'contemporary', was that the word? more practical than I was. It proved, I suppose, that arrogance was still a force to reckon with, if one could only be arrogant. And, heaven help us, I was still young enough to think that having let her have her say would be the end of it.

If her reactions surprised me, so did Em's. Em was one of those simple souls my grandmother scorned, for whom concepts like 'duty' and 'sin' were clear and precise. Any division of loyalties flustered her, and choosing my grandmother's interests over mine must have bothered her conscience. In theory, Em might have professed to enjoy the role of confessor and judge; in practice the idea of sexual sin horrified her, although in deference to her advanced maidenhood, I imagine Joe Penhire had shown some tact, glossing over the worst details, leaving them for my grandmother to fill in. In her heart I suspect Em faulted me more for involving her than for doing, well, whatever it was I was supposed to have done. Moreover, each time she began to scold, in general terms that is, remembrance of my grandmother's past silenced her. The more she tried to shift the blame, the more she showed her ambivalence. And that confused her most of all.

'The Tregarns tried to kill your great-grandda,' she cried, 'more than a hundred years agone. Claimed he were skulking on their land. Still had some that were for sale; didn't want your great-grandda buying it. Your great-grandda could have had all of 'em hanged as murderers, if he hadn't asked for clemency. And then, as thanks, didn't old Gaffer Tregarn spit out he'd liefer hang than be shut up in Bodmin gaol as proof of gratitude.'

She sighed and thrummed on the table-top with her gnarled fingers that years of hard work had bent crooked. I sensed her pity for a wrong more recent than an old murder attempt. I knew she grieved for it, even though she would never speak of it. I knew she feared that I might be caught in the same trap.

'They'll hang Zack and his nephew too, before they'm through,' she cried. She clasped her hands as if in prayer. 'Know what Phil Tregarn's just done? Comed up to Joe Penhire afore the pit, in front of everyone. Scarce could walk, and never said a word; just stripped off as if there were but the two of them; squared up good and proper, tho' the other men bet his uncle's thrashing'd slow 'un down. When Joe Penhire comed at him, wrestler's style, at a trot, stepped aside and let Joe pass; twice played 'un the same trick to make 'un mad; each time moving off the grass closer toward the pit. 'Twere already raining, pouring down, and the clay were clammed up treacle-thick. Joe's a champion wrestler, not a pass he don't know. Playing with 'un's like goading of a bull. Third time round Tregarn tried to step aside but got caught waist-high and flipped down, so hard he broke his ribs.' At my gasp of dismay, 'No real harm. Ambled forrard then, did Joe, with a girt grin, waving to the crowd, sure of hisself. Not many gets up when Joe's got 'em pinned. Tregarn heaves up to his knees, catches hold Joe's neck and pulls, head over heels the pair of them. Lands Joe on his back in the clay, he teetering like on the brink. Needed men and ropes to pull Joe out, as if he were a horse; made him out a laughing stock. Sent him slinking home without a word. The Penhires've been champion wrestlers since Cornwall began. Never thought a fisherman could best 'em, a disgrace that'll make 'em smart.

'Not that I have truck with 'un,' she hastened to add.

'But 'twill make Joe hold his tongue. And keep Tregarn out of sight. Quarrelled with his uncles too, they say. Found some lodging place up on the moors. Be out of action for a while, licking his wounds. And serve 'un right.'

Her voice lacked conviction even to my ears. She did not add, 'He be waiting there for you,' but she knew I thought it. Why else did she speak of Phil if not to give me news of him? She did say, 'Ruffled the pit owners something fierce, on edge these days in any case, nervous as cats, frightened of more trouble. Fined the two of 'em; threatened 'em with losing of their jobs, threatened 'em with the police if they moves out of line. As for wrestling, well, 'tis forbidden since, every meet cancelled, every championship, all that the pit used to sponsor, no more wrestling then for the season. That'll be another disgrace the moorlanders won't live down.' And like everything else she said, admiration and bewilderment struggled in her voice.

Several things now happened in quick succession. I put them down as they occurred, not necessarily in order of importance, although each was linked in some way. First the weather. Em had mentioned the rain, which now began in earnest, rain so fierce the soil itself seemed to sluice off in brown streams. Gales followed. Winds of hurricane force cracked branches off trees and slates off roofs, and uprooted the stand of oaks on the cliff. The sea itself seemed to boil with the highest tides of fifty years, and three boats went down before they could run to shore. These storms isolated me at Tregaran more effectively than my grandmother's threats, and kept Phil confined in his moorland hut, neither of us able to get out although of course I wanted to, worried sick how he was. And when the winds had blown themselves out, before I could leave, my grandmother sallied forth to take the law into her own hands.

Why I should have imagined the battle won I do not know. Nor why I thought she would remain passive. In fact, like a great full-sailed ship bellying into the wind, she set off to redress the harm she felt had been done. And since Joe Penhire had already been dealt with, she started first with Phil Tregarn.

Where she got the money is still a mystery to me. But she must always have had a small income, perhaps from some mine, as Phil had guessed, at least enough to keep us fed, for the estate itself could not have produced anything, years of mismanagement having reduced its worth even as farming land. Now she must have expended all her remaining wealth in one final, desperate bid. Or perhaps she sold the few things that she had hoarded, or had some stocks left over from the Crash, if they were worth anything that is. Or more likely, I think, she persuaded friends to give her cash, or obtained some banker's loan, using her plans for me as collateral. I could picture her at work now, wheedling and cajoling. And whatever the method used, suddenly there were carpenters to repair the roof; a telephone was installed, upon which she lost no time in making contact with old acquaintances from whom she had been cut off for so long. Clothes appeared for me, modern clothes, short and silkily sleek. Taking them at first for a bribe, I flung them in a wardrobe, and only afterwards tried them on, despising myself for weakening even as I became aware of how well they fitted me.

Finally, a great luxury, a car and driver were hired to take her about the countryside. Soon she was out every day, paying calls on other country houses, making her presence felt, involving herself in social events as if she had been doing this all the while, without a six years' interlude. And all with one avowed purpose: to bring me out, is that the expression? to introduce me to the public and put me on display, like some statue that a sculptor is

101

about to unveil. The most important encounter was one she did not win.

I never heard about it at the time, this second struggle on the moors. It was private, held in the small cottage where Phil had taken lodgings with an elderly widow. He only told me about it later, when other events forced him to do so, and my grandmother, naturally, having lost, never spoke of it at all. Since I think it should be told in place, I'll let him speak of it in his own words, exactly as he did afterwards. I won't try to reproduce the other things he said, or left unsaid, the contempt, the frustration that she caused, or his grudging admiration of her cleverness.

'Drove up through the mud,' he said, 'or near enough as she could get. Sent her driver in to fetch me out. And when old Mother Polgoon insisted that I couldn't move, damned if she didn't come in herself, with a hat so tall it almost knocked the pans off the kitchen shelf, and her chauffeur hanging on for dear life to haul her in. Brushed Mother Polgoon aside like chaff, pushed past into that back room where they had set up a cot, blocked the doorway, staring in.

'Didn't say naught for a while, just leaned on her stick and looked me up and down as if I were for sale. I felt a real fool too, lying there with ribs bound up like a roped sheep, and the room so small you couldn't swing a cat. "Well, Phil Tregarn," she says, "I hear you'll take on anyone. Try this for size. My granddaughter's not for you. And since she's under age, we'll see what a spot of gaol might do to calm you down."

' "Had a grandfather once," I told her, "put in gaol himself for thrashing a trespasser off his land. I'd be in good company I reckon. But since I'd not like to accuse a lady of intruding I'll ask you to leave before I forget myself."

'I started to heave myself out of bed, wrapping a cover

102

round my nakedness. "Wait," she cried. "No need for quarrel. 'Tis gone far enough as is. I've heard about you, young Tregarn. Is it true what they say, you want to make something of yourself? Looking for a fresh start perhaps, but don't know where to begin? Or where to find the cash."

'She went on staring at me, as if she couldn't turn her eyes away. "You're like your uncle, boy," she said, sudden like. "Don't ruin your life with false regrets, as he did. Begin new, some place else. The money'll be there, when you want it, in the bank, in your name."

'"And in return? Who're you trying to buy this time?" And when she had the nerve to pretend she didn't understand, "I'm not for sale," I said.

'Well, she might've had the sense to go then, but she didn't, not right off. "I know what you think you've got," she said. "A handsome face and a set of balls. Perhaps so. But she's a chit of a girl to waste them on. Plenty more where she came from. And there's plenty more like you. You'd better sell while the offer's good."

'"Get out," I said, and then I did stand up. Didn't care how I looked, nor what she saw. Let her stare all she wanted. She shrugged. "Seen it all before," she said. "Men's nakedness is nothing new for me." Again she looked me up and down. "Got a good body there, boy, despite its hammering. But it won't last, if you don't look after it. And lusting for her won't last either. Too big a gap between your life and hers, too much passion there to wait, and nothing for it to grow on."

'And when she was gone, stumping out with her stick, like a great black shadow, I dragged myself out the back and vomited over the wall, as if 'twere tearing my heart out.'

I never knew what effect this meeting had on her, whether she were shocked by it, or impressed, but the results of her other interviews soon brought results. In a short while her calls were returned; cars began to pull into our drive; the telephone rang, reluctantly answered by Em, who held it away from her mouth and shouted into it as if it were an ear trumpet. Invitations arrived, for teas and dinners and drinks, for 'cocktails', American style, a drift of little white pieces of cardboard, all formally engraved as was the custom for even the most casual of events. The car and chauffeur were trundled out daily and I was dragged along with them.

I see myself clearly now, sulky-mouthed, long-haired (most of my contemporaries wore their hair cropped short), long-legged and gawky, still too tall and awkward for my new clothes. I watch myself trail behind as I had done those years ago, nothing to say, nothing to add to a conversation that centred about horses and dogs, or the price of things, or local affairs, nothing world shattering or relevant. Who was there to talk about books, or the state of the universe, or politics, as Phil Tregarn had done? I see my grandmother, valiantly keeping up a stream of chat while covering up my silences; I see my hosts and hostesses pretend not to notice. Vivacious still, full of charm, my grandmother eclipsed me at every turn, the sort of woman of whom people said, 'Isn't she marvellous? At her age.' To give her credit I think she tried to make me part of things, but I was stubbornly resistant. All I wanted was to be left in peace; all I waited for was him. I still believed we would triumph in the end; I still felt that virtue was its own reward. My grandmother waited too, knowing differently.

Here I must mention one of the places we began to visit, an old county house, recently restored by its new owners. They were the sort of people my grandmother would once have ignored, a large and cheerfully vulgar family who had come to settle in Cornwall a few years before. Their delight in being rich was only matched by the pleasure in their new title, and they made sure to mention both frequently and unabashedly. Sir Edward Gatering, the father, was a stout, redfaced man, middle-aged and hearty, fond of striding about in tweeds, which he believed suited his role of country squire. When I heard that he had just bought the main part of the mine where Phil worked, I was intrigued despite myself, a fact my grandmother noticed, although perhaps not knowing the reason why. She herself made no secret of her thoughts. 'I knew Carnaze House well once,' she used to say each time we left. 'When I was a girl, it was famous for its hunt balls. These Gaterings,' she would rub her fingertips as if shaking off crumbs, 'may not know a huntsman from a rat catcher, but they're wealthy enough to buy us up, horses, hounds, huntsmen and all.'

Sir Edward had two things that interested her, and like a hound herself she did not mean to lose their scent. One was money, the other sons. And although I guessed what her plan was, I thought the idea preposterous. I underestimated her too, I think. I never realized how tenacious she could be, when pressed. And I never realized the worth of what she was offering.

Chapter 6

The third thing was the most important, in real terms that is. I am speaking of the strike in the claypit, the strike Phil Tregarn organized and Sir Edward Gatering put down. I heard it mentioned first during one of our visits to the Gaterings, a biased account, since Sir Edward was now the biggest owner and took his position seriously. I am not sure how much he knew about Phil and me, perhaps nothing in the beginning, although afterwards I suspected he knew more than he revealed, and there was no doubt he identified Phil as the ringleader. The news of this strike troubled me. Of course I was afraid for Phil. It was clear to me that if real trouble broke out he would be blamed. But I also was afraid for myself. I felt torn between him and his opponents, and I resented it. I rejected everything that made new obstacles to our happiness, and was angry that he seemed not to mind. But most of all I wanted Phil in his entirety. I did not mean to share him with a group of men whose rights and wrongs meant nothing to me. I should have guessed how deeply committed he felt; I should have trusted his judgement.

Phil made no attempt to hide his involvement, but he relied on me to understand. And if I look back now to that period, I see the strike as part of the universal unrest that was already invading our quiet corner of the world. I am speaking symbolically, for it was purely a local affair, at first that is, and, ironically, it was not politics that brought things to a head, it was stubbornness.

I have mentioned before how strange, perhaps mysterious, the claymining community used to seem, keeping to itself, intermarrying, abiding by its own rules and laws.

Even Phil, who had been working there all these years, had remained an outsider, ignorant of their ways, never making friends, until he went to live with them. Only then could he understand their unique mix of generosity and pride. I know what he felt because he wrote me. Well, we had no other way to communicate, he still injured, I shut in, under my grandmother's careful watch. I have kept all of his letters from that time, only a few, somehow sent through the post, and somehow reaching me without interception. (Perhaps my grandmother thought he couldn't write and so never expected he would try! Otherwise she never would have let those letters through.) Today their creases are almost worn thin with frequent handling, but I know the contents by heart, those first and only letters I received from him. I used to read them over and over, looking for proof of his feelings for me. I was still too young to take the act of writing itself as a gift, his way of sharing his new life. Instead I remember my dislike of what he wrote, seeing it too clearly as a threat, agreeing with my grandmother and her friends that meddling in claywork affairs was a mistake.

'Until now,' Phil wrote, 'I never really knew how the clayworkers lived. Now, contrariwise, they've accepted me, as if by beating one of them I've proved myself.'

His handwriting was large, the letters carefully formed and rounded like a child's, the sort of writing that digs determinedly into the page, like cutting out runes in stone. The style was surprisingly terse, just like the way he spoke, so that I could almost imagine his sitting in front of me and talking. It was the opposite of my own literary style, and although in time I came to admire it, then I was disappointed. I was looking for a love letter; it was a different sort of emotion that he described.

'They live near the pit, as close as they can get, and they eat, sleep, talk, think clay, as if 'twere glued to them, as perhaps 'tis, like another skin. Their cottages are 'tithed';

that means, linked to the job. Lose the job, your home's lost too, and no likelihood of replacing it. Up here, the pit controls everything. It owns the houses, and the people who live in them; it built the lines of shacks, leaning together like pit props, and it keeps 'em filled. Mother Polgoon (she likes to be called that) is better off than most. She lives at the end of the row, facing the moor; she gets the brunt of the east wind but has more space, an added-on lean-to, where I live. Otherwise 'tis like the rest, one room up, one down, and a privy at the back. When her husband died she should have been turned out, except her son took his father's place and rose to be a "captain" or foreman at the works, so they let her bide. But she never had a penny for the way her husband died, not his fault, an old tip collapsed and buried him. So to my mind she deserves some luck. She likes nursing me; it gives her something to do and makes her feel important.'

There was a blot of ink at this point as if he had shaken his pen impatiently. It made me imagine how he would have paused here and grinned, expecting me to contradict him. 'Now if 'twere you,' he would have said, ''twould be different. I'd not want you by my bed just as a nurse. I'd want you in it.'

'The neighbours resent her tho',' he continued. 'Say she puts on airs. Poor thing. The truth is having a lodger gives her more cash than they have, and they're envious. Their wage is small, less than it was five years ago, under four pound a week, too low to keep a family. They put their children in the pit as soon as the law allows, or sooner, while the women, all crippled up with rheumatism, work in their "holdings" as they call their plots of ground, although God knows what they hold, the soil's too poor and thin to grow much. But all the cottages have their little strip of "garden", for potatoes, onions, things like that. They make a good "leeky" pasty here, made of leeks that is, without the meat. Sometimes in wintertime those greens are the only thing they have to eat. That, and the pigs they keep, the sties jammed up against the house. I thought a fisherman's life was hard, and Zack's place was no palace, but at least most fishermen own their boats, and the sea's free for whatever anyone can catch. These clayworkers own nothing at all. And they live in fear of losing even that.'

'The second thing I've found out,' he wrote another time, 'is what stirs them up. They don't care for ideas. I could talk for a week about workers' rights; wouldn't mean a thing, water off a duck's back. But touch them where it counts, they'll fight like tigers for what they think is theirs. They may be slow and quiet; cantankerous, suspicious even of each other, and jealous, like children, not knowing what's good for them. But when it affects all of them, they're as tight as ticks. Know what started it? That match with Joe. Not what we fought about, of course, Joe never told them that, and they'd think it daft; nor who won, they don't seem to mind that much. What's riled them is the way wrestling itself has been put down, forbidden like, to keep the peace. They don't see it that way at all. Wrestling's their favourite sport, the only thing they care about. It's their obsession, just as you are with me.'

There in the last sentence was what I had been looking for. But I felt, I can't explain, that it had been tacked on, just to mollify me. Although I did not actually let the thought clarify, I began to wish that he would write less about these new friends of his, and more about us and our plans. I make no excuses for my childishness, as perhaps it was; it was what I felt. And it nagged in secret.

Phil's analysis may seem odd in retrospect, capricious even, lacking substance. And of course the reason may seem trivial by modern standards, although workers since have often gone on strike over even lesser things. But in the summer of 1934, amid the welter of workers' claims and socialist ideas, the Cornish miners chose to revolt over wrestling and its ancient laws. Yet it was always more than that. Unable perhaps to agree among themselves, they chose Cornwall and Cornish rights for their stand, a splendid Quixotic gesture that suited them.

Today it would be true to say that the clayworks are run like big industry everywhere. Its offices are nondescript, miniature skyscrapers of brick and glass, dominating the landscape; its lorries rumble along new roads; its fleet of cargo ships clog the small ports. But there was a time when it might have become what Phil envisaged, a Cornish venture, controlled and managed by Cornishmen, providing work for other Cornish when the fishing and tin-mining disappeared. And whatever the outwardly simple causes of the strike, this greater issue underlay them.

I have said I heard about the first protest from Sir Edward Gatering, and he himself made light of it, finding the country simplicity of these locals amusingly different from his own northern mill hands. But it was not a matter to laugh away. Soon everyone was talking about it, and offering advice, a better way to kill off unwanted gossip than my grandmother's bribes. No one ever remembered the miners holding a rally before, certainly not one to protest. They had always hidden what they felt, like animals hiding pain. And their version of a protest meeting was so odd that no wonder it puzzled Sir Edward.

It seemed that when the work day had finished, they had not gone home as they always did, but had just stood about in small groups, outside the pit, on that white quartz track I remembered. They didn't say much, waiting there in their clay-caked clothes; only muttering approval and nodding their heads when one of their companions stepped out from their ranks. He would strike a stance, make a few typical wrestling passes and withdraw, as if taking part in some elaborate ritual dance. No one actually began to fight; everything was kept within the letter of the law, but the way the men mimed the wrestling moves (if that's the word) almost with an Oriental grace, showed what they were feeling. It was as if they wore masks, these stiff, heavy men with their stiff, heavy faces. Cornish wrestling is a special skill, suited to the men who invented it, and adapted to their own style. Like everything that comes from the roots of things it had its own special beauty. And that mutter of approval came from the heart; was forced out like the rumble of distant thunder, deep and foreboding. It made the local pit owners flinch.

Sir Edward didn't volunteer what he thought of his fellow partners, but his silence was suggestive. I already knew a little about them from what Phil had said and guessed the rest. Most of them were small-town businessmen, (wasn't that Phil's name for them?) cautious, shortsighted men, whose only concern was to get out their money's worth and run. They would have considered themselves kind, God-fearing; would have been horrified to think women and children went hungry because of their meanness. Didn't they support the Chapel generously? Didn't their subscriptions pay for special treats, like summer outings, and picnic teas for the workers' families? Their sentimental hypocrisy must have irritated Sir Edward as much as it did Phil, as much as their habitual deference to the gentry class, who had previously given them their financial backing. It was strange, I suppose, that although Sir Edward was on the other side, the young man who was opposing him would have understood his harshness. But it shocked Sir Edward's associates.

'Never had a strike in any of my mills,' Sir Edward had told them as he afterwards told us. He was standing then in his drawing room, legs apart, hands clasped behind his back, facing us, his guests, who listened with rapt attention. I am sure he had stood in the same way, spoken in the same way, to those partners of his, talking in his loud north-country voice that made him sound reliable and solid, despite its strange flatness. 'Always nipped trouble in the bud. Picked out the ringleaders first and sacked them quick. That put the wind up the others.'

It appeared that his companions had hesitated, not used to such blunt speaking. 'No use to pussyfoot,' he had told them, unperturbedly. 'Since the great strike of '26 the bastards have had us on the trot. But here you've got the whip hand. Houses belong to the pit, you say; put them out, then where'll they live? Sack them, where'll they find other jobs? Oh, promise them anything you like, those wrestling rights, if that's what all the fuss's about, but don't *give* anything. Promise, but never give, I say. Stand firm. And mark my words, they'll soon come round.'

Sir Edward did not add why the others had hesitated. 'Scared silly themselves,' he would have said, with a sniff. 'Frightened of falling over their own shoelaces.' In this instance he had maligned them. Their hesitation had come not because they disagreed but because they knew their fellow-Cornishmen. One had blurted out the reason. 'Heard they were singing at the pit afterwards,' he had said. 'When they come out with "Trelawney", they've set their teeth.' And at Sir Edward's stare, 'Trelawney was a clergyman, imprisoned in the Tower, centuries ago, for defying a king. The Cornish rose to free him.' He had actually begun to hum himself, 'And shall Trelawney die? And shall Trelawney die? There's twenty thousand Cornishmen will know the reason why,' until someone nudged him in the arm, and he faltered into silence. 'But it's a sign,' he had insisted. 'They mean business this time. And although they'll have their wrestling back, that's not all they want. Put a foot in the door, never get it shut.'

'Show we mean business too.' Sir Edward's response had been brisk and practical. 'Call out the law. A show of force never hurt anyone.' And when they still wavered, 'Please yourselves,' he said, 'but I don't invest in mines that workmen rule. Better a show of force, I say, than being murdered in our beds.'

At that, he had looked around his drawing room at us, his friends, as shrewdly as he had looked in his study where this business meeting had originally taken place. 'I know you are impressed,' that look said. 'Wealth, luxury, you envy it. I got it by being tough. I don't give in.' And strangely enough, the man who would have understood him best was the one who was about to fight him.

'Takes a brave fool to defy a gun,' Sir Edward had finished. 'This Phil Tregarn now, he doesn't impress me as having that sort of nerve. Too young for a start, a fisherman out of his depth.' And he had laughed, a splutter of teeth behind his dark moustache, while the rest of us had smiled. 'His uncles can't control him you say; let's have a go at him ourselves.' And whatever his partners had thought they had agreed, as did his visitors in his drawing room, among whom were my grandmother and myself. And to my shame I did not contradict.

Now Phil and I had not met since that last night, partly because of the events that I have explained, partly because I had been waiting for him to sort out his own life before settling mine. And partly because of my grandmother. I could have defied her, but that would have been hard. In those days, even at sixteen, girls did not leave home. I had no money, no job or training, and nowhere else to stay in Cornwall even if I had wanted to. But one evening when she was indisposed, and had cancelled our social calls, I slipped out at dusk and went up on the moors. I was not only looking for my love that night, I was curious to see what he and the miners were about. And what I saw had much the same effect on me as it had on Edward Gatering's associates.

That evening, the miners had gathered in a natural kind of amphitheatre. It was close to the thicket where Phil and I had had our original rendezvous; in fact if we had continued downhill we would have come out on its upper slopes. I do not know what had shaped this great half-circle; perhaps it was part of one of those old hill forts, but the story was that the Methodist reformer, Wesley, had often preached there in the early days of the movement, and the place had always had a special religious significance for Methodists, which most of the miners were.

They had filled the lower part of the amphitheatre, seating themselves upon grass ledges cut into the hillside, leaving their families to spread out on the sides higher up. I don't remember exactly what was happening at the mine. I think it was functioning as usual, but there was talk of the miners closing it themselves by refusing to work there any more before the owners closed it first, and tempers were running high. It was frightening and yet exhilarating to hear a normally reticent group suddenly find its voice. From time to time one of the men would force himself to his feet. In his characteristic stiff-kneed stride, he would go to the centre of the amphitheatre floor where a make-shift stage had been built out of pit timber. Clambering up, he would begin to speak, often such an incoherent jumble of complaints and demands that it would be hard to sort out his meaning. His efforts would be greeted by cheers and applause, again a novelty that would bring him back to his senses perhaps, for he would blink rapidly in the makeshift lights and grin half-embarrassedly, before stumping back to his seat. Most of the speakers had put on their 'Sunday suits', the black heavy serge that Phil himself used to wear, and their best white shirts without the collars attached. I can't explain, but something about them touched me, like turning great lumbering cart-horses out to play, or loosing puppies in a room full of fragile objects, as if you knew they were bound to knock things over in their awkwardness. I was torn between wanting to laugh and cry. But when Phil appeared, the mood changed.

He walked slowly, almost as if by living among the miners he had begun to imitate them, and it was not until he clambered on the stage himself that I realized this was the result of the fight. I thought he seemed thinner; it was difficult to pick out his features, for the light was dim. Lanterns and kerosene lamps had been set at intervals and the wind made them flare. But when he began to speak one sensed that this was no longer a makeshift affair, with people dressed up, like a play. The women hushed their children; the children stopped their squirming and sat still, and below them, the miners crossed their arms and leaned back as they do in Chapel during a sermon. And I thought, suddenly cold, they're listening to him as if he were the man their forefathers believed.

His voice was not loud but it carried. The lilt of it was very pronounced and yet the sense of it seemed as hard as granite, even though afterwards I couldn't remember any of the arguments. I don't even think they mattered. What did matter was the energy he put into them, the force. It flowed out of him like a stream, his very body seemed to tighten with it. His intensity would have suited an evangelist sermonizing on a Mount; or a poet, one of those Cornish bards who write about the past. I don't think he even mentioned politics, although he might have. I don't remember any socialist catchwords for example, or slogans. He didn't sound at all like the Labour party candidates I heard later, dry as dust scholastics, who tried to use intellectual details to win support. He used facts of course, but they're not what I remember. Rather he reached deep into a feeling that was more fundamental than mere logic. It united his listeners in a bond, that sense of Cornish pride which seems to well up sometimes, almost without awareness, as if it is always there, waiting to be tapped. I remember he did say, 'If we could do it once we can again.' And I did hear him claim that we were more than the sum of us and, somehow, in context these ideas made sense. Yet it awed me, as if I were getting a glimpse of a different side of him, one that had nothing to do with me. And below me, the miners strained for every word, silent and intent in that August night.

I should have explained that I had come late to the meeting, and had been careful to keep myself out of sight, at the very top of the amphitheatre where a mass of bushes and stunted trees gave natural cover. I was leaning forward too, to concentrate, when someone came up behind me, so unexpectedly that I jumped and would have slipped on the steep side, had not a hand caught hold of me. 'Look out,' I heard a man's voice say sharply, 'you're on the edge.' And then as I recovered balance and stepped back, 'Well, well, here's a surprise.'

My first impression of him is very clear and I can still feel the dislike it left in me. He was not tall, stocky, dressed in a way that I was too unsophisticated to recognize as smart, dark trousers, dark jersey with a high rolled collar, casual shoes, the sort of informal clothes which the then Prince of Wales had made fashionable when he came to visit Carlyon Bay. But I did know they must have cost the earth. His voice was an educated one, I mean there was nothing of his father's northern brashness to it and it was actually the most pleasing thing about him, deep and slightly husky. Nothing else pleased me at all, the square-jawed chin with the cleft, the square hard face with its hint of a moustache, the sleek fair hair, parted in the centre. Most of all I remember how he smelt, of shaving lotion, hair cream, fresh starched linen, things like that, which, again in my ignorance, I found offensive. Phil never smelled of anything except himself.

'Are you alone?' The low voice was abrupt, the tone casual, yet I could tell somehow, perhaps by the tightening of his hold or a hint of excitement that broke through, that the question was not a casual one. It disturbed me in a different way. I didn't answer, merely tried to break his grip which had moved from my wrist to my upper arm and which tightened as I struggled. 'No need for panic; I'm here to help a lonely maiden in distress. What's your name? And why's a pretty girl like you by yourself?'

I can't explain either how these words offended me, not in themselves but the tone he used, too glib, too condescending, with a kind of false friendliness that belied itself. I was a fool ever to forget it. But when I whispered furiously for him to let go, what did he think he was doing? something about me must have alerted him in turn. 'Sorry,' he said, releasing me and standing back. 'No offence; didn't know.' Didn't know what? I thought, trying to pull my sleeves straight, trying to crane round him, for he blocked my view, too irritated to complete the sentence for myself, that I was not one of the village girls, about to be bowled over by him; that I was one of his own sort with whom he must proceed more carefully.

He peered at me through the darkness, well, perhaps he couldn't see much of my face but he knew the feel of a silk dress, and he knew what my accent sounded like. 'I'm new here,' he said suddenly, 'came down this year and been abroad. Finished university,' he added when he saw I looked blank, 'got treated to a trip to Italy and just come home. And you, who're you, where do you live?'

And when I told him, still curt and furious, the way he repeated my name told me that he had heard of me already. 'Joycelyn Tregaran, eh,' was all he said, 'then we're practically neighbours. The old man was talking about your grandmother and you the other day. Sorry to have missed you. Schools were in June and were so exhausting I felt I had to get away. Exams I mean. Catch up with you in the end they do; three years of fun and then two weeks of hell, that's the Oxford examination system for you. Got a third, that'll do, keep the old man off my back, knows I'm no ruddy scholar.'

He laughed at his joke, all the louder because I didn't.

The laughter gave him away, was coarse, almost vulgar. Oh, he himself was smooth all right, smoother than his father was, amusing, his accent right, his patter glib and smart, his clothes reminiscent of good schools and wealth. I suddenly liked his father better by contrast. At least Sir Edward never made pretence of being other than what he was. I felt that his son (I remembered now hearing about him before, this eldest son), I felt that George Gatering was all sham. If that suave mask broke, there would be something quite different underneath, something terrifyingly blank because it would be nothing like the outer man. And the veneer itself was bought, by money and influence, the way one might buy a car or a boat, or a house to impress. Or a woman.

Perhaps I am wrong; perhaps I didn't think all those things that night, perhaps they came to me later. But I do remember the dislike. And the feeling that he knew more about me than he let on. *My father was speaking of you.* What exactly had his father said? And if anything approximating the truth, why didn't George Gatering mind?

'I'm here to listen to the miners,' I told him, deliberately rude. 'So move. I can't see round you and I'd like to hear what's going on.'

'Sorry,' he said for the third time, stepping aside, 'but I think the show's over for the moment. Bit of a ham that chap, I'd say. Thought I'd stroll over too, to get a decko for myself. A character they tell me, one of those rough diamonds you find in country places these days, full of hot air like balloons. Or would you call him an ignorant savant, who has the gift of the gab but doesn't know what the hell he's saying?'

He didn't wait for my reply; he knew I wouldn't say anything. 'Dangerous gift that,' he said in a sneering way, 'saw plenty of it in Germany last year, you know. Never trust a fellow who talks too much.' And he laughed, self-deprecatingly.

He still kept his tone light and casual, social chit-chat, although underneath he was probing, testing, curious. He couldn't have known three-quarters of what he said went over my head. But I knew enough to sense that he was waiting to catch me out, so I forestalled him. 'I'm here to listen,' I said as pompously as I knew, 'and if you'd just keep quiet, I might.'

But he was right, it was too late; the speechifying was finished and the platform was crowded with miners who were deep in conference. Phil himself had disappeared, or was lost somewhere in their midst. Even as I watched, the women began to collect their wraps and shawls and gather up their children like broody hens. The men however did not leave yet. They massed together, a thick dense black against the growing darkness, and first one, then another began to hum, like a giant orchestra tuning up. When they broke out in full voice it was the most splendid thing I had ever heard.

It affected George Gatering too. 'My God,' he muttered, as if startled, 'my God, they do sing, like some damn Greek chorus. Didn't believe my old man; he said it so scared the bejesus out of his other partners that they urged him not to antagonize them.' He stood staring down himself, as if mesmerized, until he saw that I was preparing to go back the way I'd come, not willing to be seen by anyone else.

He turned then and quickly caught up with me. 'Well, Miss Tregaran, if that's what you came to hear you've had an earful. But I think my father's wrong. I think that in that mood those men would outface a regiment. As they may have to, if my father has his way.' He took my arm again. 'Another reason to leave,' he said. 'You'd not want to be caught up here then, dangerous for everyone. So if you're ready I'll walk with you.' No 'By your leave', or 'If I may', just a blunt statement, which actually I preferred to his glibness. Except he spoiled the effect by adding deliberately, 'Not a good idea to be roaming about like this, with the men all worked up, and God knows what troublemakers on the prowl, looking for more gossip.'

It was a way to let me know precisely what he'd heard, and what I might expect if I didn't cooperate, and, more important I think, that he was willing to cover for me, although why the last was something I didn't understand then. And all expressed in the inflection of his voice, the thrusting forward of that square chin which one day would develop into his father's jowls, in the sharpness of his prominent light blue eyes, as shiny as the glass eyes of a doll, bright with anticipation. And, heaven help me as a fraud, that day I went along with him, using him as the means to avoid further disgrace.

And that is why my grandmother accepted that I had disobeyed her again, and how and why George Gatering first came into my life. But why he remained there is sometimes a mystery, even to me, who permitted it.

It wasn't that I liked him at all, quite the opposite in fact, although most of the time I remained indifferent to liking or disliking. I never considered him in a personal way, or wondered what he saw in me; I never thought of him as a man, or felt any attraction for him, although I could see that other women did, and often when we went out, watched how they pushed themselves at him. Completely uninterested in him, I never thought he might be interested in me, and since he concealed his own feelings until it was too late, I did not understand that my reserve intrigued him, causing him to see it as a means of attracting him, a greater sophistication than I was capable of. The truth was I was naïve. Caught up in my own passion, presuming he knew of it, I also presumed he escorted me as a means of passing time, as a kind of joke. There was no doubt he had little enough to do except loll around or roar through the country in his motorcar. I never looked for him again. If he came, I shrugged and accepted it. And there was this advantage: with him about, my grandmother left me alone, anxious I suppose to ensure that there should be no upset to any budding involvement, as if I were the sort of girl who could slip from one love to the next like changing clothes. But there also was this, and I fault myself for it, that although I did not encourage him, neither did I discourage. That first day, I had seen at once what his usefulness would be, and I let myself hide behind it. It's not right to use someone to gain some end, but I did. It took attention away from where my true thoughts were, and that for me far outweighed any disadvantage. I repeat, I was naïve. George Gatering was not the man to let himself be used, and if there were any advantage to be gained, he would be the one to enjoy it.

He came many times in the next few days, a real suitor could not have been more flatteringly attentive. He would drive up to the front door of Tregaran in a cloud of dust and smoke from his little sports car, and sit there with his lighted pipe, languid and elegant I suppose are the words, in his white flannels and college blazer. And fuming at his impertinence, yet not knowing how to turn him away, I would wait upstairs to the last moment, making Em come limping up to fetch me. Her smiles, her, 'He'm here, he'm here,' as if his car were a chariot for a god and he were the god in it, were part of the deception's price I paid. And in the end, although I swore I would refuse, I always did come down; I always did go out with him.

My grandmother would make an appearance too, at a window or door, waving to us, the perfect grandmotherly pose. And in the evenings when I dined with her, for now she allowed me to eat with her (so she can keep check on me, I used to think, or so she can make sure my table manners aren't a disgrace) she would question me about him: where we'd gone and what he'd said, with an avidity she never tried to hide. The few times they ever met they got on splendidly. Had they been closer in age, I could have imagined that they would have enjoyed each other; their underlying coarseness would have been a bond. But when she asked me all those pointed questions I never knew what to tell her; I didn't really remember where we had been and we certainly never said much, the noise caused by the open car windows and roof luckily making conversation impossible.

One day tho' remains vividly clear. Summer was already drawing to a close and he had driven inland away from the threat of rain. He never asked me what I would like to do; sometimes I almost imagined he wanted me there just to sit and fill a space, like some cardboard figure. He always chose the route, the time, the place, and since I didn't care I let him. We must have gone through a dozen little villages, each grey and dusty and deserted, not even cats asleep on the stone steps. I was sunk down in the front seat. I hated it when he drove fast like that, changing the gears loudly and spinning the wheels to send up great dust clouds. The car, the noise, the dust all made us seem offensive, an intrusion where we weren't wanted. The last village was in one of those valleys or combes on the edge of the moors, its little straggle of houses grey and quiet, its dark slate roofs sleek like a seal. Nothing had happened there in a hundred years, nothing ever would, and we, with our clatter, were only a momentary flash, without substance. That day however was different. For one thing, there were people about, people actually walking, talking, shouting to each other, in a holiday mood. All of them were making their way to a field at the village edge where the gates already stood open. I could hear the faint sounds of a brass band, always popular at village gatherings, and from time to time there was a swell of clapping, as if someone had finished a speech. I thought George Gatering would drive on, but to my surprise he suddenly slowed and turned into the entrance of the field, making the old man who was collecting tickets jump aside. I felt even more embarrassed. Especially when he ignored the old man's shouts and pulled in smartly under the hedge to park. 'What's all this then?' he asked. 'What sort of pagan rite are we witnessing today?'

And when I told him, 'Village feast!' he laughed, his eyes china-bright, in the way I had come to distrust. 'My God, it sounds as primitive as southern Italy. Here, take that,' to the old man who came scuttling up to protest, 'that'll pay for the parking and two cups of tea, and what else, two sticky buns?'

He tossed a coin into the outstretched hand, waved aside the thanks, took me by the arm and made me come with him as he now began a tour of the field, rather like some medieval lord, smiling and waving while I scowled in his wake. Village feasts were common in Cornwall before the war; after all, it was a land of saints and religious fervour. But they were organized for women and children and were not so much religious as edible. People went to them for the food: saffron cakes and biscuits, sardine sandwiches and bread and jam, washed down with mugs of milky tea, thick with sugar. The religious part came with the hymns, which the band was continuing to thump out, interspersed with homilies from the local vicar. It was the sort of affair I instinctively avoided, and now I realized why. I hated the way people looked at us, or didn't look, pretending to act normally as if we weren't there, all the time revealing how much they were aware. I hated the way George Gatering acted towards them, as if playing a part. I couldn't decide if he did so mockingly, out of spite, to make fun of them for his own amusement. He walked up to them now as if he knew them and expected them to know him. He behaved as if this were important, shaking the bandsmen's hands (to their amazement), patting babies' cheeks, like some sort of candidate.

'What do you think you're doing?' I hissed at him when I had the chance. 'They'll think you're mad.'

'I'm practising,' he said in his cool way. 'I'm just beginning.'

'Beginning what?'

'My future.' We had returned to the car and he swung open the door on the driver's side, leaving me standing. 'Got to get used to being a country squire, like my old man. Spend the rest of my life at it.' He looked at me again with those sharp little eyes. 'And so will you.'

He was easing his thickset body under the steering wheel. 'You aren't new to it as I am. And when you inherit twice as much, won't you be glad of a little practice? And don't we make a nice couple, two bright young things, seeing to the peasantry?'

He spoke coolly, an ambiguity beneath his mockery, but the real meaning was clear. I felt myself grow red. Yet what could I say? He couldn't think that I was attracted by him; he hadn't really shown he was attracted by me. But I remembered my grandmother's enthusiasm and I knew what she would be thinking and planning.

I said again, 'You're mad. They don't want us here, acting Lord and Lady Bountiful.'

'Don't they? Does it matter what they think? Anyway I thought you enjoyed playing with the farmhands.'

It was an insult and yet he said it in such a way as to take the sting out. He was good at that.

'And if I do, what's it to you?'

He shrugged. 'Nothing, everything, depends on the point of view.' He made an impatient gesture. 'Do get in,' he said. 'Unless you'd rather walk. That would make another nice scandal wouldn't it? Local heiress left stranded.'

I said, 'What are you after? Why do you go out with me?'

He shrugged again. 'What do you want me to say? That I'm smitten with you, head over heels with your beauty, your gift of speech, your sophisticated ways, that sort of lie? Or to tell you the truth. I'm bored. And so are you.'

I began to say angrily, 'You're talking nonsense. Take me home. Don't come for me again,' when he broke in, 'Don't be more of a fool than you need be. What else is there for you? You're weighted down with that land, like an albatross. Not everyone'll want to take it on. And not everyone likes tampered goods. Think of that before you get on your high horse.'

He watched me closely. I must have grown pale for he reached over and threw open the door. 'Don't fuss,' he said, just as my grandmother might. 'Doesn't matter to me. I like a bit of spice to tart things up. So don't play the prude for me.'

Chapter 7

That night George Gatering dined with us for the first time. My grandmother invited him, of course, without consulting me, either because she sensed something was wrong or perhaps because he hinted that he wanted to come. Despite the quarrel, or rather because of it, he remained good-humoured, returning later, driving back in his evening clothes, laden with gifts, with wine and flowers and compliments, meant for her, as if he were paying court to her. And perhaps he was, or rather she to him. I remember thinking, they don't need me, as I sat between them across the dining table, like the point of some strange triangle which stretched an expanse of white, and observed their antics from a great distance. To symbolize the importance of the event, we were eating in the dining room, the only time it had been used, I think, since the sale. Except for the table itself, which had been too large to move, the room was bare, but tonight it did not look so forlorn as it usually did. True, we sat on kitchen chairs, but the curtains had been drawn to shut out the rain, and the candles in the wall sconces had been twisted in such a way as to hide the damp stains underneath. My grandmother sat at the head, I on her left, Gatering on her right. She sparkled at us as if there were twenty guests. And if George Gatering noticed how incongruous we seemed he never said so. But he noticed; nothing ever escaped those china-blue eyes.

The first drink lubricated my grandmother's charm. Soon she was revving herself up, encouraging him, swapping compliment for compliment. Each time he remarked he liked something – Em's food for example, for she had cooked a splendid meal (which makes me suspect the whole thing had been planned, otherwise where would she have obtained the food? My grandmother never would have wasted it on chance), the room itself, my great-grandfather's drive, where the car was parked – she congratulated him in turn on what his father had done and was doing at Carnaze. 'Such an improvement,' she lied unabashedly; 'it had sunk into a ruin before Sir Edward came,' as if the same couldn't be said of Tregaran. I'm sure her fulsome praise didn't deceive, but that was something else that he pretended not to notice.

My grandmother matched his stories with her own, each anecdote more ribald than the last, frankly revelling in the vulgarity, relishing it. She sent Em trotting up and down to replenish the wine from the stocks above. 'Pity you're thirty years too late,' grandmother confided, tossing her head like a girl and tapping the bottle. 'To try Tregaran cellars, that is. The Tregarans had a good nose for drink; my husband could out-swill anyone.' And when he offered gallantly to attempt to take her husband's place, sending her into childish giggles, she had him pour them both another glass 'in anticipation'. That's something else they have in common, I thought, toying with my own untasted wine. But he's flirting with the wrong woman. And I observed him with ever-growing distaste, his red face and braying laugh grating on my nerves. It was only afterwards I realized he was on edge too, twitching, fidgeting with his tie and studs. But that was afterwards, and had nothing to do with me.

The first time I became aware of his unease was when there was a strange clatter outside. It sent him jumping from his chair. 'Who's that?' he snapped, just as if he were in his own home and he had been expecting someone. I thought Em had dropped a dish and was about to say so when I heard the second sound, the clanging of the doorbell, like to wake the dead, all the more deafening because Em was refusing to answer it. I felt a shiver down my spine. Before my grandmother could protest I was out of my chair too and down the hall, George Gatering in hot pursuit.

The hall was long, running back to front across the house, and was dimly lit with just one bulb. I caught a glimpse of Em as I went by. She was crouched in a corner, her apron thrown over her head as if keeping out ghosts, the broken plate at her feet. The bell was still ringing as I drew the bolts and threw open the door, letting the rain blow in and drip on the floor. Outside on the terrace Uncle Jack was peering back at me.

He seemed bigger, burly in his oilskins and hat, like an oak tree athwart our door, just as I had seen him last athwart his own. The rain sluiced off his back and ran in puddles around his boots. 'Where's he at?' He squinted from me to Em. 'Where's my boy? They said he comed this way and I wants to get hold of him.'

'Who the hell's that?' Gatering's voice was slurred but he got the sentence out. He began to push forward, his shirt front gleaming, his tie straight, his fair hair neat, the picture of a gentleman. 'Did my father send you?' he began. Jack Tregarn brushed him aside as if he were some kind of gilded moth.

'I want Phil,' the old man insisted, talking fast, his voice full of menace. 'Afore the law gets hold of him.' And at Em's soft moan, 'Get over, missus, you must have heard. The mine's been closed, the gates be barred, and the men've come out to tear 'em down.'

'Good, good!' Beside me George Gatering visibly relaxed, suddenly becoming his father's son. The veneer cracked, the steel showed through. 'Well done,' he said. There was a triumph in his voice. 'I knew the old man would win. Just as he predicted. Let them make one wrong move, he said, I've got 'em fast. If they've attacked the gates then they've given him the excuse he wanted.'

He might have gone on to explain but Tregarn interrupted him. 'Wrong or not,' he said, 'can't be right to goad ·men on, shutting 'em out from their place of work, and baiting 'em to fight back. Don't have truck with miners myself, never did, but bain't fair play those sorts of tricks. And bain't fair neither to call in special constables to do your dirty work for you. So if you be young Gatering, tell your da I've even less truck with him. And he'll have me to answer to, if my lad's come to harm.'

Some of this tirade was lost on the younger man. I could sense his frown. 'Who's this old chap?' he must have been thinking, 'who's "this lad" of his?' when a third voice broke in, shrill as a bell, trembling imperiously. 'Get out, get out,' my grandmother screeched, 'you've no business here. And if he's about, take your precious nephew with you.'

She had suddenly appeared, moving faster than I believed possible, stumping along the wall, using her stick. She must have recognized Jack Tregarn's voice, and perhaps he recognized hers. I have no idea how long it was since they last met but the emotion that I had sensed before seemed to gather about them, doubly charged. I saw Tregarn start and peer again into the hall, as if searching for something.

When he found it he gave a little half-whistle. 'That's never you, Evelyn Tregaran,' he said, sharp as a tack. 'Well then, you know me. Last time I set foot in this house you turned me out as if I were dirt, not fit for your shoes. I've not forgotten that. But I've a reason to search for my lad. And she's the one he comed to find.'

He stabbed out a stubby forefinger at me. 'Heard he were looking for his girl,' he said. 'Silly bugger, what good's that? She's found someone else, I told him. And she has. Didn't take you long, did it?' He turned to me. 'Didn't take you long to cheat.'

'You're mad.' George Gatering had recovered himself

129

and was pushing past. 'You heard the lady of the house. Leave, before I throw you out.'

'She'm no lady,' Tregarn spoke very clearly, every word distinct. 'We've known each other too long for lies. And neither is that other little tramp. Bitches, the pair of 'em.'

He ducked abruptly as George rushed forward with his fists clenched. Then with a heave he grabbed Gatering by the shirt front, letting him dangle until the gold studs burst and rattled to the floor like cartridge shells. 'You bain't nothing but an adventurer yourself,' Tregarn said, gritting out the insults, the veins starting on his neck like cords. 'You and your da, no match for real Cornishmen. Out of my road, I know the way without your help; knowed it afore you was hatched. Go back yourself where you belong. We don't need little men like you cluttering up our land.'

They were of a size and shape, yet he seemed to tower over the younger one, holding him up, then dropping him, spilling him like a sack of wheat. 'And when I find me boy, don't think I shan't tell him.'

'Ruffian, bastard.' On his knees George Gatering was swearing in a gush of obscenity, fighting for breath, trying to struggle back into his shirt, clawing for his tie. 'Just let me get my hands on him.' Then recalling where he was and the part he was supposed to be playing: 'Mrs Tregaran, my apologies,' – the veneer in place, the pretence begun. 'Let me take you in.' She was not even listening to him; was leaning on the wall beside Em, a look on her face I had never seen before. It made her old. Despair was its name, and it was something she had long lived with.

Snatching an old mackintosh from a hook I followed Jack, shouting to him to stop. The wind took my words and blew them away, blew the rain into my eyes, drenching me before I had taken a dozen steps, reducing my shoes to pulp so that I might as well have thrown them away too. There was no sign of anyone, only darkness, wind and wet. I ran along the drive towards the road, the accusations cutting colder than the wind. Behind me I heard the car start up with a spurt of gravel; the wheels spun; I had the sense to duck behind a tree before the headlights picked me out. But George Gatering was not looking for me. I knew now what he had been waiting for and where he was going, and why. And as soon as he had passed I followed in the same direction.

I knew the short cut to the moors by heart; even so, in the dark I slipped and fell on the slippery stones. The wind was so fierce it tore the breath out of me. It lacked the force of all those other things that Uncle Jack had hurled at us: the closing of the mine, the miner's strike, Gatering's treachery, and my own, so muddled up with Phil's coming to Tregaran that however hard I ran I seemed not to be running hard enough. I couldn't imagine what Phil had wanted, if indeed he had come to find me, or what he must have thought if he had seen George there, or what he would do if Jack kept his threat to tell him if he hadn't. Even less could I predict what George Gatering had in mind, or what his role was. I only knew things looked black. But the lesson I had learned when I was ten gave me courage. *Fight back*. I meant to keep on fighting.

By the time I reached the open moor the rain had eased into a drizzle but the mist had thickened. I would have been totally lost had not a brightness begun to burn through the fog, and for lack of any other objective I followed it. And as I picked my way through the water-logged grass this light resolved into a ring of small bonfires built at intervals like beacons, around the confines of the pit. Even from a distance I began to distinguish the outline of figures massed against the glare and hear occasional shouts, eddying in gusts. There was no doubt in my mind that Jack Tregarn's news was correct, the miners were out in force, and somewhere Phil would be with them. And somewhere, on the other side, would be George Gatering, equally intent on stopping them.

I also began to make out other things that seemed out of place, two lorries for example, parked across the gravel path. Together they formed an effective barricade. Behind them steel gates had been barred shut. They were new, at least I supposed so, never having noticed them before. Coils of barbed wire were strung over the top, making climbing over impossible. The same strands of wire had been wound in loops along the gorse patches which edged the lower slopes of the sand tip continuing presumably around the whole pit, turning it into a fortress. 'That be Gatering work,' a woman shouted at me as I came up to the first set of wires. She stood, arms akimbo, threatening. 'Proper no man's land. All 'tis needed is the guns.' Behind her a group of children were throwing wood on to a fire, dragging up timber as large as themselves. I don't know who the woman was and doubt if she could have known me but even if she did it no longer seemed to matter. I went on, going more slowly, weaving through these outer ranks of women and children, some of whom seemed too young to walk, although their mothers had set them down on the ground, letting them fend for themselves. In the flickering of the flames the women's faces had a set expression I was to remember afterwards, the strained look about the eyes which suggested familiarity with fear. I was surprised to see them there at all; I hadn't thought that they would actually appear in person to support their men, or bring their families with them.

The men themselves had begun to approach the first of the lorries and were standing beside it, deep in discussion. Now they started to rock it from side to side, trying to tip it off the road, jumping up and down on the wheels and smashing the glass to get at the brakes. Eventually it began to roll, sliding down the embankment in a spray of mud, lurching on its side with a thunderous crash that sent the wheels spinning. And before it had settled they had rushed past the second truck towards the gates. There was no way round or through the gates except to undermine them. And so without delay they settled down to dig, a line of them, taking turns, first before the gates, then spreading out along the perimeter to tackle the other posts that held the wire. Most had brought their tools with them, picks, shovels, iron crowbars; some used only their hands. I came close enough to see the gleam of sweat on their bare backs, although the night was so cold. They worked hard, feverishly, as if fearful of being stopped. Digging was their occupation and they were good at it. I thought, it won't take them long to get those posts down, then what? For inside the barbed wire fence, on the other side of the gates, a different obstacle confronted them, a more difficult one, a group of men.

They wore official blue uniforms, and were spaced at intervals, guarding the gates. Even I could see how nervous they were. They paced about, keeping at a safe distance. From time to time one would break away and duck into a kind of shed, perhaps trying to make contact with head-quarters, presumably telephoning for help, for there were new telephone lines strung outside the hut, dangling in loops. And perhaps help was assured, for now they suddenly re-formed their line, and began to advance, keeping in step, their truncheons at the ready. The fires flickered down, the women beside me suddenly sucked in their breath, only the diggers kept up their steady work, paying no attention, until the blue line was level with the gates, just on the other side of the wire. Then one by one the miners downed their tools, wiping their foreheads.

Someone must have made a joke for they all began to laugh. The tension eased. I think myself, even then, that had they had time to talk, these Cornish miners and the police force, both sides probably would have come to some peaceful agreement, had not a new sound cut across the air, plainly audible in the silence.

I didn't recognize it at first, a general thrumming which gradually evolved into several different ones, of motors revving hard uphill, followed by the noise of larger vehicles changing gears. And as everyone now turned to watch, over the crest of the moor, approaching from the direction of the main road, a convoy appeared. The heavier vans were in front, rumbling from side to side, their wide wheels tearing up the clumps of grass, and spinning the mud in waves. Behind them came a small sports car, which I immediately recognized. It too weaved in and out, bucketing over the cart ruts.

The woman beside me pursed her lips, spat out the word perhaps they all had come to dread, 'Reinforcements.' It echoed like a wail, as now more lorries came lumbering into view, each loaded with another complement of men in uniform. We could see them clearly now, seated in rows on the open trucks, holding on as they bumped along, ready for action.

Then the women and children started to scatter, running like sheep; the fires, untended, began to go out; it was the turn of the miners beside the gates to shift back and forth indecisively. Only a few held firm. And as the convoy ground to a stop and the constables inside scrambled out, two figures came into focus before the gates. They were both miners and seemed to be struggling with each other, one appearing to restrain a second who grasped a stick. I was too far away to see who was who, or what the scuffle was really about, but I noticed the other miners backed away although both they and the constables inside the gates continued to shout advice. Then the picture blurred. A third figure leapt forward upon the two, there were more shouts, a general swirling effect, and finally a series of sharp cracks like a bottle bursting.

I didn't know anything about guns then; I didn't even

recognize the sound. The women did. They screamed, and began to run in earnest. Abruptly everything snapped back into focus again: the running women, the startled miners, the uniformed officers, ducking out of range before regrouping to converge upon the gates, where finally, only two men were left, one lying on the ground, from his clothes obviously a miner; the other shouting and cursing as only George Gatering could, the rifle fallen between them.

Another great wail went up. 'Who's hit?' was repeated back and forth at intervals, like an echo. 'One of ours, or one of theirs, who be it? How bad?' No one answered. The moor seemed alive with darting things, like a sea of fish. Within moments everyone had disappeared, gone underground like animals, seeking refuge in their own bolt holes. The uniformed men, the 'reinforcements' George Gatering had brought with him, milled about, only gradually taking charge. The constables inside the gates cautiously ventured out, while others scurried into the hut to report, congratulating themselves upon their 'victory'. As for myself, bewildered by this quick chain of events, uncertain what they meant and knowing myself left alone upon the moor, I gave way to panic too. I began to run, and almost without my meaning to, found myself heading for the path I'd come up, like a frightened animal.

Tregaran was bolted up itself, dark and quiet, but I knew how to get in and up to my room. My heart was racing so loud I thought it would beat through my chest and awaken everyone. But when I had stripped off my wet clothes and crawled into bed, fatigue so took hold of me that I immediately fell asleep, the dreamless sleep of the exhausted, so deep that when I woke, five minutes later, five hours, who knows, I came struggling up from some place where I had been drowning. I had slept in the same room all my life; I could not identify anything in it, not bed, not window, not door, not myself. For a moment I knew the terror of someone whose memory is lost. Then I heard the sound that must have awakened me and recognized it, a sliver of sound, scarcely that, the shifting of a window pane.

Carefully, without noise, I turned my head. There was a hand on the casement pulling it wide, a dark head followed, then shoulders, a heave, the body was inside, long clayed legs and muddy feet, sliding across the sill.

'Are you there?' the voice said. 'More importantly, are you alone? Or are you expecting someone?'

The voice was slurred, sounding almost drunk, with a hint of violence like a flash of light. I reached behind me for the lamp.

'No,' it said, 'leave be. No need to wake up the house for me.'

I could see that his hair was plastered to his skull, and when he moved his boots made squelching sounds, and his sodden clothes dripped. He must have been running fast, plunging through the undergrowth, criss-crossing the moors, looking for some bolt-hole himself. And then, almost angrily, I thought, why's he come here?

He stood there on the matting, his hands crossed on his chest as if he were hugging himself. 'Comed before,' he said, as if speech hurt. 'Seed his car, and you with him. Heard of that already, see, how you openly go off with him. Thought I'd check it for myself. Before I left, that is.

'Never meant to come back now,' he said. 'Not my style, sharing things. But thought I owed it you, as courtesy. Although 'ee didn't show me any.'

I could make out his expression now; it shocked me as much as his words.

'What's wrong?' I cried. I sat up, winding the bedsheets around my nakedness. 'What happened at the mine?'

'You don't deny you were with 'un,' he said. 'Well, if you were, ask 'un yourself; he knows. His father planned it.'

And when I still sat there, cocooned in my bed, 'Out-smarted us,' he said, 'made us look some fools. Thought we had bested 'em at their own game, working slow but not on strike. Nothing wrong with that, is there? But when they shut us out, turned us out, and we struck back, well that's something else again. That's destruction of property, trespass with intent, riot, all those little things they can get you for, charge you for and pen you up. To say nothing of being armed.'

'Who was shot?'

'No one you knowed, and he weren't hurt.' He brooded for a moment. 'I could have killed him myself,' he burst out, 'silly bugger, traipsing out with his gaffer's gun. Hadn't been used in thirty years and he didn't even know 'twere loaded. Could have got it off of 'un quiet-like; could have talked 'un round, if that other fool hadn't rushed at 'un and scared 'un into firing. Couldn't hit a barn at twenty feet in the normal way of things, hit hisself in the foot, gived the other the chance to shout out like he's being killed. Decided then 'twere time to leave, nothing more to be done, so I got out quick before they charges me with murder.'

'And who was the other fool?' Although I'd guessed.

'Who?' he mimicked me, 'why who else but Son George of course, carrying out his father's commands, the general on a white horse. Except wouldn't have happened that way at all, not with violence it wouldn't, if he hadn't brought up all those other troops; if he hadn't interfered.'

He said, 'I'd grabbed the gun; t'other poor sod would have given me 'un without protest, 'twould have been finished in an instant. But no, Son George was determined to be a hero. So there you are, mine's closed, miners shut out, and work stopped. Nothing for it but to cut and run. And won't Son George boast!'

The bitterness was back, lying there like a scarlet wound, jagged and raw. 'So what else he's got to boast

137

about?' he said, 'that he's prevented a riot, that he's stolen my girl?'

He lurched towards the bed, swaying on his feet, trying to steady himself against the footboard. 'Half a mind to show him different,' he said. 'Let him know what it feels like. Save I've never fancied other men's leavings.'

He was looking down at me, his beautiful eyes blank, devoid of colour, his face blank, like a page where the writing has been bleached out. 'God, but you'm some gorgeous,' he said, suddenly quiet, without the bitterness. 'A man could lose his sense over you. You'll take some getting over.'

I wasn't listening to him; I was looking at the floor where the mud and clay had puddled into dark stains; I was looking at his hand on the bedrail, dark and wet. Ignoring his protest I turned up the lamp, seeing now how those stains dissolved into brown and red. 'You're hurt yourself,' I cried, jumping up. 'Fool yourself, why didn't you say so?'

He didn't contradict me, stood there swaying on his feet. 'Told you the poor sod couldn't aim,' he said. He grinned. 'Nicked me, that's all. Now if it had been Son George, he'd have blown my head off.'

He was a tall man, heavier than he looked. And stubborn. It took me all my strength to persuade him to lie down on the bed. I was afraid he'd fall before I got him there and then I'd never get him up. He was shivering, with delayed shock I suppose, with cold, perhaps with relief as I covered him with blankets and pulled off his boots. 'Careful,' was all he said, as I began to ease his coat off, 'got to last me for a while. Don't cut 'un.' And for a moment he closed his eyes as I had done, perhaps sinking as quickly into as deep a sleep.

But when I spoke of hospital, doctors, for I could see where the bullet had hit, high on the arm, a long ragged tear, 'No,' he said, 'that's where they'll watch.' He twisted

138

his head to look. 'Just make me a pad until the bleeding stops. Had worse before, won't harm none.'

And after I had done with tying the knots as tight as I could, using most of his shirt, 'That'll do,' he said. 'Now for us.'

He was still lying with his eyes closed but his good hand shot out and gripped mine. 'What is he to you?' he said. 'Let's get that straight before I leave.'

I cannot reproduce the feeling underlying those few words, the menace, the pain. It struck me hard. I could not even argue. How will he believe me, I thought, with the example of all those other years of treachery? How can I convince him? Instead, 'Leave?' I challenged him in return. 'And where exactly are you leaving from?'

His reply jolted me again. 'Portsmouth,' he said. 'Some of the other lads plan to take ship. There's a train first thing in the morning. Starts from Truro; gets them there in time to sail with the tide.' He hesitated. 'All the younger men, that is.'

'The unmarried ones,' I finished for him. 'The ones without responsibilities, I suppose, who think they're free to up and go, without a thought on those left behind. Like you.'

He didn't answer.

'What makes you think you're free?' I cried. 'Just because of what your uncle told you? Didn't you think he'd got it wrong? Didn't you know I don't want Son George about? I don't ask him here? I never knew he planned to go to the mine or interfere. How could I suspect he was involved. I never want to see him again. And I don't want you to leave.'

I cried, 'Stay here until things quiet down. They'll never look for you here. In the cellars, that's the best place. You could hide there and be perfectly safe. Then go on to your uncle's. He came looking for you too, you know; he wants you back. If the mine's closed, then work for him, go on his boat. He'll take you in.'

It was easy enough to talk. Talking made things seem right, put them into perspective. He listened without comment.

'Christ,' was all he said, after a while, rubbing his hand across his eyes. 'I'm that fool myself to think I could be free of you. Look, tonight I came here first to find out; to see how things were; I spoke to Em; she could've told 'ee that at least. I wanted to explain what might happen, the dangers like, if things went wrong.'

He cried out passionately, 'I should have knowed. I should have stopped 'em; I could 'ave. And yet I were mad, too. I wanted to get even with Sir Edward, see; I wanted to tweak Son George's nose.'

He was looking at me with his eyes their most vivid blue. 'You'm right,' he said, 'I'm trapped alright. Trapped, besotted, done for. But you'm done for as well; you're stuck with me, girl, no way out for you.'

He said, 'Always did wonder how 'twould be, lying in bed with a naked girl. Always did fantasize. First, I thought, she'll take my boots, then my coat and shirt; doesn't leave me with much else. So suppose you start now with my belt, unbuckle it and draw it off. Then what's left of my shirt; made a right old mess of that. Then there're the trouser buttons see, undo 'em.' But as I reached he caught my hand and drew it down inside against the skin, where the flesh was warm and pulsatingly alive.

'Always thought she'd hold me there,' he said, his voice quickening, 'always thought she'd take me up and draw me in. That's what my naked girl would do.'

He had been stripping off the sheet, loosening it, until it fell in folds. 'There,' he said, his mouth at my neck bone, underneath the ear, 'always thought she'd have fantasies too. Hold me, she'd cry.' His arm was about my waist, the

140

fingers moving up each breast towards its tip, sliding down the spine, untying each bone until I was disjointed and limp. 'Touch me, she'd whisper, soft as a dove, lower, lower, where the flesh be white and cream; open me she'd say, like a flower, make me come alive. I do long for 'ee she'd cry, only for 'ee.'

He reared upon me, long and hard. 'And so do I,' he cried, 'so let me in, no room for anyone but me.'

Afterwards I lay crooked in his arm, empty, drained, a husk, listening to the sound of his breath fanning my cheek, hearing, far off, the constant suck and surge of the sea. Perhaps we both slept. But when he turned to me I felt a rush of hope, almost as strong as that passion previously.

'Alright girl,' he said, 'you win. I'll try to do as 'ee ask, tho' it goes against the grain to duck and hide. But for 'ee, I'll bide. Zack'll know how to arrange things; he's been on the lam hisself a dozen times.'

'And you'll work for him.' I almost clapped my hands. 'You'll go on the boat; there's a score of coves where you could bring it in and I could be waiting. We could get a cottage for ourselves, further down the coast where no one would know us.' We could do this, could do that; I urged ahead, arranging an impossible future. He let me talk and plan his life, what I wanted for us, what Jack would want. I never thought it was not what he had meant for himself. Yet he never once said, 'And when the winter comes, what then?' He never asked, 'How will you be able to live with me, how would they let you and how could I keep you if you did?' He only smoothed my hair, smiling to himself as at a dream. But after a while, 'Hush,' he said, drawing my head down to his chest. 'Listen.' I could hear his heart and mine, beating together. 'In, out,' he said, drumming with his fingers on my skin, 'in, out, in harmony.'

He rolled over on his sound side, his eyes sparkling in

the lamplight like a cat's. 'Hold the beat,' he was whispering. 'Never let 'un go. What do it matter then what be outside, if we keep time within?

'Bain't that enough, Little Miss Prim,' he said. 'You wants to have all things laid out, level and straight. It's not without that counts; 'tis all within.'

His hand was cupped over my heart, the fingers thrumming their own tempo. 'Hush now,' he said, 'keep to my tune. In, out, in, out, slow at first, now quick, quicker.' He held back, looking down at me. 'Now,' he said, and the rhythm broke over me like wine.

It was still night when he left. 'But not by the way I comed in.' He laughed at me. 'Don't 'ee know how difficult 'tis to climb with one hand?' He was pulling on his clothes anyhow, as I was mine. 'I told 'ee once long ago, perhaps 'ee've forgot, that when I comed to this house I'd come like everyone else. Well, perhaps I comed in a back way like, but I'll go out the front.'

I'd not forgotten what he said – *when I want something*. And I thought with a rush of pride, I'm the something! As for my fear that we'd been heard, 'Who else is there to hear?' he asked. 'Only two old women, fast asleep, dreaming perhaps of old past loves, like the one we have.'

He took my hand; reluctantly I followed as he went down the stairs, the boards seeming to creak in protest. He strode along the hall as if it were his until we came to the door and he drew the bolts. Outside the air was mild and sweet, laced with the smells of rain and wet grass and leaves. It was that hour before the dawn when you think the sun will never rise, and for a moment we both paused on the steps, looking instinctively towards the sea. I thought suddenly of that ancestor we shared. Had he stood like this, that last time, straining for one final glimpse, listening for it? And even afterwards, did he hear it in his inner ear, like the sound in a shell, that rush of the waves, that hidden music Phil spoke of?

142

Perhaps he felt my thought. He put his hands upon my shoulders as we came down from the terrace past the cellar door. 'Be that where 'ee shut in them other maids?' he asked. 'Christ, no wonder they had fits. I'm a miner, see, who works on top but the underground don't worry me. Yet I'd not like to be shut up there; I like a place to breathe.' He said, simply, 'I like to see a way out from where I'm put. I'll not endure prison life. I'd rather die than be locked up.'

Was it the morning wind that made my hair stir; what was it that sent shudders down my spine? He felt it too, that silence that means someone walks upon your grave. He held me again then, not saying anything, just holding tight. 'You'm some sweet Miss Prim,' he was whispering, 'and young, like a creature full of trust. You make me think of my Alice when she were left alone. I can't promise 'ee the world, my love; life's not like that. But as God made me I do believe that what we makes of ourselves stands firm like rock and cliff, so that naught can weather it. Just listen to what's within.'

He shifted, perhaps anxious to be gone, and I wanted him gone too, suddenly afraid for him in the open. 'Think of it this way,' he said, and I knew he was beginning to smile, trying to make me do the same, 'imagine you'm in that cellar alone. But imagine too that I'm there as well, keeping watch for 'ee all night. You'd not be afraid then, would 'ee? You'd like it. You'd welcome it, now tell the truth, if I were there.'

He was tickling under my ribs to make me laugh, laughing himself, smoothing down my spine. 'Perhaps I were there that last time,' he said, solemn as a judge, teasing me, 'perhaps that was what kept the others there all night long. See what you missed.' And, 'Oh God,' he said, 'see what I'll miss.' Holding me, laughing at me, encouraging me, forcing me to react to him, ousting all those apprehensions. And in the end that was how we parted, with laughter not with tears. But like the first time, it was not the end.

I watched until he had pushed through the hedge where he had scrambled as a boy. I heard his soft goodbye, then the rustle of grass as he went down the lane towards the headland. Before daybreak, I thought, he'll be back with Jack. They'll meet as friends. I thought of him climbing down the cliff past the upturned boat, the dog silent this time on its chain. I saw Tom open the cottage door. 'Come in, me dear,' he'd say, his face lit up like a moon. 'We've been waiting for 'ee to come home.'

And when I could no longer hear his footsteps I turned round myself and came up towards Tregaran House, openly, through the meadow where the grass was knee-high and still so wet that it left great splotches on my skirt. Across the horizon now, far off, was a smudge of red where, as in a flicker of an eye, the sun would suddenly spring out of the clouds like a ball. I thought, the whole world smells fresh, reborn, and new. Everything will be alright. On the terrace by the door a shape stirred; I saw the red spark of a cigar end, and above the scent of grass and leaves smelled the tobacco smoke.

George Gatering was still in his evening clothes, a white scarf tied around his neck. You'd never imagine he'd been running and scuffling in the dark. Even in the shadow I felt his smile. 'So there you are,' he was saying in a normal voice, as if we had agreed to meet and he had been expecting me. 'You've kept me waiting. Knew I couldn't have missed you.'

His voice was casual but the words were double-meant. I looked beyond him up the drive, where the vague outline of his car showed. It was tucked almost out of sight against the hedge. How long had it been there? How long had he? Careful, I told myself, stall for time; give nothing away.

'You know where I've been,' I struck first. 'And you

144

know who with. But that was earlier. Now I've been down to the beach to watch the tide. It's quiet there, and . . .'

'Quite,' he said. He flipped the cigar butt away. 'And that's a lie.' He grinned. 'I know both who you were with and what for. And where you had it.' He jerked with his thumb above his head. 'But no one else does, no one else has to, do they? Unless you want them to.'

He seized my arm in the familiar painful grip. 'No one,' he emphasized. 'Except you and me. I swear. If you do what I want.' His intensity frightened me. And his sudden laugh, harsh, knowing, was unlike his usual raucous tone. 'You wouldn't want the world to know,' he went on, 'too dangerous for him; too dangerous for you, aiding and abetting a wanted man. To say nothing of abedding him!'

'My grandmother,' I began, but he cut me short. 'Grandmother has more to lose than anyone,' he said. 'Remember that.' He gave another laugh. 'There's a verb for you to learn. Recite it after me. I know, you know, she knows, but all the rest of the world won't know. If you keep your part of the bargain.'

And when I started to ask 'What bargain?' — 'One already made and signed and sealed, my dear,' he said. 'Bugger grandmother, bugger you. She'll give in, with or without your consent. She wants the house all tidied up, you see; I want the land. She gives me the one, I'll restore the other; you're thrown in to make up weight. And that's the best marriage offer you'll ever have, sweetheart; that's your dower. One you can't refuse.'

I remember trying to say no, but the sound wouldn't come. I remember beating him off with my hands, like a bird. 'Come now,' he said, 'two can play at that game. And I'll win. You'd not want your love in prison would you, merely because you wouldn't cooperate?'

Before I could stop him he had thrown both arms around me, swooping down like a bird himself, kissing me on the mouth. I can't tell how dreadful it felt to have his tongue thrusting where my lover's had just been, or how his lips scorched like fire. But when I struggled it almost seemed to please him. He kissed me harder, pressing me against the wall, shutting off breath. And when I still resisted he drew me up the steps, half-lifting me as he himself had been lifted earlier. 'Two can play at the same game,' he repeated through flattened lips. 'Just watch. And I'm better at it than you are.'

His back was to the door; he held me easily with one hand, feeling for the bell. 'No one makes a monkey out of me,' he hissed. 'I saw Tregarn here. I saw him on the moor by the gates. I'll swear he was holding the gun when it went off. I'll swear he aimed at me. Just say the word, I'll raise the alarm, and have him caught before I've finished telephoning. And if he's hiding in those damn woods I'll prise him out, even if I have to chop down every damn tree myself.'

He was watching me closely. I closed my eyes, suddenly seeing the trap I'd made. 'But if you agree,' he tempted me, 'I won't tell. Word of honour. He goes scot-free for all I care. Just you keep your part of the pact; I'll keep mine.' He suddenly grinned again. 'No one knows who you went out with tonight. But they'll all know who brought you back.'

Before I could stop him he grasped the bell and kept his hand on it, pulling it, jerking on it as if to break the chain. Lights were coming on upstairs; there was a scuffling in the hall. Em was opening the door, her hair in long plaits down her back. 'We're home,' he was crying up the stairs to where my grandmother stood tottering on her little feet, like some Chinese doll. 'We're back. Sorry about waking you up but we want you all to share the news.' His hand was tight around my arm, my body drawn into his embrace. 'Want you all to give us joy,' playing the part of an ardent swain. 'It's agreed, Grandmother T, just as you hoped,' with his great raucous laugh and his calculating eyes, butter not melting in his mouth. Didn't he look like a king, accepting surprise and relief! I was looking at my grandmother and she at me. *We'll find a husband to take care of you.* And so she had.

It's not over yet, I thought, Phil'll be back.

But I was wrong. He never did come back. And then Em told me why.

'Never fooled me one bit,' she said. 'I opened the door to you that morning, didn't I? 'Twasn't locked on the inside. And your bed'd been slept in. Someone had been in, then out, to come back in again.'

She wouldn't look at me. I don't think I ever knew until that moment how hard she could be. 'No use crying over what's broke,' she said, 'the damage's done. Thank the good Lord you've found someone to pick the pieces up. But Tregarn's gone. Had to get away, he did, the police out hunting for him. Got a price on his head, dangerous criminal at large, wanted for violence, what's new about that? Went up country they say, by train, then overseas by boat, where, if he keeps his mouth shut, who's to know who he is. Needed money to go off quick. But,' her eyes narrowed innocently, 'where'd he get the money from?'

And then she told me where, about grandmother's offer to him and the money in the bank. Not of course as it really had been, but as she wanted me to believe it. Love can't be bought. Now I saw money could buy everything. And after that there was no point in asking anything, no point at all. And so the second parting of my life began, the second exile from love and happiness.

Chapter 8

The Bible says Rebecca waited twice seven years for Jacob; sometimes I think I waited almost as long. In the beginning I could not believe it real that Phil had gone; he seemed to hang there in the air, almost, not quite, tangible, as if, if I could just reach out, a mighty effort on my part would pluck him back. The worst was not knowing where he was; the not knowing drove me mad. That first week, first month, I haunted the post office, going there openly, morning and evening (although the postmistress had eyes like gimlets and trumpet ears and a tongue that clacked non-stop). No letters came, no messages, nothing.

Sometimes I convinced myself that the next post would bring me an address where he could be reached, or name a place where we could meet. The following day I was equally sure my grandmother had already intercepted all my mail so I would never find out. Once, certain that he had returned, I ran all the way along the cliff path to where I could look down at that jumble of a house. Even to me it seemed forlorn, as if two old men sat on either side of an empty grate and stared at space. I never went there again for news; pride kept me away. And always at the back of my mind two thoughts hammered incessantly in my brain: I don't take other men's castoffs; he used your grandmother's bribes. Somewhere, I thought, between those statements is another kind of truth. But I do not know how to get at it.

I went over and over the events of that last night, setting them out like a deck of cards, laying out each incident as if to find the missing piece that would explain what made him change his mind. As lovers do when they part, when either death or absence or death of love divides them, I tried to reconstruct what had been said, left unsaid. Had the possibility of happiness blinded me, so that when he told me, 'I can't promise you anything,' I misunderstood? Had he always meant to leave and been ashamed to confess? Had he used George Gatering as an excuse? Or in the end had it been Zack who met him at the door; not Tom. Had Zack said, 'Go on, boy, while the going's good. Time's running out. You'd be some daft to throw away what the old woman gived. As for she, them Tregarans's poison to us.'

There was a song I remembered from childhood. Em used to sing it and now it echoed in my head, like a sound that couldn't be turned off.

> Sister Ann, Sister Ann, is there anyone coming?
> Nothing but the wild wind blowing and the green grass growing.

I remember standing in the windows overlooking the lawn and seeing the rain slant across the fuchsia bushes, tattering them to shreds. I remember thinking, nothing can hurt me like this again. I remember telling myself that time would pass. But at my age time seemed to stretch to eternity. Only numbness helped. Numb, I did not feel pain or loss.

In due course time did help. Sometimes a whole day would pass without my remembering. Gradually I forced myself to kill off memories as surely as if he were really dead, and that was a terrible thing for me. But when it was finished with, then at least I was free of him. And truly numb, impervious to hurt.

And gradually too, my misfortune merged into the greater one as the whole world began to lurch towards the madness we call war. Almost without noticing, Cornwall was drawn into that chaos, as now the twentieth century closed round us, forcing us to adjust to that monstrous shadow that was eclipsing us. Sometimes when I look at photographs of that time, those sepia-coloured images of cricket teas, of tennis games, of picnics on a lawn or hunt balls, behind those vapid smiling faces, I see a look of strain, similar to that I'd seen in the miners' wives. Suddenly the young men in white flannels, and college blazers and silk scarves seem to bleach away like Cheshire cats; first their sleek black hair fades, then their trim little moustaches, then their smiling mouths, until only the outline of the smile is left. And when it is gone they are all gone too, swallowed up in that blank whiteness.

Village lads began to emerge in uniform, swaggering in front of the girls, speaking up, or back, to their 'betters' for the first time in their lives, as if wearing khaki gave them unexpected courage. And women everywhere surrendered their men, no one was safe, no one immune to loss.

We learned a new vocabulary: words like ration books, gas masks, air raids. The cliffs were mined; the beaches closed, although Tregaran Cove was left intact; foreigners from 'up country' filled our villages and towns, speaking with strange accents and making even stranger demands. Cornwall's quiet assumed new importance, making it a safety zone. Even the crown jewels were stored in Bodmin. And the more people poured in for safety, the more quickly the quiet was lost, never to be found again.

I remember how the sky was lit by the fires of bombs when Plymouth burned, like a giant Roman candle on Guy Fawkes' Night. I remember when the fishing fleet went out to France to help in the rescue at Dunkirk. Tom did not go, but Zack did. He went alone, managing his boat on his own, not the rowing one that Tom had been in, but the big one. Beneath its unpainted sides and deck the motor was still powerful and fast. He went alone, and came back alone, and never spoke of it to anyone. But it was the last time he went to sea. Afterwards, he drew his boat up onshore, alongside that other rotting hull, chained it like the mangy dog, and left it for the children to point out the bullet holes. And when we saw the survivors come ashore, grey-faced with shock, huddled in blankets, we knew what true numbness was, and why Zack for one never spoke of it.

My grandmother shut all knowledge out. Like others of her age and class she could not accept another war after the one that had killed her sons. When the little pleasures she had come to enjoy, the motor car, the chauffeur, the round of Edwardian festivities ended, she shrugged and withdrew into her shell. But the rest of us couldn't afford that luxury; not even I who tried. Everyone had a radio, or wireless then; everyone listened for the news. And news bombarded us.

Tregaran was 'occupied'. It was too large to be left for private use and I doubt if we could have managed otherwise. First came evacuees, women and children from up-country towns, sent to the country to be safe. They hated it. Hated the loneliness; hated the quiet; hated the lack of all those amenities they considered 'civilized' (whatever that word meant to them). When they were gone, the army took us on, using the house for a military base, head-quarters to a succession of companies, each of whom stayed a while before moving on. We were reduced to living in a few cramped rooms, although my grandmother kept her own. Surprisingly, Em preferred the new kitchen; I stayed in the old. We seldom used the great living room rebuilt from the old picture gallery, turning it over to the officers for a mess. It was another irony, I suppose, that when the restoration work was complete, just as the whole building had been freshly decorated, it should have been carved up again for offices, storage files, sleeping areas for men who often worked so long they were too tired for sleep. Sir Edward Gatering must have been relieved that at least the refurbishings were crated up, all the furniture, rugs, pictures his money had paid for, stored away for the 'duration', another new phrase we had to learn. In fact, it was thanks to him and his son George that we civilians were allowed to remain in Tregaran at all. But perhaps thanks had no part in it; after all George owned us; why shouldn't he protect what was his?

Did I forget to mention I was married to George? For me, Son George (I always thought of him as that) was only one more adaptation we were forced to make. He had planned to get Tregaran, and he did. He got the land for his own use; my grandmother kept the house, restored to her taste, with herself kept on as chatelaine; I was thrown in for ballast. And, in a nutshell, that was the story of my marriage.

I do not remember ever consciously feeling this arrangement unfair. In fact I never thought of marriage in emotional terms. All was strictly business, meaning as little to me as any other business matter. If in some ways it seemed remote, as distant as those other events which were disrupting people's lives, I hope I will not be misunderstood when I say at least their calamities were real; mine were not. I might even confess that, in some ways, for me the war came as a relief. It took Son George away for a start, carried him off for long intervals to London where there were fortunes to be made and finally put him in a 'posh' regiment, where he was found a cushy job. His absence left me in virtual charge of Tregaran, and that I liked. To my surprise I found I was better at administering than either he or my grandmother, and this new competence gave me a confidence I'd lacked. And it kept my mind off things.

In all fairness I should add I felt I had no reason to complain of George. I had understood the nature of the contract we'd made, and if I hadn't he would have been more than willing to expound. And I could have refused. Once my lover had gone who was there to protect, except myself? If I accepted, it was not because I was tricked, or because I had a change of heart, or because I was afraid. George Gatering never really overwhelmed me with his personality, although people may have thought he did. Quite simply put, I accepted his offer because I chose to do so. And I chose because it was not worth the effort to refuse.

The marriage, if I can use that name, took place then, before the war, when I was seventeen; the 'society event' of the year, they called it, 'Cornish heiress marries industrialist's son', that sort of thing. The headlines never mentioned that without that industrialist wealth there would have been nothing to inherit, but I imagine people guessed. And if the Gaterings struck a hard bargain, my grandmother more than matched them. She and Sir Edward certainly enjoyed themselves. Together they made plans with the same precision he managed his mills, their enthusiasm hiding perhaps its lack in their respective offspring. Sir Edward especially revelled in the publicity; publicity was good for business. I shouldn't have to explain why he did us proud: Tregaran patched up for the event, the gardens cleaned, Jim Pondhue in a second glory of content, all in all a vast display of Edwardian opulence, as mistimed as it was extravagant. No expense was spared to summon forth the local tenantry, to wine and dine the local gentry, to arrange the honeymoon abroad, everything calculated to ensure the perfect trappings for the perfect young couple. Just as Son George had prophesied. Except it was all a lie.

For whatever was said or done in public, in private there was no pretence. Nothing was changed from what he had first offered, a marriage of convenience, is that the phrase? and my grandmother and his father both knew that. If I made no secret of my indifference, neither did he. And if our families hoped that, given time, we might settle down, they were deceived.

He was a lacklustre lover at best, and, after a few half-hearted attempts when he was drunk, not even that. Perhaps the fault was mine. I know I must have disappointed him. Expecting something 'hot' (his phrase), at ease with whores, titillated by the thought of rescuing a 'fallen woman', he found in me that most dull of objects, a woman in love whose love had jilted her. In fact, from his point of view, far from seeing me as a victim he would have claimed that he was one, having sacrificed his sexual freedom and preference for a respectability which had turned sour. And if I myself had married him on the rebound, in hope perhaps of some recompense for loneliness, or even to satisfy my own sexual lusts, I too would have been disappointed. Neither of us had anything to give to the other, to ourselves, and that's the truth. Long before the war broke out our marriage was a failure. But I swear it never had a chance of success, and neither of us had expected it to have. And that is exactly why I married him.

I do not ask to be pitied. Pity and remorse meant little to me in those days. Cynicism is catching, like the flu. I steeled myself to become as cold and cynical as he was. I believed myself inviolate, a wall of ice. And in truth that barricade was only penetrated a few times. But on my wedding day two things broke through. I pride myself only that no one could have known their effect on me.

I have said that the wedding was all display, calculated to gratify snobbery, having nothing to do with love or happiness. Sometimes I think it must have seemed like the end of an era, the last of Edwardian complacency before the storm. There were the usual trappings of finery, of dress and veil (which I thought a mockery and said so). The wedding list was long, as long as my grandmother and Sir Edward could devise; the ceremony picturesque, in a small picturesque church, selected for the benefit of the photographers. I remember little of the event itself, a blur of grey and white, and an unexpected rain squall, which caused the floral wreaths to sag and sent a flood cascading on the ladies' hats. As long as I spoke, was silent, moved, according to rote, I could survive. But when it was done and the organist was thumping out the wedding march, there was a commotion at the back of the church.

'Hurrah,' someone was hollering in a rich baritone, 'long life to 'ee, and to Tregarn. Long may the house of Tregarn flourish and grow; long may Tregarn be remembered,' and other such nonsense. There was a ragged cheer from some of the guests, quickly suppressed when they realized their mistake; the rest swiffled around *en masse*, ignoring the bridal pair and concentrating on the object of disturbance. And as we progressed down the aisle, virtually ignored, under the banks of roses and fern, I saw Tom beneath the porch.

He was dressed in his fisherman's gear, a necktie knotted outside his coat, and his boots caked with mud. His face was working with effort. 'Time 'twere done,' he called out to me when I came up close, 'time things were put to rights.' An usher tried to hustle him out but he grabbed my hand, his stump waving in the air to claw out thoughts. 'Long life to 'ee, little maid,' he said. 'The first time I seed 'ee I thought, she'm the one. God bless 'ee Miss Joycelyn, for all ee've done.'

Now whether he knew the truth and deliberately chose to distort it, or whether it had become confused in his addled brain, I knew sarcasm was not in him. His grasp on my hand was as warm as that time we sat side by side in the boat and, strange as it may seem, his greeting was the closest I ever came to a loving blessing.

It caused a scandal of course. There was no hushing that up, although at the time, out of tact, no one discussed it openly. Certainly it dampened my new in-laws' enthusiasm. I know Sir Edward was furious, suspecting some kind of deliberate sabotage, and afterwards Son George tried to have Tom shut away, on the grounds he was dangerous. He used his father's influence as magistrate, but when Em told me I was outraged. So that too was hushed up and Tom was left alone. But I never forgot.

The second incident was at the reception itself, when I was standing on Tregaran steps counting the moments until the end. A guest approached. She was slender, attractive in a flapper way, with dress cut off above the knees, and blonde curls fluffed out under a cloche hat. 'Fancy,' she minced the word, leaning towards me in a familiar way, 'however did you land him?' She had a well-bred whinnying voice, the sort that set my teeth on edge, and she nodded meaningfully towards the groom, dapper in his morning clothes. He was red-faced and jovial (although by now I knew enough to be suspicious of that mood), surrounded by a group of friends, all of whom were as drunk as he was. 'Never thought anyone'd catch him,' the young woman went on. 'Always thought Georgie Porgie was too smart. What did you have to offer that I didn't, to persuade him to make you an honest woman?'

She laughed to take away the sting, but the sting was there. She pulled off her hat, drawing the curls over her ears in a gesture that was also familiar. 'You know his college nickname, of course,' she went on. 'At Wadham they called him the King of Tarts.' She smiled. 'But then, don't they say reputation maketh the man? I'm sure you've got all his little peculiarities well battened down. I never could.'

She laughed again. 'You don't remember me, do you?' looking at me with appraising eyes. 'We haven't met since the day you locked us in. Sneaky little thing, weren't you, to play us such a trick.' And sneaky aren't you now, her look said, to have tricked him.

'Oh, it's all under control.' I gave an equally brittle laugh, involuntarily moving back. But I thought, that's what it is all about for them, a game. I deal, I play, I win; everyone saving face, everything a paying off, everything for a laugh, to be a sport. He can do as he pleases, I thought, take you as his mistress again, as I presume you meant me to believe. I don't care a damn. He did, and I didn't. And that sums up my life with him. And how little it mattered to me in any case since I was dead, and never would come alive again.

The third time reality touched me was when the evacuees were in the house, a group of London children whose terror at bombs was only matched by their terror of us. None of them had been away from home before; some had never slept in beds; they sat on the cots we had provided in the hall and glared. 'Like rats,' one of the other 'lady' helpers said, sotto voce, loud enough for them to hear. She gave an exaggerated shudder. 'No doubt they've fleas. Look out they don't bring bubonic plague.'

I doubt they would have understood even if they had been listening, but on a sudden impulse I took as many of them as I could and went down with them to the beach. I have said most of the cliffs had been mined or sealed off for military use but Tregaran Cove was left open for some reason; Son George's work perhaps, or perhaps because later there were so many soldiers in the house it didn't need special guarding. I thought it had never looked more lovely, the water sparkling in the clear sunlight, like a blue lagoon. Although we had been warned not to go out-of-doors (stray planes had been sighted; troop trains were on the move; strafings along the coast had been reported) I tried to coax the children to run and play at the water's edge. They didn't want to. The sand got in their shoes, and they were mesmerized by that expanse of empty sea. And so we dragged up wearily to the top of the cliff again, where they stood in sad despairing rows like sheep before they're dipped. I myself was looking out towards that shimmering horizon when a throbbing sound behind my back grew and grew until the earth seemed to rock with it. The children recognized it instantly; that was something they did know. Wordlessly, they threw themselves down, hands over ears, or rolled under the bushes, or pressed themselves against the cliff. I turned and looked at the plane, black and huge, so close I saw the pilot's head and the crosses on the wings, as it swerved along the coast, then out to sea.

Afterwards they said it was a miracle. 'You were lucky,' they said, implying also I had been a fool to have exposed myself and the children to such risk. Luck played no part in it. I had seen the plane, the pilot; I felt the impact of the bullets before they came, and had known no fear. I had no feelings left, you see, nothing to be frightened of. And that was what really frightened me.

And so the war continued, disrupting our lives, changing us as it changed the world. Soon going into the village meant asking first who was bereaved, whose house should be visited, whose sad story heard. It was the lack of a funeral that bothered many of them in their mourning. 'Methodists do love a funeral,' Em used to say. They couldn't accept that their son or husband or anyone they loved had died and been buried far away. And that was something I could understand; something I could grieve for.

Food grew scarce, even in the country which had always relied upon producing its own. Allotment gardens became a common sight, people eager to till more land. Our former gardener, Pondhue, took on a new lease of life, and dug and planted as if he were thirty again and had the strength of two men. We kept chickens, ducks, pigs (which my grandmother never knew about), and gave the surplus to the 'authorities'. Everywhere now there were authorities: on blackout curtains, fire-fighting, pig-killing. We all loved the story of the two Cornishmen who, trying to kill a pig on the sly, thought of chloroforming it to reduce the noise. When they and their helpers never returned, their wives found the pig merrily alive, its would-be butchers lying unconscious side by side. That was something to laugh at; mostly we mourned.

My grandmother's wine soon disappeared but she found a new source of supply. A visit from the officers who boarded with us became obligatory, like presenting credentials to royalty. To my surprise this custom became popular. 'A grand old lady', several called her, as reverent as if she were an institution. At first I acted reluctantly as her go-between, or procuress, if that is a better word, but when I joined up, as many girls my age did, I enjoyed serving as liaison officer for the various companies stationed in the house. That knack of organization (inherited from my uncle, I suppose, since my father never had it) stood me in good stead and I was pleased to make my contribution to the war effort. I learned how to file and then to type. Soon I had a half-dozen local girls working for me, arranging the logistics of feeding and billeting. There was an official billeting officer on duty of course, but he was always harassed and forever lost among the maze of Cornish roads and glad of advice. I started to like the feeling of 'helping out', 'running the show', other new expressions we learned. And I suppose, without my noticing, or meaning to, I began to put down new tendrils myself.

I never meant to grow at others' expense; I never knew I had. But one day after the arrival of troops had become commonplace, a troop of Indian cavalry came to stay. Usually the officers lived with us; the men were billeted in the village or put up in the large Nissen huts which began to appear all over Tregaran grounds. In this case, I suppose to keep us segregated, only the horses came to Tregaran, and I got in the habit of watching them when they were turned out each night. The orderly in charge was a little man, huddled under a large turban. He wore a top-coat and scarf and mittens, and his nose and chin were pinched and wan, although I thought the season unusually warm.

'Aie, Madam,' he told me once, speaking into his muffler, 'they are beautiful, isn't it, see how they run.' He leaned forward over the gate, watching them himself. 'That one,' he pointed with the stem of his pipe at a handsome bay that held its head and tail high and pranced, as if walking on tiptoe. 'It misses its mountains, memsahib, it knows the difference.' He looked at me with his mournful brown eyes, suddenly throwing his turbaned head back as if he were one of his horses. 'Aie,' he repeated, his lips blue with cold, 'they need a place to breathe, a place to look out from. They don't like being shut up. Nor do I.'

His words suddenly brought back another evening which I thought I had buried; another man, who had said the same thing. That night was the first time in years that I cried, lying alone in my old bedroom. That night was the first time in years I did not feel an exile in my home.

And so more men came and went, our moors and cliffs became training grounds for campaigns overseas; and we became used to the routine. It scarcely varied; I came to know the procedure by heart. One battalion would depart; another arrive; there would be a spate of telephone messages and the duty clerks would look grim. Then the lorries would be heard, grinding up the drive my great-grandfather had been so proud of, escorted by jeeps and armoured cars. The lorries drove in convoy, in clouds of dust or sprays of mud depending on the weather. The men inside were always the same too: hunched uncomfortably on the hard wooden seats, facing each other, cradling their guns, uncertain where they had come from and equally uncertain of where they would arrive. Their destination reached, they clambered stoically out, formed lines, wheeled away into the night, to be quartered in the village, while their officers climbed down themselves, stretched, and made jokes about being at Land's End.

I was watching one such group, leaning over the terrace for a breath of air myself, when I first became aware of their curious looks. It dawned on me how strange we must seem, and I began to look about myself, seeing Tregaran through their eyes. That famous drive was reduced to a mass of ruts, its edges flattened out of recognition, the rhododendron bushes (which two officers had already gone behind to pee) broken off or uprooted. Wooden scaffolding and girders barricaded the façade of the house and the windows were sandbagged shut. Along the terrace itself other wooden structures had been built, added piece by piece like wasps' nests, dividing it into a dozen cubicles. The view had long been gone. You wouldn't even know the sea was there, blocked by a row of galvanized huts. Temporary buildings they were called, but Son George already had his eyes on them; they'd do nicely for the estate afterwards, he'd thought. The woods too had almost disappeared. He had cut them down before the war; unused timber a wasted resource, and where he had replanted he had put in firs. Firs don't look right where oaks and elms have been; they hide the contour of the land, and kill the undergrowth, but they made an efficient backdrop for a line of steep-roofed wooden shacks, that looked as if they belonged in the Alps. As for the inside of the house, it too was so divided up that it had come to resemble a rabbit warren, through which one wandered along corridors flanked by desks or boxes or more sandbags. I thought, if I had come here myself, I might not even recognize it.

'So where're we at then?' The speaker was a red-headed first lieutenant. He was stabbing at the map with a pen, trying to rouse a laugh from his companions, most of whom had already scattered about other duties. 'Here or there, or Goddamn somewhere else? Thought we were supposed to be saving England; we might as well be in Nova Scotia.'

His voice was flat, his accent hard, the vowels dragged out where ours would have been soft. He himself was short and eager and young, his uniform unbuttoned and his belt undone, his behaviour more casual than an English officer's would have been. I strained to see the insignia on his shoulder patch, something unfamiliar, Canadian I thought.

'Hey, there's a honey.' He nudged his friends and one by one they all turned around. Their interest was flattering but I was used to it and it never bothered me. 'Say, lady, if you're a native, what's this place, if it has a name, that is? And what in hell, heck, is it?' He gestured hopelessly. 'A castle or something? And what do people do for fun?'

The others tried to hush him, been a long day they apologized, but I laughed. 'Try the pubs,' I said. 'There're several in the village. And say you've come from Tregaran House; they'll take care of you.'

'Tregaran eh?' He mangled the word, peering down at the map. 'Now that's familiar. Doesn't it sound, who is it, what's his face?' The others cut him short, wanting to know my name, trying to find out where I lived, what I was doing there. It was my turn to cut them off. 'I live here,' I said, smiling so they wouldn't feel hurt. 'And my name is Tregaran too.'

And it wasn't until afterwards that I realized what I had said.

That evening, I don't know why, I felt tense, ill-at-ease, as if somehow I had betrayed myself. I went down to the beach again. I avoided the usual path since that would have meant going through the meadow where the huts were, but followed the course of the stream on the other side of the fence. Son George at least had left the beeches alone, I don't know why. (I think his ideas of management were worse than any Tregaran had known. He wanted to be owner of an estate; he liked playing at squire as his father did, but he treated the land like a barrow boy, selling all he could for profit and touting the rest.)

The old road itself was so overgrown you wouldn't have even known it was there, but the stream was still running underneath. I never liked listening to it, as melancholy as windchimes on a wet day, but by following it I had discovered a new way out to the beach where it spilled over the cliff in a small waterfall. For some reason I found myself taking care not to be heard. Bushes grew all the way to the edge and the sound of the water would have drowned any I made. But I needn't have bothered to walk quietly. Others had got there before I did, and were making enough noise to waken the dead.

I don't know why I was angered at first, but I was. I was not used to seeing people on what I still thought of as 'my' beach and as far as I knew none of the officers had come there before. I kept back, out of sight, just above the green-scummed pool where the stream ended, and watched them. They must have come along the usual cliff path, although that too was overgrown, not clearly visible. And there they were, playing on the beach, walking on the sand, throwing rocks into the sea, completely at home. It was still light; the sun had set but the twilight would be long. Some of them had piled their tunic jackets in a heap to make a goal and were throwing a ball about, a strange oval sort of ball, in a game that seemed to involve a lot of running and pushing. Others were stretched out on their backs, eyes closed, their shoes and socks thrown anyhow, as casual as if they were in their own backyard. One had gone alone along the water's edge, for the tide was out, and was jumping among the rocks to hunt for stones. He picked them up, as if examining them. Some he kept, the others he sent skimming across the bay so that they skipped over the waves in little splashes of white. Everything was tranquil: the water flat, hardly a ripple stirred and the seaweed among the rocks rose and sank as if it breathed. My anger went. I felt ashamed of it; they were so much at ease, so enjoying themselves like the boys they were, I wanted it not to end for them. I wanted them to stay there, far from the war, and be at peace.

The man on his own went further out, beyond the rocks on to the sand bar, his shoes slipping from time to time on the green weed. I thought, suddenly amused, if he doesn't look out he'll be caught, and sure enough after a while I saw the surge that marks the turning of the tide. I was debating with myself if I should come out from hiding and shout a warning when one of his companions did. It was still not dark, that colourless grey before the light quite goes, and his ball-playing friends, led by the red-haired lieutenant, had given up their game. They had come down towards the sea, and were pointing to the channel that was beginning to fan out behind his back. It was not deep but widening fast, almost too wide to jump.

'Hey, hey,' the rest were mocking him, chanting as if at a football match. 'Time to go, man, time to go.' He stood balanced on one foot, trying to take his shoes off, then gave a laugh, straightened up and jumped. There was a splash; he was in right enough, up to his waist, and he stood there laughing back at them, his dark hair ruffled over his eyes, catching the last light, water dripping everywhere.

'Knew I never liked the sea,' he was saying in his lilting voice, 'knew I'd had enough of it, on the ship for days on end. Knew I should keep clear of it. Always brings me bad luck.'

'Then why'd you take us here?' one asked. 'How'd you know about this place anyway?'

'Ah,' he said, and smiled. I couldn't see his eyes or his face, it was too dark, but I knew he was smiling. 'All in the past.'

He waded ashore, his shoes full of sand, his clothes streaming, the others eagerly giving him a hand. How good it was, they must have thought, just to be rescuing someone from the sea, just to be helping a friend who'd fallen in, who wasn't wounded, or dying. Or dead. I stood transfixed.

The light was fading, the glow was gone, in a few moments it would be night. I could not even see the group on the beach; I could not hear anything they said. But this man, the one who had fallen in, surely he wasn't who I thought he was, surely he was too tall, surely the shoulders were too broad? The accent was different too, the tone, the words. But the lilt was there. How could he have come back? Impossible. And if he did, why hadn't he let me know? And I thought, if it is you, this is the third time I've caught you, Phil Tregarn, and this time I won't let you go. But I don't know what to do with you.

I turned and ran, afraid of accidentally meeting him, afraid I wouldn't. I can't explain how trepidation and delight surged through me. It was like having frozen hands and feet; when they thaw a tingling begins, painful at first, then deliciously warm. It would be easy to check if I were right, in theory, that is. I had only to read the adjutant's records to find his name. But I couldn't bring myself to creep through those tunnels of desks in the dark, in case it wasn't there or in case it was. I sat in my bedroom, looking towards the sea. You couldn't drown the sound at night, that sullen suck, that soft swish and fall. I thought, I am looking out at a place which only came alive when he was here; I am sitting in a room whose only happiness came from him. But I also thought, so many years have passed, so much has happened to change us, can it ever be the same? I thought, somewhere close he is asleep, or is he like me, awake and wondering? I thought, how does it feel for him to be in this house at last, to lie under the roof that his ancestors built? Why doesn't he come and find me? Why must I always make the first move? He didn't come, and he never did sleep at Tregaran, perhaps out of pride, and in the morning I found out why.

His name was on the list all right. I went to look. P. W. Tregarn, Captain. Well, I thought, he's Son George's equal at last. And then, still inconsequently, I never knew he had a second name. I did all this, read the lists, put them away, as detachedly as if it were part of my regular work. Only my hands betrayed me. The third time I dropped the papers to the floor the duty clerk looked up and grinned. 'Got the jitters?' he inquired. 'Too much coffee, too many late nights.' If only those had been the cause. I found the name and rank easily enough but not the man himself. He had already left the night before, for 'manœuvres'.

When the troops moved in and out like this, the reason usually was for special training that Cornish terrain could provide. No one was supposed to know exactly where these army exercises took place, but everyone did. 'Top Secret' was the name for them, but if you wanted to find out you had only to ask the village girls. They could tell you the time and date, down to the exact hour of finishing. They used to cycle up in twos and threes, lean their bikes against a hedge and wait, wearing the new nylon stockings and the lipstick which they dared not wear at home. It would be easy enough to follow them.

The training grounds consisted of a vast track of moorland further east than Phil's claypit, all of it fenced off with barbed wire, with new roads cut through the heather and a part levelled for a landing strip. Sometimes small planes came in and took off with surprising velocity; sometimes there was gunfire and artillery. Much of the surrounding moor was supposed to have been mined, and great cement blocks had been erected at intervals to deter parachutists. From time to time a flock of sheep or cattle broke through the fence and there would be a rescue effort, which no one took very seriously until a dog was blown to bits. After that, 'unauthorized personnel' were kept to the roads and had to be checked in and out. Why did I fill my thoughts with this trivia as I rode along by myself? Why did my thoughts flutter like moths? What was I hoping to achieve?

I had borrowed the bicycle and a clean uniform skirt and blouse. The clothes were too big and the olive drab unflattering. The bike was too small and although I knew the direction I kept getting lost. There were no signposts now, to confuse the enemy, and the old roads wound in and out like a fishing net. But when I came to the wide new road then I made good progress. My excuse was a flimsy one at best, but fortunately the guard at the gate was a local man who knew me, so I didn't have to use it. He let me through with a casual wave; all I had to do was mouth the Colonel's name. Once inside the camp I headed for the main hut where I knew, thanks again to the adjutant's list, that Captain Tregarn was duty officer.

The new road was like a slash through the moor, wide enough for three cars abreast. On each side of it were rows of tents, dotted here and there like brown mushrooms, although if you looked at them from a distance you saw some kind of order to the rows that made you think of a Roman fort. In the early afternoon, for I had timed my arrival carefully when the camp would mostly be empty of men, the lazy swirl from fires beneath the mess tent suggested that cooking was already under way. But in the distance there were angrier-looking patches of smoke and sudden black puffs, accompanied by loud explosions, that dispelled any idea of this being a Boy Scout camp. I suddenly began to feel frightened. This was no place for me, no place for a woman in man's affairs, no place for love in the midst of war.

The main hut was set in the centre, marooned in a shadowless incline, an ugly oblong building sweltering in the sun. When I knocked at the door of the outer room, still in two minds whether to turn back or not, the red-haired lieutenant of the evening before swung round, startled at being disturbed. He had his feet on the desk and was leafing through a picture book, of Italy as it turned out, which may have given away a host of army secrets.

'Well, I'm damned!' he exclaimed, or words to that effect, suggestive both of pleasure and surprise. 'Never thought you'd turn up. We don't see many of your kind.' He made an elaborate pretence of dusting off a stool for me to sit on. 'So what's your pleasure?' he went on, leaning forward in a parody of expectation, 'what can I do for you?'

I've said I had a flimsy excuse prepared, but I forgot it. I told the truth. 'I've come to see Philip Tregarn.' And when he looked at me, eyebrows cocked facetiously, 'My cousin.'

'Your cousin!' There was no doubt of the surprise. His voice dropped. You could see him thinking back, making the comparison of names again. 'Well, then,' he said, 'you're in luck. He's just inside.' He tipped his chair and stuck his head round the inner door with the same casualness that I had noticed previously. 'A visitor, sir,' he said. 'Someone to see you.' And at the obvious question, 'Someone you know, your nearest and dearest, I suppose.'

There was a startled curse, the sound of a chair scraping. I went in to find Phil Tregarn on his feet, furious at being disturbed.

He had been sitting behind a desk, sheaves of papers were strewn on all sides; he had the tired look I had come to know from men who had been working all night. But he knew me even in that dreadful wartime gear, with the too-long skirt and faded blouse, from which my arms stuck out. And I knew him.

He was taller than I remembered and yes, his shoulders were broader; he had filled out from boy to man. I almost

168

said to him, 'You've grown.' In his shirtsleeves, tie off, hair standing on end, where he had been pushing his fingers through it, he almost might have been his old self. And the fury was the same.

'How'd you get here?' His opening remark was not promising. Nor was the second. 'You've no business here.' Nor was the third. 'My God, I never expected to see you.'

'Why not?' I spoke calmly; you wouldn't think the world was crashing about me in flames; you wouldn't think the wounds were beginning to bleed. 'You've come back; you were in my house last night.'

The lieutenant had been lingering in the doorway, fascinated. Now he tried to put in a good word. 'Cousins,' he began, when Phil turned on him too. 'Cousins.' Fury exploded in that word. 'Just call me a poor relative. That's all. Get out. And take her with you.'

We stared at each other without speaking. For a moment I almost hated him. How dare he come back into my life; how dare he disrupt what I was trying to rebuild; how dare he ignore what he had done to me?

And perhaps he felt it. 'Well, sit down, now you're here,' he said grudgingly. 'Dick, bring her some tea.' But he didn't sit down himself, he prowled about, back and forth with the loose stride I remembered, as if he felt penned up, like a tiger in a cage. He fidgeted. I never had seen him do that before, with papers, pen, glasses. He must wear glasses then. I suddenly thought, my God there's a difference all right, Phil at a desk, like a bureaucrat, and caught that glint he flashed at me, much as he had done that day on the moors long ago when he said, 'I can read, you know.'

I took the cup Dick brought, slopping the tepid contents over my lap from nervousness. When he had withdrawn, stiffly offended, pointedly closing the door after him, I set the saucer down with a shudder as if I could see my fortune in the leaves.

'It's no good,' I heard myself say, 'I've got to go.' I didn't know my hands were trembling again. I didn't know the tears were rolling down my face. 'It's too late.'

There was a loud whooshing sound, a crash, an explosion that made the whole building rattle, and the sound of rapid machine-gun fire ripping across the roof as if we were really under attack. I felt myself start to shake and when I looked up I could see his hands were shaking too.

'Why did you lie?' he said. 'Why did you lie, Mrs Gatering? About your name, about him. Why did you marry him?'

And into the awful silence that followed I screamed back, 'Why did you leave?'

Then the world seemed to break apart again, a series of explosions, like crackers going off, more shots, a regular barrage of artillery fire, a bombardment. It made answering impossible, if there had been something to answer. It seemed to rock him back to his senses, for when the noise abated somewhat he said, 'You can't stay here. You shouldn't even be here. There's a war going on outside, men are shooting each other, learning to shoot, be shot at.' He didn't add, learning to die, but I could see he was thinking it. 'This is no place to chat,' he said, into the lull that followed. 'You've got to go.'

Then as the noise began to build again, 'Look, you seem to know what these practice affairs are prelude to; you probably know what happens when we've done with them.'

'Yes,' I said, the image of that half-concealed Italian book unwillingly flashing across my mind.

'And you probably know how long they last.' At my nod, 'And the leave we have after them, before the real thing starts. I'll lay on a car, fetch you; tell me where to pick you up. Just to talk. We've got to talk.'

'Yes,' I said. But it wasn't talking that I wanted. I couldn't keep my eyes off him, taking in every line, every stretch of him. I thought, I'll die myself not touching him, not having him touch me. Having him so close and not reaching out was the hardest thing I'd ever done.

He must have sensed what I was thinking. Perhaps he felt so too. 'Just get out of here.' He almost groaned. 'Leave now.' He pulled open the door. 'And you, you bag of worms,' he shouted to the other man, 'if you've done with eavesdropping, escort the lady out, and see she gets safely away. Pronto, understood?'

Perhaps he realized how different too that made him sound, used to giving orders now, expecting them to be carried out, authority. He hadn't had that before, now he did.

'I am a gunner, after all,' he said, not without a touch of irony. 'I'll be out there tomorrow having a turn, going through the same exercise. But I suppose you know that too.'

'Yes,' I said. 'That's why I came today.'

'Christ,' he said. 'Christ Almighty, but you take the cake, Miss Prim. How long's it been, and in you walk and start again, as if it were only yesterday and nothing had changed.'

'You came back,' I said.

'Not by choice,' he said. 'I came where the army sent me, that's all. And stop crying.' He suddenly shouted at me. 'I can't bear to see you cry.'

'I'm not,' I said. But I was.

The young lieutenant had pulled on his cap and buttoned his army blouse, and was ready. Under an increasing barrage of noise he took me towards the gates, tactfully not looking at me, and in the intervals of quiet carrying on a conversation with himself. It was eerie, trying to walk normally like that while the earth seemed to crumble beneath your feet, while your head seemed to float off with the noise, so that even silence seemed deafening. But it wasn't the noise that made my feet stumble and trip as if they didn't belong to me; it wasn't the clouds of dust blowing off the moors that made my eyes water. And it wasn't fear or hope I felt, nor misery. It was just looking into an abyss and finding that I was already there.

Chapter 9

I was in the abyss, but I also was in the air, like one of those Indian horses prancing along. The only way I can explain those shifts of moods is to show how the world had come alive, each texture more vibrant, each scent more keen, everything standing in sharp relief, as it sometimes does after rain. Without my meaning to, without being aware that I had noticed, I could have named every paper on his desk, every stain on the scuffed wooden floor, every cobweb on those closed windows, where heat and dirt had left long smears. I could have numbered every hair on his head; I could have traced every line of that sensuous mouth, closed up so tight against me.

And I wondered if he, in turn, had noticed me; would he have seen I'd cut my hair, would he understand the strain I felt?

The week passed. An invitation was issued in his name, very stilted, very military: Captain Philip Tregarn presents his compliments, eighteen hundred hours. I arranged to be at the turning to the moors, not out of sentiment as much as privacy, and I was late. I couldn't have borne being there first, and having to wait. He arrived by jeep. Somehow that seemed more fitting. A car, with him in it, would have seemed incongruous. And I suspect he thought so too, for when he had helped me clamber in, his first words were, 'Not sure how to drive this thing, so you'd better hold on tight. A little habit I've picked up, but on the other side of the road.' There was a hint of the old mockery in his voice, but it still was formal, too formal I realized, as if he were playing a part.

We skidded off. I sensed his glance at me, but I didn't

look at him. Yet I was as aware of him as I'd always been. He was dressed in uniform but had thrown his cap and jacket in the back. With his shirt sleeves rolled up, he might have been any young man out for a spin on a summer evening, except for the colour and the stars on the shoulder tabs that gave him away. And when he asked, 'Where do you suggest? I thought of somewhere quiet for something to eat and drink,' I almost smiled. That image was even more incongruous, that he was asking me to recommend a restaurant where presumably he would order food and wine and would pay for them. What had we known about such things? We scarcely had ever been indoors together, certainly never to eat. I would have laughed if I hadn't wanted to cry.

'I don't know of any,' I said truthfully. 'Most are closed. The food's dreadful anyway and the pubs are crowded.'

He didn't say anything, just continued driving along the narrow roads. There was little traffic at that hour, because civilians couldn't have petrol, and the army avoided these smaller lanes. The hedges had not been cut and fronds of grass and Queen Anne's lace kept sweeping along the jeep's open sides. We were going fast, not out of control but faster than was safe, and I could feel how tense he was, like a piece of metal that's seized up. When he jammed on the brakes and said, 'This is ridiculous,' I almost cheered. 'We didn't come for a tour of the country-side.' He sounded angry. 'You must know some-place. You've been living here long enough.'

'Turn here,' I said, suddenly desperate. 'Anywhere will do. Just drive down here.'

He spun the wheel. We bumped along a rough cart track, which ended abruptly at a gate, beyond which stretched an empty field of corn.

He drew up, switched off the motor, leaned back, stretching out his legs. They looked even longer in combat boots with the tops laced over his trouser cuffs. And he looked more formidable. I studied him stealthily. There were new lines, new marks of fatigue; his face was tanned, but much thinner; his eyes still that startling blue but with dark shadows underneath. I thought, he's been pushing himself as hard as his men, just as they all do. And the old protective feeling swept over me.

'Cigarette?' he asked, studiedly polite. He reached behind him for a pack, American style, tapped one out, flicked a lighter professionally. Although I didn't know how to smoke, I took it, and gasped as my lungs filled.

Suddenly he gave a laugh, stretched over, took the cigarette out of my mouth, stubbed it out and threw it away. 'Well,' he said, and now there was no doubt of the mockery, 'let's give up trying to impress. It doesn't work, and serve me right. But although I'm sure there's something worthwhile in that field out there, it'd help a bit if you looked at me. People usually do look at the person they're talking to.'

'I've nothing to say,' I said.

'Begin at the beginning.' He stretched his legs again, as if studying his boots. 'With your marriage, for instance.' He added, whiplash quick, 'That's the first thing that counts; that's what we've got to talk about, Mrs Gatering.'

I wanted to say, 'It doesn't count at all.' I even opened my mouth, then shut it. How could I explain in a few sentences the whys and wherefores, the cause and result; how could I unravel all that loneliness and heartbreak and despair? Instead, seeking wildly for some reply I stammered, 'And how about you, what about your marriage?'

'I'm not married.' The reply was brusque. Then, as if to explain, 'Never got round to it, I suppose; never had time.'

He twisted in his seat so that he was facing me. 'But your marriage exists,' he said, 'it's real enough, it won't go away.'

'I don't want to talk about it,' I said.

'You've got to . . .' He was puzzled. 'It was your choice,

although God knows why. I've tried hard enough to understand. After all, it changed my life; it drove me away.'

I couldn't bear it any more. 'But that's why I married him,' I cried, 'because you'd left; because they said you'd never come back; because I thought I'd never see you again.' I took a deep breath. 'Because, with you gone, nothing mattered at all.'

I was shaking so violently that my teeth were chattering, and when I couldn't stop, he put his jacket round me, until the familiar smell, the warm feel, seemed to wrap about me like a benediction. After a while I heard him ask in quite a different tone of voice, 'Who said? What "they" do you mean?'

'Em,' I said. 'She told me you'd gone; she told me you'd used grandmother's money and run.'

Into the silence that followed, 'I could have understood the running part, but not the leaving without a word.' I added, 'I knew it wasn't safe.'

'And you believed that of me?'

Then he told me the truth, how Zack had taken him in as we had planned, had hidden him, offered him his old job back on the boat.

And how the very next day Em had gone through the village with the news of my engagement to George.

'What was I to think?' he asked. 'I'd seen him there with you, there'd already been talk. That first time, that evening when I came, drew the heart out of me. So I thought it must be true. Zack bought me a ticket and I went. But I'd come that night to ask you something else.'

I wanted to ask, 'And you believed that of me?' but I didn't. For then he told me what my grandmother had done, and what she had offered him.

He said, as if a thought had just come to him, 'Em can't have lied to you, and lied to me, just because Evelyn Tregaran told her to. There must be something more than

176

spite. Your grandmother can't have wrecked two lives, just to get her own back.'

I wasn't listening. It was what he'd said before: 'I'd come to ask you something else,' that caught my attention. And all in the past, all finished with. I cried out, just as I had once before, 'It doesn't matter, does it? It won't change what we once had.'

Behind my words I seemed to hear others he'd said. 'I don't care for castoffs.'

He tried to smile. 'Here we are,' he said in his old way. 'In some pickle. You thinking the worst of me, me thinking the same of you. Me never wanting to go, you never wanting me to leave. And now I'm back, we're still in the same quandary.'

We sat in silence, miles, years apart, while the summer twilight began to creep over the fields, bringing its long soft shadows. There were briar roses in the hedge and the dew enhanced their scent. Overhead, where the light was still bright, swallows were darting to and fro, searching for gnats. He said, 'When I was in the States (that's where I went, Michigan, the Midwest, where the mines are) they sent me all the details of your wedding. I've got 'em still, the papers, kept them deliberately to convince myself it was real. Otherwise I'd not have believed it.'

He said, 'It was hard enough in Michigan without that, a hard cold place, hard cold men. No time for sentiment. But you had to admire those people's strength. They'd lived through a Depression too; they were hurting for jobs. Yet they pushed ahead to make something of themselves. Sometimes I think the lower down they sank the harder they pulled themselves up. And in the evening there were classes, night schools they're called, where you could go no matter how old you were. I learned a lot. Those mining towns were full of smart men who knew exactly what they were doing. Then just as things were going right, diploma, offer of a job, the start I'd been dreaming of, the war began and that was that. Nothing to the rest. I went to Canada, joined up, was sent to North Africa with one of the first Canadian detachments, was promoted in the field, was sent back here. It was strange in the desert, all that heat after the cold, but it was stranger still to find myself in Cornwall. Tho' I think I always intended to come back when I had done what I meant to do.'

I thought of the contrast with my husband, who had been educated merely because he was rich, and had gone to the right schools and spoke with the right accent. And who didn't care if he passed or failed. And I suddenly felt a great respect for the man beside me, who had achieved as much through hard work and courage.

'And did you like it there?' I asked, for something to say. 'How does it feel, being back?'

He shrugged. 'Always preferred cities,' he said, 'perhaps because I was born in one. As for being here, it's a different return from what I imagined.'

He said abruptly. 'I want to show you something. I don't expect you've been there. It was a place that meant a lot to me. Do you mind a tour after all?'

He reversed down the lane; we started forward. He seemed to have no hesitation now about which way to go and when he said, with a grin, 'This is quicker than a bike, especially with a girl on the handlebars,' we both laughed and suddenly felt more comfortable.

The church was in a small village tucked beneath the moors in a valley or combe. I was surprised. It wasn't the sort of thing I'd have thought he liked. It was old, the graveyard overgrown, the granite headstones covered with lichen. And the church itself was grey and worn, its floor slanted and green with mould. But there were candles in the candlesticks, and a fresh white altar cloth, and the brass flowerpots had been filled. 'You'll never guess who was married here,' he said, surprising me again for I had never thought of him particularly interested in the past and certainly not affected by it. 'A strange tale and a strange place for it to happen. Zack's got it all written down. Our common ancestors. Your great, great, however many greats it takes, grandmother; and my equally great grandfather. Her name was Tregaran. She was daughter of the man who first stole our estate, and he was son of the man who was robbed. They say he married her to be avenged, and fell in love with her, but perhaps that's an old wives' tale. Their grave is somewhere hereabouts, although now it's all tumbled down. Tho' why they ever chose here, anyway, and why my ever so great grandfather came to live here, is a mystery. But there's a tomb on that wall, a knight with sword and shield, and another here, in chain mail, of some Crusader, all my forebears. And somewhere on the moors up yonder, a battle was fought in some civil war in which a grandson of that first pair determined to win his inheritance back.'

He said, 'You see what a tangled history our two houses have, all done for land or wealth, or revenge at losing them. But when I was young I used to think it was for love. I used to come here,' he went on, 'when I was a lad, waiting for you to grow up, and plan how it would be when I was rich and famous. And now you've grown, and so am I. I'm twenty-seven. The world won't stop for me. I meant to ask you properly, before I left, to wait for me, and so I would have done, had not pride kept me quiet. And now whatever I'd like to ask, can't be right, not with the war. Not with both him and me in the thick of it.'

He said, 'And now, my love, I'll take you home. I've got a few days free. It isn't much but let's enjoy each day as it comes, just you and me, like we were before. If you're willing, that is, to take a chance on getting to know me again.'

But I already did. We were not lovers, perhaps would not be again, perhaps never would be at all but I knew he desired me. There was a look, a tone, a feeling to him.

And I knew the same thing in myself. But I also knew that what I had sensed from the start, his fastidiousness, was that the word? his sense of honour perhaps, would come between us, and that was something he must fight out with himself. Well, adultery, divorce, had become household words since the Prince of Wales had brought them into the open, but I could see they would go down hard with him, for all that he had been living in America (where, some said, they were accepted as a part of daily life). And I could appreciate that fastidiousness, even though I felt none of it myself.

Along the way he spoke easily of his life in America, with a wry affection. 'You can't turn your back on your own,' he said when I asked why he had chosen to enlist. 'Not had to, wanted to. My friends in the States called me Americanized, part still Cornish, a proper half-breed. Perhaps I am; perhaps I don't belong now to either place; perhaps I still don't quite fit in. But it wouldn't have been right not to have volunteered.'

We were coming up to Tregaran now, and he was avoiding the ruts in the drive. 'Always did think it was too large,' he said, pointing to the house. 'Work of men not quite sure of themselves. But to my mind, none of us really owned this place, not house, not land. They were simply lent to us, and when our time was done, we passed them on. But here in England the landowning class thinks it's theirs by some God-given right. Oh, I know the war has changed things a lot, "mucking in", don't you call it that? Brothers in adversity. When peace comes it'll revert to what it always was, they up there, the working man down here, and never shall the twain meet. And the sad part is it's as much the fault of the working man as anyone's. He prefers having someone over him telling him what to do, ordering him about.'

He let me out so I could slip ahead alone. He drove on to park the jeep; a sentry was snapping to salute; he was climbing down and approaching the terrace steps where I was waiting for him.

'I apologize; a long-winded answer,' he said, with a half-embarrassed grin. 'In Michigan they claim that if you ask a Cornish Jack something, say where's the letter box? or how do you drive in a nail? you have to listen to a sermon first.'

I hesitated there in the semi-dark, then took a chance. 'Why don't you come in?' I asked. 'Em's long gone to bed, and my grandmother seldom leaves hers these days. She hasn't been downstairs since the war began. That young friend of yours, Dick, he's the only one to know who you are or care; there're always plenty of stray officers about.'

The invitation wasn't exactly elegant, but that didn't seem to faze him. 'Dick's all right, he'll keep his mouth sealed,' he said. 'So if you'd like me to, I'll come.'

We wound our way through the maze of wooden partitions, into what had been the hall. He held the door that separated our part and we went down into the old kitchen. Unlike the rest of the house, it had changed only slightly. The old iron stove, which had to be blackleaded every day, was gone, and so were the pots in which Em cooked. But the deal table was still in place and the hard-backed chairs, and the great stone slabs on the floor. When I left him to round up some food (not much, for Em still controlled the pantry keys, and was zealous in her duties), I heard him pacing back and forth. 'Strange isn't it,' he said when I came back. 'I suppose my family built this floor. God knows what's beneath it tho', Celtic crosses perhaps, with Celtic bones.'

He resumed his pacing. 'Is this where you spend your time?' he asked. 'What do you do?'

'I read, I listen to the radio.' I tried to think of things that didn't sound too dull. He reached across me and played with the switch. When the strains of some popular music filled the room, he sat down at the table, tapping out the tune on the oilskin cloth.

'Where's Son George?' The question upset me, although the old nickname made me smile. I didn't want to talk about him.

'Away in London, I think,' I said at last.

'Don't you know? What's he doing? Is he in the army?'

'He's supply officer,' I said, 'for one of the Guard Regiments. Sir Edward got him the job, and he's been sitting on it since.'

He didn't laugh. 'Then he could come down to visit you? How often does he?'

'I don't remember.'

'When was his last leave then?' He was leaning towards me across the table, drumming on it impatiently. 'A month, two, three months ago?'

I said distinctly, so there would be no mistake. 'His last leave was spent in London.'

'He doesn't want you to join him?'

I didn't reply.

'The fool,' he broke out. 'I don't understand him. And I don't understand you. What's he doing, leaving you alone? And there you sit, Patience on a Monument, making tea, getting a meal. I never thought of you as domestic before. What's he done to you?'

I took his fingers between my own to try and stop that incessant drumming. 'It was all over with a long time ago,' I said. 'Be calm, listen to the music; you've lost the beat.'

Our hands touched, his gripped mine. 'Oh Christ,' he said, and there was such misery in his voice it made me wince. 'I wanted you to wait for me. And now 'tis too late. He's got there in between.'

'He was never anywhere,' I said. 'There was no one there but you.'

And we sat together, just like that for a long while, as the music went on and on.

The next few days passed in a blur. We lived for the now, putting past and future aside. He visited his two uncles; I think he spent his nights there, and they, almost recluses themselves these days, accepted him as if his leaving were only yesterday. I had to work, but in the late afternoon he waited for me in the curve of the road, parked neatly off the verge, out of sight of any casual passerby. This discretion, almost second nature to us, was perhaps unnecessary. There were many strangers about; people were preoccupied; gossip almost seemed a thing of the past. For gossip you need time and leisure to enjoy it. No one had that these days.

I let him drive where he wanted to, not as it had been with Son George because I didn't care, but because I cared so much. Most often, taking advantage of the long evenings, we went up on the moors, ranging east and west along that central spine. Once we climbed to the top of Roughtor where the wind almost blew us off its peak and took our words and scattered them like chaff. On the way down we turned aside to look at a menhir or standing stone and he walked around it, measuring it.

'How in heaven did they dig that up?' he asked. 'How did they transport it here? What's more, how ever did they hoist it upright?' He eyed it thoughtfully. 'Another Cornish mystery,' he said. 'When the war's over that's what I'll do. Find out all of its secrets. Isn't there a verse like, about all its treasures being gathered up and cherished?'

He looked at me, looked away. I felt myself blush. I knew what he was thinking. It was the closest we had come to letting reality intrude. And having let it in, there was no way of shutting it out again. And perhaps that was what made us careless.

We kept up the pretence of parting before the gates; I going ahead; he arriving later on his own. There were other officers he knew, young Dick for example, billeted at Tregaran; he could always find excuses to visit them before discreetly coming to visit me. And since we merely sat and talked, actually there was no reason for secrecy. But that night we were silent as we drove along, too many thoughts, too many possibilities tempting us. Neither of us noticed the large staff car parked in front of the main steps, and we met too soon, on the terrace itself, as if we did not want to lose sight of each other, even for a few moments. The sentry saluted; Phil pushed the door; I turned to speak. And saw my husband standing in the hall, surrounded by a group of fellow officers.

I had not seen him for several months, and he looked more like Sir Edward Gatering than ever, rotund in his dress uniform, his face shining with perspiration, for the night was warm. When he saw me he tapped his baton on the wall, sending down a shower of plaster. 'Place's a mess,' he said, as if I were supposed to fetch a dustpan. 'God knows how we'll ever clean it up. Surprised to see me I suppose?' He turned to Phil. 'There's women for you,' he said, 'weeping and gnashing of teeth when you're gone; not even a smile of welcome when you return.'

There was little risk that he would recognize Phil, not in the dim light of that blacked-out hall, nor was there any reason for him to associate this tall Canadian captain with anyone he had ever met, certainly not with that violent young miner who had struggled with him outside the pit. And even if he had, he was too drunk to remember what he knew. But I was scared, and felt the sweat start, cold and clammy on my skin.

In fact it was the drunkenness that saved us anyhow. Drunk, George became garrulous, expansive, loud, eager for an audience, any would do. He fastened on Phil, using him as the butt of his remarks, addressing him as if he were an old friend. I think in any case it would not have occurred to him that I might have come in with him, for that would have meant I must have been out, and he had long believed me incapable of attracting anyone.

'Come upstairs, *mon vieux*, old man,' he said in his expansive way, gathering up his entourage, like a broody hen with its chicks. 'Let's have a drink, something *à boire*. All in the family, you understand; glad to have you in my house. *Bienvenu*.'

He led the way unsteadily, into the new sitting room which had been reconstructed from the old picture gallery. I have said it was seldom used, except as an officers' mess and they tended to avoid it at night when it was hot. The windows were too big to black out so they had been blocked with sand bags that kept them dark but prevented air from circulating. The place smelt of stale smoke, and was always close and damp. I had never liked the change, and the bare floors and few scattered chairs, some still covered with dust cloths, gave a temporary look, as if the builders had momentarily disappeared, leaving half their work unfinished.

'*Asseyez-vous*, sit down, drinks on the house.' Whisky had made George affable. He flung off his cap, loosened his well-polished belt, and unfastened the buttons of his Savile Row tunic. He sank down into an armchair, his feet on a table in front of him. When he tapped his cane, tap, tap, tap, some orderlies hurried in with glasses, whisky, a bowl of ice (a Canadian innovation, since we never used any). The other men, a handful of Canadians who had been trapped by him and who had the air of being rounded up against their will, helped themselves, raised their glasses, gulped the drinks down. Son George's hospitality had them obviously confused, especially since he persisted in lacing his remarks with a smattering of French, as if all Canadians were French-speaking.

When he continued, in the same patronizing way, urging them in French to make themselves at home, his accent atrociously British, they obviously didn't know what to make of him; proprietor of the house, it seemed, captain in a prestigious regiment, popping up among them unexpectedly, and now sinking fast into that most dangerous mood of all, belligerence, masked by affability.

I took a seat as far away from Phil as possible, and silently prayed that he would have the sense to keep quiet while Son George drank himself into oblivion. But George revelled in the audience. He became increasingly talkative, embarrassingly lewd. I must confess that the years had not worn well on him; the high freshness of his youth was gone and he seemed bloated rather than solid. After several jokes, so off-colour that even his guests didn't know where to look, abashed at having a woman in their midst, he suddenly began to resent their lack of enthusiasm.

'Drink up, *mes amis*,' he cried again, tossing them a bottle. (He never explained where the drink came from. I presumed it was the Canadians' in the first place since they were quartered there, but they were too polite to mention it.) 'There's a war to win. Bloody thing's been going on too long. Made me leave my wife to guard my home, *oui, oui*, like a bloody medieval bitch. When the lord's away the ladies play. Except mine never played at anything.'

He hoisted his glass and drank the contents at a gulp. One of the things about George's 'binges', as he used to call them, was his remarkable stamina. I'd never really seen him out of control, but he could be terribly offensive. I saw several of the other men exchange glances, clearly not wanting to be caught in a domestic row. George watched them through narrowed blue eyes. 'Bugger you,' he said in his most refined English way. 'Half frogs anyway. Well, wife, you'll be pleased to learn that I've been transferred.' He raised his glass. 'Join me in a toast,' he ordered his companions. 'I've just got my own company.' He drank, adding darkly, 'And we all know where it's going, don't we, although no one will admit so. And when I'm blown to kingdom come, won't my charming wife be sitting on my fortune.'

He slammed the glass down so hard it smashed into a cascade of brilliant fragments. 'But, God damn it, it's not fair.' He suddenly shouted at me as if we were alone, 'God damn, biggest mistake the War Office ever made, taking me off the General Staff. Suppose they think they're doing me a favour. Father pulled the strings to get me on; he'll have to again. And you've got to help us.'

This maudlin confession was the finishing touch. One by one the others made their excuses and drifted off until George's audience was reduced to four: myself and Phil, at opposite ends of the room, an unknown young Canadian, who had got himself trapped behind some chairs, and another drunk, asleep on the pile of rugs. George himself glared round at us with blood-shot eyes, like an enraged bull.

'So we're all in the same boat,' he cried, 'comrades-at-arms, brothers in adversity.' He gave his loud laugh. 'Was in Italy myself before the war. All that pasta, all that wine, all those Italian whores with hairy legs. Wonder how much that's changed.' He added in a quite different sort of voice, as if he were posing a serious question, 'What do you fellows do when you're gone, I mean, when you've left your women behind? Lock them up with a chastity belt, go on a crusading rampage yourselves? Or are you both faithful and all that? True love.' He sneered, smoothing back his receding hair. I noticed how his hands were trembling, 'Don't have anything like that to worry me; my wife's so chaste she won't even let me in.'

The drunk hiccoughed and rolled on his side; the pale little Canadian blushed and again made ineffectual efforts to remove himself. Phil got up. 'That's enough,' he said. 'Pack it in. Go somewhere and sleep it off; then come back and apologize.'

'Sleep, but not to dream.' George spoke in a falsetto, his idea of parodying Shakespeare. 'Sleep, but not in her bed.' He began to laugh again. I wondered why I'd ever thought his voice attractive; like him it had coarsened with the years. 'I like my women ripe and willing.'

He shouted at me, 'Damn your eyes, look what I did for you. What have you ever given me? Don't think I mean to die in some piffling campaign just to make you a rich widow. By God I paid a price for Tregaran, and so'll you. Tomorrow, tell my father you're expecting his grandchild. He'll move heaven and earth for me then, get that transfer revoked if it's the last thing he does, nothing too good for his son when he hears that news.'

'He knows I'm not,' I said. 'You haven't been here in a year.'

'Old fool can't count. Or if he does, make up some lie. Tell him you came to visit me in a fit of wifely zeal. Just make sure he realizes how important it is that his grandson's father remains alive, safe and well in Merry Olde England. You can always fake a miscarriage later.' He added, 'Or perhaps by then we'll have had time to make it real.'

I'd never known George so earnest, not since the night he told me how much he wanted Tregaran. I thought, my God, he's scared. Suddenly the war's become real for him and he's frightened of being killed. But I couldn't do anything about that.

I said, 'It won't work.'

'It'd better, that's all. Or I'll beat the shit out of you until it does.'

He began to pull himself out of the armchair, levering himself up like a beached whale. To this day I don't know what he meant to do, perhaps not rape his wife in front of everyone, even if he were capable of it, but I never had the time to find out. Phil took him by the slack of the shirt, held him like a dog by the front, just as his uncle had done. 'Bloody swine,' he said in disgust. And when George flailed at him, 'Just sleep this off.' He set George carefully down on his feet, curled his fist. One well-placed blow laid

George out, collapsing him neatly back into the chair like a balloon that's lost its air. 'Always this pleasant, is he?' Phil asked the world in general, and to me in particular, 'Jesus Christ, is that what you've put up with all these years?'

Strangely I was unmoved. This scene was not so unusual as it seems, although George's revelation of his inner turmoil was atypical. Normally he never showed his feelings; I almost thought he hadn't any. I think I might have felt sorry for him. 'It's alright,' I said, 'he'll find some other women somewhere when he wakes; he always does. Usually not locals, I'll grant him that, *noblesse oblige*, but he certainly never lacks for them. He'll not come near me. He never has.'

'The hell he won't.' Phil took my arm, dragged me after him, pushing aside the Canadian boy who looked sick, down the stairs two at a time, through the hall before the startled sentries could scramble to attention. Outside, the night air was doubly cool and fresh in contrast with that pent-up atmosphere inside. 'Whose is this?' We stopped in front of George's car where a sergeant was dozing at the wheel. Not waiting for an answer, Phil jerked open the door, hauled the poor fellow out, bundled me in, and got in himself. 'Priority,' he snarled to the chauffeur's ineffectual bleating. 'Let the bastard walk, if he can find his bloody legs.' He turned the key left dangling in the dashboard, floored the accelerator, the powerful engine leapt to life. 'For once Son George's outranked,' he said, still with a snarl. 'I've got him licked, experience, service, combat duty, the lot. Let him wallow in that.'

I said, mildly, 'And suppose, when he comes to, he finds you've stolen his wife as well as his car?'

He slammed on the brakes so hard I could have been hurled against the glass if he hadn't caught me. 'Not stolen,' he said in the same savage voice. 'She always did belong to me.' And his mouth came down on mine, hard and possessively.

When we started up again, 'Off-hand, I only know of one place to go,' he said. 'In fact no one else knows I've been staying there. But you may not like it.'

I understood at once what he meant. 'They'd never want me in their house.'

'They're growing old,' he said. 'They sleep early, wake late. What I do with them is their affair. What I do on my own is mine.'

He was driving fast. The headlights streaked along the quiet hedge. Sometimes when we rounded a corner, twin specks of light reflected back at us, small nocturnal animals caught crouching in the long grass at the verge. 'I'd like to take you there,' he said. 'I can't explain why. To make my peace with them; perhaps, to make my peace with you. To set at rest all those cruel happenings that tore that house apart, so that things can be put to rights as they always should have been.'

We were following the inland road, keeping the fishing village on our left, its quiet streets, and empty houses along the quay, its few moored boats, mute testimony to the way it was dying without its men. The pubs had already closed. Sometimes we passed one, each with its crowd of soldiers in uniform loitering outside, surrounding the young village women like a hive of bees. That was something else that had changed; before the war the pubs were the men's preserve; the only women who went there were what Em would have called, 'no better than they should be', 'grassy-backed' as the Cornish say.

Most of them did not even bother to look up as we went by, except one drunk who tried a salute and fell off the steps. Then we had crested the last hill, were turning seaward again, along the smaller road that bordered the course of another stream, similar to the one at Tregaran

Cove. And where it widened at the foot of the cliffs we came to a stop.

The freshening breeze brought the smell of seaweed and salt. I could hear the slap of the waves against the rocks. The house itself was a black shape against the starlit sky. From the landward angle it had a simplicity it lacked on the seaward, a solid mass of stone and slate. 'Funny, isn't it,' Phil said, 'your family's gone up as mine's gone down. I don't know how old this house is but Tregarns have been living in it over four hundred years. Yet their name is forgotten everywhere else, even in that village we went to.'

He paused again. 'But you're as welcome here, as ever that great-grandmother.'

We picked our way over the shingle between the boats. There was no barking dog and the windows were dark. But when we stepped over the threshold into that old room I could smell the same wood smoke and feel the warmth of centuries of fire on the hearth. He took my hand, just as he had done that first time and willingly I followed him, through the dimness where furniture loomed in shapeless lumps, up the twisted staircase cut into the side of the house. We took off our shoes, treading carefully to make no noise. I was thinking, he has done all this before, when he looked round and smiled. 'Been out on the tiles many's the time,' he said, as if he guessed. 'Never lied about that to you. Haven't been a monk neither all these years. But I've never brought anyone here before.'

Just in front of his room, where the door was so low he had to stoop to go in, there was a niche in the wall. It held an old copper jug full of flowers and as I brushed past their petals fell in a shower of white and gold. 'Tom puts 'em there,' Phil said, 'in memory of my mother, I believe. She used to pick 'em herself when she lived here.' He put out his hands to smooth away the pollen; they caressed along my shoulders, down my spine, holding, touching

191

me, as he backed into the room bringing me with him. I felt the quivering start, along the veins, the tingling through the wrists to fingertips, the pulse of desire.

He unfastened the buttons of my blouse, one by one; felt for the waistband of my skirt; pushed down the underclothing so that it fell in folds. He held me away from him and, naked, I let him look. 'Your skin still has that same gleam,' he said, smoothing it now here, now there, 'but 'tis your eyes that speak. They give you away, dark and mysterious, like moorland pools.'

He stroked my hair, gentled me, whispering words I couldn't hear as I undid his shirt and slipped my hand against the warm skin. He caught it and held it with his own, the two palms against his heart. 'Listen,' he said as it quickened with mine, 'don't you hear it, keeping time.'

We were in another room, another age. How many other lovers had stood like us, listening to the thrumming of their blood, following each other's lead, turn and turn about, until the tempo leapt and broke?

I think of all the intimate things lovers do with each other in the dark, sleeping together afterwards in one bed is the closest. In sleeping there is trust and confidence, contentment as well as love. And when I woke before the dawn, I still was in his arms and he in mine.

We watched the day brighten the walls of that small whitewashed room, with its old black beams and its bare wood floor. The window opened inland so that the sound of the sea came in drifts, like the soughing of wind in trees, reminding me of Tregaran. He shifted his dark head on the pillow to look at me. 'Many's the time,' he said, and there was the same wonder as I felt, 'I used to lie here and think of you. When I come back, will you be waiting for me here?'

He smoothed away my tears. 'I promise you I'll be back,' he said. 'Not a bullet in the world can hit me. Not with you here. You'm like some spell for me.'

panting, as if the climb up the stairs had taxed his strength. 'Tom don't hear naught, but my ears be sharp enough.'

I was distressed how much he had changed, shrunken into his clothes, only his eyes as fiercely alert, like his nephew's. I sat up in bed holding the sheet to my chin.

'I know what's underneath,' he said, ''tain't the first time I've seen a woman in bed. But since he's brought you here, then bide. I won't step between 'ee again.'

He leaned against the doorpost. 'Been a long haul for 'ee,' he said. 'There's been talk. None of my affair, I thought. If it's turned out like last time, serve 'ee right. But I see things aren't the same.'

He said suddenly, 'Too much killing in this world, too much blood and pain to waste breath on. Got to believe some things worth salvaging. Never thought to see the lad again; never knew what it meant until he were gone for good. Blamed 'ee for all of that as well. But 'tis water 'neath a bridge. He's back. And if he's spared he'll return as long as you want him to. Don't want to risk losing that on my account.'

We looked at each other, understanding the unspoken armistice that he was offering. 'But be warned,' the old voice went on. 'When he'm gone again, watch your back. I shan't interfere, but that's not to say she won't. She's been queen-pin around here far too long; thinks the world revolves around her plans. 'Tain't so no more; can't keep the lid on everything. So poke about yourself a bit, find out what's what. There's something still not right.'

His voice was the echo of what Phil had said, was the echo of all my childhood dreams. 'You may not like what you find,' he was adding, 'but you were always for after knowing. And you'm the one best fitted for the job.'

I shut out the part about leaving; I shut out the risk, concentrated on what was important now. 'Alright,' I said to the old man. 'I'll try. On one condition.'

'What?' There was such deep-rooted suspicion in his

voice, centuries of it, I thought, discouraged, it'll never yield to me.

'Take me in,' I said, 'believe in me.'

He stared again. Then slowly, like the start of a sunlit day, a smile began to spread across his face, starting in the corners of those dark blue eyes and fanning out. 'Get on with 'ee,' was all he said. 'Breakfast be on the hob when he gets back. And next time tell him that car of his be loud enough to shake the house into its grave. And I ain't dead yet.'

And he gave a laugh, so that for a moment I almost thought he was his nephew all over again.

Chapter 10

We breakfasted well: crusty bread, sweet milky tea, fresh eggs (which I was sure Tom had filched), homemade red-currant jam, all luxuries since the war. Tom grinned at us round the chimneypiece, standing on tiptoes and giggling. He had become plumper with age, layered with rolls of fat like a Buddha, seeming to expand the more his brother shrank. Yet both brothers appeared as fit as ever, although they seldom left their own property. We never asked where the eggs came from and Tom never asked where we did; he had accepted us as a gift from the gods. And if afterwards he questioned Zack, that was their business.

Nor did Phil speak of George again, except once. He never told me, for instance, that when he had gone back with the car he had found George gone – a little matter of prudence it seemed, a strategic withdrawal, sparked by the colonel-in-charge, who, hearing of the brawl, had sent compliments to Captain Gatering, with the request he bugger off before there was another row; there'd be no drunkenness in his Mess if you please, to say nothing of other behaviour unfitting to a gentleman. Nor did Phil mention that Captain Tregarn had received a similar reprimand. So George had left, making no attempt to see me again as far as I could tell, and certainly making no attempt to see his father or my grandmother. (And to be fair to George, I should point out that whatever the reasons for his transfer to a fighting unit – drunkenness again, or possibly some sort of fiddle with supplies – once in Italy he acted appropriately, enough to be wounded and survive.)

But when I tried to explain, 'Leaving George I leave

everything, you know. Grandmother's already changed her will and deeded Tregaran to him as part of the bargain they made.'

'Don't want her money or her house,' Phil replied. 'Only you.'

We were sitting on the beach near his uncle's house. It was a typical Cornish June day, the sort that makes weather announcers tear their hair and brings out the perfume of the roses. Both of us were dressed in old clothes, fishermen's jerseys and baggy trews that smelt faintly of fish and oil. I knew we were living on borrowed time but we didn't speak of that either, sat there throwing pebbles into the sea, sifting through the sand for shells, or when the sun came out, sometimes lying on our backs with our eyes closed. I'd never known such happiness before in familiar things. And when he turned on his side facing me I thought, this is meant to last; nothing should take this moment away.

'Fact is,' he was saying hesitatingly, 'I'm not so badly off. A captain's pay is adequate, and then there's what I saved abroad.' He laughed. 'Compared with what I was,' he said, 'I'm bloody rich.' He reached over and pushed my hair back. 'Fact is,' he whispered, 'I'm the richest man in the world. When I come back we'll be married, find a place of our own, start all over again. You won't mind being a miner's wife? You won't mind life in a cottage with a parcel of kids? Fish and chips and cabbage leaves?' He grinned. 'And me.'

He suddenly sat up, sobering. 'But we shouldn't make plans until I return. Let Gatering [I noticed he never used the old nickname again] get on with his war first. Poor sod, he's in for a surprise if he thinks it's all loot and lechery. But it's not my way to hit a man once he's down. Wait until I return; wait until I'm here to help; then we'll make a clean break.'

He used George in part as an excuse; he said, 'until' and

198

'when', but he may have been thinking 'if'. The 'ifs' of those times screamed at you. You could see them behind people's smiles, behind their eyes, locked away into their brains. But that too was something we didn't speak about. It was enough for him to say, 'All week I've been generous and let you work, now today your place's with me.' It was enough to know we were together on his uncles' beach, away from the rest of the world. All over Cornwall people were saying goodbye; this was our day of home-coming.

The place to cross Tregarn stream was where it spilled over the wide sand flats. Beyond it, on the other side, the cliffs came down to form a point, and beyond again, there was another tidal beach. The rocks there were flat and smooth, made to trap the heat so that when the sun came out they steamed gently, drying out the seaweed into long green strips. The cliffs themselves were riddled with caves, not natural ones but man-made. Trickles of rusty water, stained with tin, emerged from the openings of these old mines, and if you shouted inside, the reverberations splintered hard as stone, echoing and echoing, deeper and deeper underground until the whole cliff shook.

Phil was proud of those caves. He showed me the marks where the old pilings had stood; he traced out the veins of ore, trying to teach me the names of each layer of rock. When it rained we went inside, feeling the way along the wet sides where the line of whelks and mussels dripped at the high-tide mark. It was frightening there in the dark, but when we turned a corner in the distance we could see a patch of light and the floor underneath changed into dry fine shingle. After a while we came upon an open place under a square of sky, framed by ferns and grass arched over it like an umbrella. 'Look,' he said. He pointed to half-way up the cliff where various tunnels branched out from the main shaft. 'That's where I hid after the strike. I could have remained hidden there for months. There're caves inside, big as rooms, with running water, all mod cons.'

He smoothed my hair again. 'Don't worry,' he said. 'I'll never hide again. I won't leave you. I'll always be here.'

I clung to him. I couldn't say, 'Don't go,' as once my childish self had done, not when all over England women were trying to avoid those words. I couldn't put my demands on him. All I could do was hold him, caress him, act the lover for him as he had for me. All I could hope for was to imprint his flesh in mine, seal him deep within; all I could do was let him go without regret or recrimination.

Afterwards he made a request of me. 'Visit my uncles sometimes,' he asked. 'I hadn't realized how old they'd become. Cheer them up. They're alright, live on for years. But it's sad that at the end of their lives neither Zack nor your grandmother can be reconciled.'

He didn't add, 'I wish they were. I wish I could be the link between,' but I knew he regretted so. Nor did he ever mention the date or time of his departure. We said goodbye as if it were any other day, and tomorrow he would still be waiting for me. But what he did say when he brought me back is engraved in my memory.

He had stopped the jeep in the usual place and taken my hand. At first he merely held it, turning it over and over and spreading my fingers with his own as if to intertwine them. 'I'm not a religious man,' he said finally. 'I used to think that God dealt harshly with me when I was born, although I've got over that. And He played us a cruel trick to keep us apart so long. But last night and today, I think He's made up for that.' His grip on me suddenly tightened. 'Consider this as a beginning,' he said. 'Long days, long nights ahead, for the rest of our lives.' And for that moment while he held my hand, I believed him.

I did not see him again, but I knew when he was due to

leave. I'd seen too many companies come and go not to know the signs. In any case I had only to go to my desk to read all the details myself in the papers left there, the lists of names and ranks, the requisition orders, the supply requests, the arrangements for rebilleting of the departing troops; the similar sheaf of similar forms for the incoming replacements, down to the very hour of the turn-over. So I waited up all night, until the pre-dawn chill, watching from the balcony as the lorries came and went, as the soldiers paraded out, bent almost double under their gear. I didn't see Phil, I repeat, but I knew he was there, lost somewhere in that mass of equipment and men. And perhaps, although I couldn't see him, he could see me, and that would be my farewell to him. Well, all over England women were saying farewell these days; I suppose we were no different from thousands. Yet I felt we were, as if perhaps Phil were right and God owed us some recompense. So I continued standing there, while the convoy rumbled off, that convoy that was to take them far away to some port, to some ship, to some 'destination unknown'. And two weeks later on the tenth of July, when the invasion of Sicily began, I knew for sure where they had gone.

I suppose modern war is so vast that it takes some personal touch to make it come alive. The Italian campaign became 'my' war. Suddenly all those little flags that recorded the movement of troops, those coloured charts and maps that marked their progress, became real. When the duty clerk thrust in a pin, I felt like a schoolboy, putting tacks into live butterflies. Each pinpoint became a stab to my own flesh; each inch gained, a battlefield, where my love might be lying dead; each inch back a graveyard where he might be buried. And as one by one the towns of Sicily surrendered and the Germans retreated back to the mainland, I rejoiced, thinking the struggle was over. The hardest battle lay ahead, and both Phil and George were caught up in it.

It was Phil I thought of day and night of course; Phil who was constantly in my prayers. But it was George people talked of. George was the husband they asked about, sympathized over, sent their greetings to. I tried to hide my true feelings, once more having to live a lie, and this time hating it. There was only one place where I could be myself, and I began to go there as often as I could, although I knew my grandmother was bound to find out. At first I always found some excuse because I was doing as Phil had asked. It was later that I realized how comfortable I was in Zack's house, where I was free to listen to the news, pore over atlases, trace the line of the Allied advance without pretext, where I could speak of Phil openly. As for my grandmother, I am not sure how much she was deceived or how capable she was of retaining suspicion even if she did feel any. As far as I know she had not heard of Phil's return. She did say once, when I had come to pay my morning duty call, 'You're looking peaked. Don't tell me you're worrying about your husband.'

She was remarkably alert that day, propped up in bed, her hair fresh-dyed and spread out in coalblack wisps across the pillows. She glanced at me in her birdlike way. 'Or did his last visit leave you a little souvenir to remember him by?'

It was the closest she had ever come to admitting that she knew George had been to Tregaran at all, but the thought disgusted me. 'Ah,' she said, knowingly, 'you think I'm crude. But that's life. An heir would be a nice surprise, don't you think, after all those barren years?'

She cocked her head again. 'Don't tell me I'm losing my touch,' she cried. 'I could have sworn you were moping after someone.'

Again that shrewd, malicious glance. 'I've heard whispers,' she said. 'There was talk of a Canadian.' And when I didn't respond, 'Well, girl, speak up. You're not a child. Did some Mountie come galloping to the rescue, and have you fallen for him?'

I considered my response carefully. I knew enough now not to be frightened by her, and I was sure no word of the truth could have leaked out, but I wanted to be sure. I said, watching her, 'I didn't ask George to behave like an idiot. At least my "rescuer" was a gentleman.' It was my turn to wait for a reply. 'But as you know,' probing her, trying to trap her, 'I've only cared for one man. I'm not likely to go off in the bushes with just anyone.'

She didn't rise to the bait. 'Then the more fool you,' was all she said in her old cynical way. 'I know how shamefully George neglects you; who would blame you if you paid him back? Can't you tell me who it is?'

She thrust out her head, expecting me to confess. I merely laughed, matching my cynicism with her own. And yet, I thought, suppose I had taken a lover to spite George – what would I have to lose? Nothing, nothing at all, not even this house which once I thought I loved. But I also thought, she doesn't know who that 'Canadian' is, and for once felt that fortune was on my side.

By this time the British and American troops had reached the Apennines on the mainland, that mountain range whose swift-flowing rivers and treacherous ravines were soon to become household words. And there the advance had stopped, blocked by the Germans and the snows, each side ground to a halt by the appalling winter of '44. And over them, like some enormous shadows, the massive walls of Monte Cassino glowered.

Monte Cassino, that too was a name we all came to know as we studied it in the history books, found it on the old prewar maps, heard talk about it every day. Until that December, who among us knew what Monte Cassino was, or associated it with the Benedictine monks? or ever dreamed it would be turned into a fortress by an enemy? Now it loomed into our lives like a malevolent giant that had to be battered into bits. And that was the task of the Canadian gunners.

The atrocity of that battle became real for me only when I heard about the guns, those great modern guns that can blast centuries to dust within seconds. Their noise, their incessant hammering, their reverberations, became the topic of an on-going debate. 'Ah,' said Tom when we were listening to the news, "tis the rocks, see, they'm worse than shells. They splinter, cut 'ee like razors.' He suddenly ducked, cupping his good hand over his ear and burrowing his face into a cushion. 'How they bang inside your head,' he moaned. 'They never lets up, never goes away, boom, boom, boom.' Zack and I stared at him, with pity and understanding, but I couldn't forget what he said. I remembered how the cliffs had echoed with sound that day Phil had left and tried to imagine it magnified a thousandfold amid the icefields of an Italian mountainside. I remembered the day upon the moors when the artillery had opened fire. I'm a gunner, Phil had said. I imagined him with his men, dirt-engrimed, eaten with cold, beating his hands upon his sides as he tried to hold the binoculars steady against the wind. I saw his keen eyes scan ahead; I heard his order to fire. The shells slid into place with a furtive gleam; the couplings snapped, the muzzles flared. The sky lit up, pale green and white, tipped with orange like monstrous flowers. And like Tom I wanted to cover my ears and weep.

Each day now the victory we had been expecting seemed to slip away, as the bitter cold took its toll and we shivered at home in pale imitation. That January seemed the longest of the war, bleaker than all the previous years combined, having no beginning or end. I have read since that the battle for the Monte Cassino line was one of the turning points of the war. It certainly must have been one of the cruellest. As the winter hardened so did conditions deteriorate, until the ground was too frozen to dig trenches and supplies had to be hand-carried up, as in medieval times. And always, night and day, those incessant guns, until one was deafened, blinded, paralysed, by them. In short, that expected victory march turned into a five-month impasse under conditions which would have made Hannibal flinch. And when, at last, in the spring, the line was breached and the ruins of the monastery out-flanked, as the Germans began their slow retreat, among the casualties left behind were two Captains, Tregarn and Gatering.

I heard about Phil later. George's name showed up first. At once a stream of bulletins reassured us that he would live, nothing serious, a shattered leg that was all, suffered behind the lines, 'in the call of duty'. 'Thank God.' Sir Edward Gatering wiped his forehead and looked pale. 'Perhaps now he'll be sent home. Time he came back to settle down.' He didn't look at me but his remark was pointed, as if he had added what was in his mind, 'Time to settle down and start a family.'

I smiled to myself. I wasn't the one to lecture on marriage duty. But if I were, what would Sir Edward think if I told him I was leaving George? Would he be surprised? Would he be horrified, or relieved? Would he simply draw a breath and advise George to start again? I doubted if either way he'd care much on my account; he certainly had never been close to me. And what would my grandmother think; would she care? Would she be amazed that the worm had turned? Not even that, I thought. The only thing that would count for her would be who was the man I would go away with; was he worthy of a Tregaran. And when she learns who it is, she'll certainly fight, while she's got an ounce of breath. But that climax had not yet arrived. George didn't come back, at least not then; and instead of coming Phil wrote to me.

I heard from him only when he was due to leave hospital. I had received nothing from him for over a month but that of itself was not so strange. We seldom had news of him since he left, unlike that other time when we were young, and mostly his letters were laconic to the point of austerity, about himself I mean. For one thing he never mentioned the war if it could be avoided. Like many men I think he couldn't, or wouldn't bring the war into his private life, wanting to keep the two worlds separate. But in the desolation where he'd been, there had been little else to write about. Now there was.

'I have seen Gatering,' he wrote. 'He was in the same ward, and eventually the next bed.' (This was the first mention of Phil's being in hospital and it drove me frantic. George, of course, had never mentioned him but then George would never write to me about anything.) 'He recognized me, surprisingly enough, and we got to talking. The days were long and quiet, different from outside (the only mention he made then to that hell on the mountain top).

'"Well now," says George, summing the situation up. "Surely we've met before? Didn't I invite you once to have a drink with me in my house? And didn't you belt me one to shut me up?" His leg was healing; he could hop about, so over he came and perched on the end of my bed, although the staff nurse ordered him off. "Well now," he repeated when she'd gone, "and didn't you take my wife's part?"

'He laughed. "What the bloody hell," he said. "She never took a shine to me. All she wanted was some Cornish chap, some miner's fellow with a police record, and when he went off she took me as second best. Surprises you, doesn't it, a woman like that?" He shrugged. "No accounting for taste, of course. Me, I admit liking my women rough and ready, but she's not like that at all. Underneath, she's cold as ice, holding a torch for someone else. That doesn't leave me much room for compromise."

'He leaned over, breathing confidences. "Never mind, there's compensation to be found, even in war. That's how I got this bloody thing." He tapped his cast. "Damned shell landed in the village square, blew the brothel windows in and blew me out. Well, it's there alright, only you have to have the lolly to pay for it."

'He coughed discreetly and looked around. "Even here," he whispered. "Take that nurse just now. Gave me what for, didn't she, but afterwards, off duty, doesn't she like a hero on the side! And I'm always willing to oblige."

'He winked at me. I said as distinctly as I could, "I'm that mining chap. And quite the opposite of leaving her, she's coming back with me."

'I write all this,' he went on, 'not to give distress or to worry you, certainly not to offend. No, it's to tell you to pack your things, meet me in London when I have leave. We don't need George's blessing, but he's already given it. It's time we took the law into our own hands.

'"Hey," was all George said, looking alarmed. "Steady on, no need to get worked up like that. If you think so much of her, help yourself. She's not such a bad little thing at heart, just obsessed. Tell her I said that," he added. "Tell her we'll work things out."'

I sat holding the letter, twisting it between my hands. That's like George, I thought, affable to the last. But I knew his moods. He too was different underneath. He too was not as easy as he liked to pretend. He'd not be simple to get rid of. But that was something that would wait. What was important was that Phil was alive, was whole – for a moment I had had a hideous vision of Tom – and would soon be coming home. His letter reached me at the end of May. By early June both men's regiments had been recalled, all leaves cancelled, and the invasion of France begun.

Everyone had been expecting that, for years, I suppose, ever since the retreat from Dunkirk. And everyone had guessed it must start soon, although not where nor when. All spring there had been troops along the Cornish coast, practising coming ashore in the grey dawns, their strange flat boats grinding into the shingle of our coves. I'd seen the soldiers climbing up our cliffs, swinging like spiders on their slender ropes. ('That'll mean Normandy,' Zack had once said, looking wise. 'They've cliffs like ourn; you mark my words.') Work at headquarters had multiplied, leaving no free time at all. Now abruptly, as if a switch had been turned, all that activity was finished with; the house was cleared, the county emptied back to its pre-war calm, as if someone had taken a giant broom and brushed it clean, all the clutter of the military world gone, leaving only empty files and rusty pins. Where had all those men disappeared, those large Americans who milled through our small towns like cattle penned for slaughtering? Where were those Australians, New Zealanders, those cold, homesick Indians? Where were the Canadian gunners? All scoured away, swept up and poured into boats, poured out again, while the world waited expectantly. I waited too but strangely calm. 'My' war in Italy was done; Phil had survived; I felt I could afford to wait. But to be certain there was one more ghost of my own to expiate.

I have said several times that my marriage meant nothing to me, and in a sense that was true, as impersonal as those army forms I signed and filed as part of my daily routine. But that wasn't the whole of it, by any means, and I had to admit Phil's 'fastidiousness' had had its effect on me. It might have been the dark side of our Methodist world, but I could appreciate what he felt because at heart I felt the same, possibly even more strongly than he did; it was my marriage, after all, into which I had entered knowingly. For all my professed dislike, my professed disdain of George Gatering, the sanctity of the vow still meant something to me. Then too, Phil's comment about God's making amends had remained with me. I didn't want George, and he didn't want me, but neither did I want him on my conscience. In fact I wanted that imposs-ible of things: a clear conscience and the conviction that God was on my side. I didn't think then, that God's way is to take a thing and twist it so it turns upside down. I didn't realize that recompense goes both ways. This was the real reason why I went to Tregaran Church, to make confession and find peace, in the end doing neither, as it turned out. And the excuse I used, revealing more secrets than solutions.

Let me explain. At that time the vicar of our church, Michael Towshed, was perhaps sixty years old, unchanged, in my eyes at least, from the days when I used to struggle with grammar and sums and borrow his books under his benevolent tutelage. He was still tall and lean, his habit of standing on one leg with his head thrust out giving him the look of a hunched-over heron, with a high beaked nose and waterish yellow eyes. He always dressed in old-fashioned clothes, popular in his youth, and con-cealed his straggling hair under porkpie hats that looked as if he sat on them. He had come to Tregaran at the end of the War, the First World War I mean, and seemed as permanent as the church itself. I had always thought of him as a kindly man, sensitive to other people's difficulties, and so he was, in general terms. It was only personal matters that alarmed him.

My first request pleased him. (I should also mention that to break the ice, for I hadn't seen him in years, not since my own marriage day in fact, I had professed interest in his church records, which were renowned.) I told him I was hoping to find details of old family ties in which I'd become interested. I didn't say which family and it was no lie that the Tregarns fascinated me. And it was true that during these past months, perhaps to help the time pass

209

easily, Zack had lent me a book, a prized possession, in which his family history was recorded. It contained many tales which I had heard before, the source I presume of all those old stories Tom liked to tell, and although he never let it leave the house I was touched by his offer, as a mark of confidence. And it was Zack who had put it into my head to consult the vicar in the first place. For when I'd questioned him, 'Ask the Reverend,' was what he'd said. 'That be women's work, ferreting out who married who, and why and when. He's got lists in his church stretching back to the Domesday Book. Not much he won't uncover, if it's scandal you've got your eye on.'

It wasn't scandal I was looking for, but confession. Nevertheless scandal is what I found.

'We-we-weddings interest you!' Vicar Towshed was delighted at the thought, his pink cheeks glowed and his eyes sparkled behind their thick lenses. 'W-w-why, we've got splendid ones, the best in Cornwall, almost intact. I'll look them out.'

His stutter, combined with the long vowel sounds, almost sent me into giggles. I remembered how Phil used to imitate him, and had to hide my head. We had been having tea in his study as we used to do; the sun was pouring through the open windows where his rose garden awaited him. But when I came to the point and asked about my own marriage, in abstract terms that is, he grew red and shifted uneasily in his chair, polishing his spectacles on his sleeve, his high forehead shiny with embarrassment.

'My dear,' he said at last, trying to smile, 'you judge yourself too harshly. Of course a church oath is binding, as you say, and of course we Anglicans don't recognize divorce.' He sighed, then brightened as a new idea struck him. 'Your husband's been gone a long w-w-while, you know, don't think of things that, pray God, may never happen.'

As if aware that these platitudes were not worth the air it took to mouth them, he unwound his long legs and stood up. Poor man, I suppose offering to show his records on the spot was his way of sympathy. I'd have preferred more practical advice.

The records of which he spoke were in fact remarkable, a list of births, marriages and deaths stretching back for centuries, neatly kept and stored away in a wooden chest in the belfry tower, under a banner brought from some long-forgotten war. I couldn't help wondering what trophy Phil would bring back from a worse battle than ever knight in armour fought.

The lists themselves were bound in books, stacked inside the chest like sheets or towels. Vicar Towshed went down on his knees to pull them out, dusting the cobwebs off with his handkerchief. I watched him curiously. I knew he was proud of his church and its treasures, yet he handled these almost casually. But then, in those days, no one thought of preserving things; no one feared church robberies. For the first time I began to wonder about him, why he had stayed at Tregaran so long, why he had come to Cornwall in the first instance. He was obviously a clever man, learned, a good conversationalist although so shy. When I was a child he used to dine with us sometimes; my grandmother always made a pet of him. What had made him bury himself in this quiet place?

Forcing myself to put my personal dilemma on one side, I concentrated on the books in front of me. Useless to rely on Vicar Towshed, I thought; I'd make my own peace in my own way. The first volume was dated five hundred years before, and as I tried to decipher the faded script the Tregarn name leapt out at me. How many Tregarns there were in those days, every other page referred to them. I remembered Tom's boast about peopling the countryside. I flicked through the leaves. Not many Tregarans at first, I thought, but then, as modern times approached, beginning to predominate. I found the record of my grandmother's wedding, almost as long as mine, several pages of signatures including minor royalty. I found the record of my own, my name small and tremulous compared with George's decisive one. But in between, to my surprise, no other Tregaran at all (except for my grandfather, who had died early in this century). No births, no deaths, no marriages. The lack of burials didn't bother me, my grandmother's sons would have been interred in France, but why were they not baptized? And where was my father's marriage? Where was the record of my birth?

'Surely John Tregaran was married here?' I asked the vicar, showing him the latest book that dealt with the twentieth century. 'So why isn't there an entry?'

Such simple innocence, making such a simple request; how easy it is to dig up dirt, even when you aren't looking for it.

If Vicar Towshed had looked flustered before, now he positively turned red. 'You must be mistaken,' he cried, scrambling to his feet. 'You're looking in the w-w-wrong place.'

'No,' I said. I flipped the pages to and fro to make sure they hadn't stuck. 'See for yourself.' I held the volume out so that the spine fell back. And in the crack, between the leaves, there was the jagged rip where several pages must have been torn out.

'I don't understand,' he said, biting his fingers, the stutter suddenly obliterated. 'I've kept the records here for over a quarter century. Historians would give their right arms for them. Who would dare deface these books?' He suddenly stopped, and began to gather the volumes up, bundling them back in anyhow. As suddenly, he turned to me, looking at me directly for the first time since I had asked him for advice. 'Forget what you've seen,' he said, in a strange high-pitched voice. 'I served with the Tregaran boys in France, you know. I've kept faith to their memory ever since. That's why I'm here; that's why their mother gave me this church; that's why I've been loyal to her.'

A strange remark, I thought, staring at him as he went back to jamming the volumes into the chest, almost a confession. But it doesn't explain anything, only how he feels. Unless, and here the thought leapt into my mind and wouldn't go away, unless there is something to confess, and he knows it.

I let him hustle me away, slamming the church door behind him and locking it as if afraid I'd come back. 'Goodbye, goodbye,' he cried, hardly stopping to shake hands, all his old-world courtesy forgotten, as he too hurried off. It was clear he'd had a shock, but it wasn't the shock of discovery; it was the fact that I'd made it. I thought, it's true he's been a crony of my grandmother, a kind of pet, the sort of devoted retainer she'd like to have had, had she been living in the eighteenth century. And it's true her sons knew him. He may not have tampered with his records himself, he's too honest perhaps for that. But he has a suspicion who did. And I also thought, so here we are back to the start, back to that old mystery. It's like a current beneath the surface, a slow deep current that never goes away. Haven't I always sensed it; hasn't Phil? There must be more to it than that. And this too I recognized from that first time – yet now there were new possibilities to frighten me. I didn't want to face them or their consequence. They made me feel alone, not even Phil to help. I thought, the Tregarns may have their history book, written by some ancestor, extolling their virtues, defaming their enemies, serving as their source of family pride. *Zack's got it all written down.* When it stops, what other source is there? Only the memories of two people, both full of hate, so prejudiced that their evidence is biased from the start. But if my father wasn't married here, where had his marriage taken place? Or had it taken place at all?

213

And if I wasn't baptized here, was I illegitimate, like Phil? These ideas were too complicated, too new, as if a genie had been let out to dominate the world. Even then I didn't take them all in. And fortunately, or unfortunately perhaps, once more several things happened to make me put them to one side and do what Phil had spoken of, take the law into my own hands.

First and most important, obliterating everything else, was Phil's return. It appeared he had been wounded again, not so badly as before, but enough to send him back on extended leave, whatever that meant. (Since he seldom spoke of either time I never did unless he began. That was part of the pact we'd made, to obliterate the war as much as we could, and not permit it into our lives.) I obtained leave myself, not difficult since work had slowed after that previous burst of activity. I arranged for a driver to meet the train, more complicated, hiring someone who was new to the region, and who didn't know us, and who had petrol for his car. I found a house, a cottage actually, close to the moors, near the village that Phil had taken me to, again a stroke of luck the place being empty and for rent. And on an afternoon of a wet September day, when the sea mists had come inland and shrouded us in grey like camouflage, I packed, taking only those things I'd bought myself (for I had a little money saved), leaving everything that was George's, including my wedding rings. I left him a letter too, the duplicate of the one I sent Evelyn Tregaran. In it I said goodbye to the place where my childhood had been spent, to the house that once I had felt my home. It seemed easy, at the time, to put that former life aside, like shedding a skin. I told myself there was no time for regrets or thoughts; I would never have to think again. And as I went down the drive to meet the car, splashing through the puddles in the ruts, it seemed to me that the trees shone through the mists and the late flowers bloomed amid the wreckage of those old gardens, as if the seasons themselves had changed and we were coming into spring.

Chapter 11

The train station was an out-of-the-way one, set down in a village like a children's toy, at the end of a single street. The village itself was surrounded on three sides by grassy fields; the fourth opened on to a stretch of marsh extending a good mile down to the sea. The Cornish name meant 'House on the Shore', and once the tide must have come deep inland, slanting down the narrow road and bending the fronds of the palm trees (withered proof of the existence of that mythical 'Cornish Riviera' – we might have been in Siberia!). Not even cats or dogs ventured out of doors. But when a train came in, the station suddenly became alive, as people appeared, either meeting friends or relatives, or hoping on an off-chance to find them. Others simply stood about, as if a train's approach was an event (which perhaps it was, in this quiet little place). But many had a look I recognized, that look I had seen first upon the faces of the clayworkers' wives; in this instance transfixed into the hopeless resignation of expecting someone who would never arrive.

The trains themselves appeared at odd intervals, having nothing to do with schedules or time-tables, their whistle rippling across the marsh as melancholy as a foghorn. No one seemed to know where they came from or where they went, least of all the station-master. He stood watching helplessly as people pushed and shouted and milled about like cattle at Truro market day. All the carriages were packed: with soldiers, with men in strange uniforms, with foreign-speaking officials, with more evacuees, all equally weary and dishevelled. There was talk about a new weapon, bombs that fell from the sky without warning, rockets they were called, as if they were some kind of firework. Each time one of these trains stopped (for some went past with great bangings and clatterings) I felt my heart thump in my chest. And whenever I caught a glimpse of a tall man in uniform, saw one lean down to pick up his bags, or stretch his hand out to open a door, I felt myself begin to run like a sheep in a flock. But when the bustle had died down, and the train had disappeared, puffing along the single track into the mass of rhododendrons, I would find myself left alone on the platform. After a while, to pass the time, I took to walking up and down the street. I counted the houses that lined its sides; I measured its length before it opened on to sand, 500 feet of it, excluding the cobbled part around the chapel; I studied the wild fowl on the marsh, the ducks and geese and single swan. I could have named every plant that grew along the verge where village ended and waste land began. I came to know that village stick and stone, as if I had been born and bred there, and when in fact Phil did arrive our meeting was almost anti-climactic.

By then the light was beginning to fade; the taxi driver had become fractious, and I had despaired of Phil's coming at all. I had returned to the car one last time to persuade the man to wait a half-hour more, when I thought I heard his voice. I knew there was no one there, the street completely empty except for an army lorry backing round, but I felt Phil's presence close to me. Not like a living person, it is true, rather, like a sense of warmth as if I had stepped from shadow into sun, or as if a lamp had been switched on. And my expectation was so high, the disappointment so keen, that when in fact five minutes later he did call out, I didn't even bother to turn round until the driver nudged my arm. 'There be a hofficer shouting at 'ee, miss,' he said, and I almost angrily replied, 'Well, let him shout; what can he want with me?'

When I did look back to find Phil there the first thing I

said, almost accusingly, was 'How did you get here?' all the things I had meant to say blocked in my mind as if the method of his arrival was of prime importance.

'Stopped off at Plymouth.' He was coming towards me from the lorry, a private behind him carrying his bags. He was moving slowly, planting each foot with care as if his legs might not bear his weight. 'The trains were jammed so I commandeered a truck. Carry on, we'll take over from here.' This to the soldier, while I stood rooted to the spot. 'Unless,' and now he was close enough to speak in my ear, 'unless, Miss Prim, this is to be a foretaste of our future life, you speechless, glowering at me through the rain, while I, equally speechless, stand here, getting wet.'

Then realization flooded over me. I began to talk, jabbering away non-stop, while his belongings were stowed away next to mine, while he climbed into the back of the car and we drove off, while he fell asleep, without warning, like an old man overwhelmed by exhaustion.

The rest of that drive was a nightmare. Repeatedly we got lost, twisted round by mist and rain and by the capricious windings of the roads. Each time we took a wrong turn and had to reverse, I worried that Phil would be jerked awake. The driver's frustrations grew. He ground the gears, and muttered curses beneath his breath. Once, when we came into a farmyard by mistake, I eased myself out to ask the way. I picked a path through mud that came to the tops of my shoes, and shouted questions over a barred gate. Either the farmer was deaf, or, typically Cornish, he decided to ignore me. He went on herding his cows into the barn until the driver himself went after him. And even so, it was full night before we came down a steep hill I recognized.

Our destination was at the foot of the moors, a village tucked into its folds, and the cottage I had rented lay half-way up a second hill on the moorland side. The rain was still falling, in a Cornish drizzle; the rooks were cawing in the church-yard elms, and as we rattled past, the wheels spun upon the fallen leaves, lying in brown and yellow piles. We skidded to a stop beside a ditch, where a broken gate had been propped ajar; we woke up Phil, dragged the bags out, one by one. Then the car went on, disappearing over the crest with a final snort, and we stood staring over the hedge to find out where we were.

The hedge itself was overgrown with brambles and rose bushes, bent under the rain, straggling across the weedy path. The cottage at the garden's end seemed dark and small and secretive. There was no sign of life, no lights, no curl of smoke (although I had engaged a woman from the village to clean the place, start a fire, and prepare food). It had been daylight when I had come before; I didn't remember how small it looked, or how isolated, or, when I had struggled the locks open, how damp and cold, smelling of old ash and mould like a graveyard.

'Here we are at last.' I spoke as brightly as I could, but I felt more like crying. Premonition of disaster gripped me. I fumbled for the matches, praying there would be a lamp, while, behind me, Phil leaned against the doorjamb, not saying anything. But I felt his thoughts as clear as glass. And when he flicked his lighter on, they leapt out at me, like my own.

I don't know which was worse, his look, or the chaos which inspired it. A junkyard muddle confronted us: broken tables, legless chairs, shards of dishes and pots, yellowing newspapers in heaps, a rubbish tip left in the middle of a room, as if someone had begun to collect it up and as suddenly had thrown it down.

'My God!' Phil dragged the words out as if he were stunned. And when I tried to apologize for the arrangements I'd made, 'Don't fret,' he said shortly. 'Old busybody probably forgot, too engrossed in prying round. Well, I've lived in worse.' He gave a shrug, that gesture I associated with disengagement. 'Don't count on her.

We've four walls, a roof, a floor. That's paradise where I've come from.'

He was speaking of the war of course, but I thought he meant his former home. Suddenly all those jokes, half jokes, about cottage life came back; I remembered my grandmother's jibes. Mortified, I thought, he can't believe this done on purpose; he deserves a better return than this.

I tried to pull at the outer layer of debris until, exasperated, he prevented me. 'Leave be,' he said a second time, 'don't fuss. You'll have the whole lot about our ears.'

'We should have gone to a hotel,' I began, when he interrupted me. 'That's my line. Remember when we first met. What's so wrong with this? Or is it you, that finds it wrong? What did you expect, Miss Prim, a mansion, like the one you've come from?'

There was an edge in his voice that matched my own. Careful, I told myself; say nothing you will regret. Any moment now he will erupt. And if you erupt too, then the magic will be lost. I bit down replies I could have made, let him clear a space, bending carefully as if a false movement would break him apart. Gradually he prised the hearthstone clear, built and lit a fire from worm-eaten logs, spread his coat with blankets to make a couch, and eased himself down. When he began to rummage through his knapsack for tins of food, I watched him, partly fascinated, partly piqued. I hadn't meant that he should have to take charge; I'd hoped to have managed my own billeting.

He looked up, the firelight dancing from his insignia. (I hadn't realized until then that he had been promoted.) I saw a gleam in his eye. 'Poor Miss Prim,' he said, 'who wants everything prissy nice. Who wants everything cut and dried and clean. I'm not a guest. I can fend for myself you know; I shan't melt. And I can fend for you. That's my reason in life.'

He reached out. 'You look tuckered out,' he said,

'clemmed like some badger in his bolt.' He laughed. 'Bet you've not heard that in a while,' he said. 'Bet the old chap who lived here had. Look, there among his things are his poacher's nets. Recognized them first off. Haven't seen their like in years, not since Tom hung up his.'

He was holding me, slowly peeling off the sodden clothes, arranging my shoes before the fire, hanging the garments on a line over the mantelpiece, one by one, until I was naked in his arms. 'There,' he said, leaning back, 'that's better. Let me look at you.'

I watched him watching me as his hands caressed and warmed. 'I may seem banged about a bit,' he was whispering, 'but that won't hinder us.' He smiled his wide generous smile. 'Come closer love, I've work to do.

'This is where you belong,' he said. 'No need to fret. This is what is meant.'

We had been lovers in many ways, since childhood. We had made love in many places, in different moods, in good times and bad. This was the richest of all, a depth that came from maturity and need, a comprehension full and complete. And as I surged on him and he in me or as we lay becalmed, interwound, it seemed to me that the whole house took on a colour that came from us, a shape and texture, like a garden after rain whose scents perfume the world.

There is one other thing I wish to recall from that night, while we relived our past and revelled in the future. Just before the dawn I woke to find him sitting bolt upright. He was bathed in sweat although the fire had died down and the room was cold, and when I touched his arm he jumped as if I had startled him. He turned round. For the first time I saw the scars. 'Thought we needed more wood,' he was muttering, almost incoherently, 'ought to tend the fire.' He made ineffectual efforts to get on his feet. And when I tried to help him, 'Go back to sleep,' he said, 'nothing's wrong.'

He remained upright like that for a long time while I pretended not to watch, until the streaks of light began to filter through the window pane. When he finally did lie down he was still shivering yet his skin was burning hot. 'I was thinking,' was all he said, as he stretched beside me, stiff as a board, 'I was remembering.'

After another long wait, 'Listen,' he said. There was no noise, only the birds in the trees singing as they used to do in Tregaran woods before George cut them down. 'Once,' he went on, 'last year it was, I watched the dawn. It came up red as fire across the snow under the slopes of Monte Cassino. I'd gone forward during the night to take up an observation post in the ruins of an old farm house. It'd have made this place a palace. It was the highest building left, you see, all the others, church steeples, clock towers, schools, already blown down so we couldn't use 'em. We'd crawled forward in the dark, one of my men and myself. He was as big as I am but I've never known anyone who could move like him, slithering between the rocks like a bloody lizard. The wind was cold. God was it cold, any moment the shelling would begin. My job was to give the coordinates so the guns could knock out the German ones, giving our chaps cover as they advanced. Suddenly out of that wasteland a bird began to sing. Don't know what kind it was but it sang its heart out as if it knew what day would bring.

'I had my glasses trained on the mountain opposite. I could see the tracks of the German artillery, the dark patches left in the snow by their tracer fire. I could see the lines of their trenches scratched in the cliff surface like rabbit warrens. And always towering above them those great white walls.

'Suddenly the corporal with me gave me a nudge. He'd been a poacher in civilian life before he went to Canada. Came from up Dorset way. Hadn't lost his touch. Best pair of hands I've ever known for stringing wires or cutting 'em. Beneath the walls of the house, the skeleton walls I should add, the burnt-out timber struts where we had perched ourselves, a German squad was lying snug. Might have been there all night too, resting up from some foray of their own, not knowing we were there any more than we did them. All they had to do was look up and we'd have been sitting ducks. They could have reached up and pulled us down, just like you did from that beech tree.

'Don't know how long we stayed put like that, seconds dragged like hours. Every moment I expected the radio to give a beep, crackling out some God fool command; or a stone would shift or our feet would slip. Even thought the rising sun would give us away. I saw my corporal unsling his gun, fingering the trigger carefully. But we wouldn't have had a chance, two against twenty like that.

'It was the bird,' he said. 'The one that had been whistling. Flew out just beneath my feet, a burst of colour rivalling the sun. I saw how those Germans turned to watch, as if they too had been listening. When it was gone, damned if they didn't pick themselves up and plod off. I thought they looked like country boys, might have been I suppose, stumping along in a grey file, hunched down against that cold. Five seconds later I was on the air, the bombardment began, and that was that.'

He was talking to himself, the words pouring out. I didn't know how to answer him, just let him speak. 'And when it stopped,' he said, 'the monastery still remained, intact and huge. Below it the mountain slopes, the enemy lines, were all hidden beneath a wall of smoke. And beneath the smoke our men went crawling along like insects, like bloody ants trying to undermine a giant.

'Three months we tried to take that place,' he said. 'By land, by water. Up cliffs that a goat couldn't climb, across a river gorge running like a mill race. We walked on corpses spilled to pulp like orange rinds. And in the end when Monte Cassino fell in a bombing raid, there was nothing inside. No German guns, no German head-quarters, only old monks and refugees. Monte Cassino was a sham, and we blew it apart out of pretence.'

He gripped my arm. 'Some cheered when those bombs fell,' he said. 'Some climbed up on the rocks and urged the planes on. But I thought, there go centuries of God's good will. And when a sniper finally shot me out of a roof top, not that one, another day (an occupational hazard for reconnaissance officers), my only thought was where you were and the peace that comes with you. You are my good will, my content. Everything else is all sham.'

He was talking to me directly now, earnestly, trying to make me understand. He waved his hand at the nameless tangles in the corner's angles; he pointed to the rotting stairs, up to the empty loft where the wind moaned and mice scuttled in the beams, out beyond garden and moor where the land sloped down to the coast, beyond the littoral to Tregaran House. All those things too he encom-passed, and set aside. Well, he was right of course. But we both knew now that a safe place is only safe as long as we could make it last.

We spent the next days putting order into our lives. 'Try love in a cottage and see how long it lasts,' my grand-mother had sneered. She herself had turned up her nose at it. I found it suited me. Bit by bit we cleaned things up, ripped up matting, scrubbed floors, whitewashed walls that hadn't been touched in years. It wasn't easy. 'Got to get used to fending for ourselves,' Phil said. And so we did, living on the tins he'd brought, making do.

One day we dragged out the broken furniture and set a match to it. It went up like kindling wood. But although the smoke drifted in black patches down the hill no one came to watch or give advice, not even children, who love bonfires. It seemed the villagers had turned their backs on us. And so we perforce turned our backs on them. And that was strange.

One more unusual incident from that time. In sorting out the rubbish heap I found a crumpled envelope stuffed beneath a chair cushion. It was the one I'd sent, and inside, wrapped in the letter that I'd written, was the money I'd paid out, the whole crumpled up, letter, banknotes, envelope, forced out of sight as if at the last moment someone had taken them and put them there before temptation got the better of him. I took the money and smoothed it flat. It'd come in useful some other time. But I never mentioned finding it. I don't know why, some instinct perhaps, some doubt, which told me, even then, it was better kept to myself.

As soon as Phil regained his strength he took to the moors, like a man released from prison. I don't think even I had realized before how much they were in his bones and blood. At first the walks were short and I went with him, then, as his health improved, longer, until he was out all day. It was always interesting walking with him, he had a geologist's knowledge now and an artist's eye. Often he brought his surveying tools with him and set them up, peering through them intently. I wasn't sure at first what he was looking for; it was enough to know that he did. But gradually it dawned on me that what he was searching for was his old boyhood dream, now miraculously made possible, a Cornish mine for him to own and work and modernize, develop with modern techniques.

I came to know the mines he spoke of although personally I never visited them: Reedmoor, Gainesbarrow, Greytor, old mines most of them, small, independent mines whose ownership was dubious, and some of which had not been worked in years. I knew he went down in them, spending hours crawling along the old galleries. He never told me either that when he needed help down there, digging at the old ore beds, carrying out samples to study at leisure, he preferred not to ask in the village (although being a farming community it is true that there weren't many men likely to relish working underground, and not many men free in any case). He asked Tom.

Tom had seldom set foot off Tregarn land since George's attempt to institutionalize him, but he was as strong as an ox, and when he appeared, his beaming face was worth more than twenty villagers'. Phil had bought a motorbike, and soon the pair of them became a familiar sight, Tom perched on the back, grinning in triumph like a child. Yet it was odd that Phil had felt the same reluctance to approach the village as I did. And stranger still, the village still made no overtures to us. Usually farm folk are friendly types. That first day when I had come to look at the house they had been all over me, nothing too much trouble, all eagerness to please.

'It's the moor in them,' Phil said. 'Cantankerous, moody, unyielding. Just like me.' He grinned at my protest. 'Or better put, like these rocks here; think how many aeons twisted them into shape.' He rolled them across the table top, feeling them lovingly, those chunks of stone that so fascinated him. I liked to hear him talk, his old enthusiasm tempered now with professional calm. I knew he wanted to buy a mine, work it as he had learned abroad, hire Cornish miners at a decent wage, make a success here as a Cornishman. He made no secret that it would be an uphill task, first finding a mine to buy, and then buying it. Few mines just came on the market like a house; most were sold privately, or by auction. Our finances were adequate for us, but not enough to buy a mine. He'd need loans, mortgages, bank credit. He'd need local agents to tell him when the property was for sale. He'd need local support to see the whole thing through. Yet it never occurred to me that he wouldn't succeed. I wanted him to, you see, as much as he did. And although his work took him out at all hours, I never once resented being left alone. I only wished, I suppose that was natural, that there was some way I could assist. So that when an emissary arrived from Tregaran, I suppose the thought came into my mind that perhaps a reconciliation might be possible. After all I was my grandmother's only heir; she might still relent and give me help.

Em was my visitor, completely unexpected. I didn't know how she found out my address, although later I understood, for even the lawyers had only a postal address. But one day she appeared, silently observing me over the open gate, a look of disapproval on her face, as if I were a child playing in the mud. I was alone, dressed in casual clothes, and had been trying to tear up the weeds that blocked the path. When I stood up she gave a sniff, staring pointedly at the clods of dirt. 'Just look at 'ee,' that sniff said. No word of greeting, no surprise, certainly no display of affection.

'Your grandma's been asking for 'ee,' she said, without preamble. 'She's not been herself these days.' She looked at me accusingly. 'What a thing,' she burst out, 'sneaking off like a thief.' She sniffed again, that sniff that expressed more than words. 'So where is he then? I won't come in noways but I'd like to be sure he won't be underfoot while I stands here and talks to 'ee.'

She sounded as if she thought I might lure her into an opium den. I almost laughed. I observed her silently as she now came towards me up the path, crunching the grass beneath her heavy lace-up shoes. She wore her best black silk, and her second best Sunday hat, perched over her plaits, and she grasped her black bag tight, as if expecting to be robbed. I had to smile again as curiosity got the better of her. 'How ever did 'ee find this place?' she asked. 'What do 'ee eat? You'm no cook. Whoever does the house-cleaning? And bain't that rosemary you'm chucking out? I'll take some of that. Since Jim Pondhue died the kitchen garden's gone to waste.'

'Now Em,' I said, throwing aside the bundle of plants and wiping my hands, 'you've tried to peek in those windows long enough. Step indoors and look to your heart's content while I make a pot of tea. Let's hear your news, proper like, and then I'll tell you mine.'

She sniffed once more, before allowing herself to be mollified. Her expression took on a kinder look. By the time she had come inside, propped her battered shoes up on a stool to ease her feet, she was ready to relent. I never said a word more about Phil until she did, but I saw her take in his overcoat, the military cap and jacket with the major's stars. In any case she must have seen the pipes and boots, the mining books, the geological maps, for she suddenly burst out, "Tis true then, he'm come back some gentleman? Well, 'twas always what he wanted, always did think hisself special. But what's he after then? And where's the money coming from?' She looked at me, her eyes bright. 'If he's after starting up a mine hisself, that'll take more than Tregarn's worth.'

She studied the hem of her dress, brushing off imaginary specks of dust. 'And there's Captain George back too,' she said, 'drinking hisself into the grave and taking your grandma with 'un. Don't know what's got into 'un; he be like a man possessed. All for turning Tregaran into some sort of cheap hotel, Holiday Camp, he calls it, now that the army's gone and he's got it back. All for chopping down the rest of the trees and tearing out part of the house. Your grandma's fit to be tied.'

She cried out, "Tis all your fault. You never ought to have let her change her will. Why ever did 'ee provoke her so? And why ever did 'ee think to throw George over? The Tregarns are naught to 'ee. Told 'ee from the start they was out to ruin us, and so they have. And that nephew of thurn will drag 'ee down into the mire.'

'It's over with, Em,' I said. 'I've left George. I can't come back. I don't want to. I'm going to marry the man I always meant to, the man I love.'

'Love, love, fiddlesticks,' she broke in, sounding just like

228

her mistress. 'I've managed without love very well. I won't hear another word about such wickedness.' Her face grew down into stern lines, assuming what I used to think of as her 'Methody' look. 'Master George'll have it all,' she said, 'lock, stock and barrel, won't he just. And nothing any of us can do unless you stop him first. Don't throw it all away like that. You were her heir before he was. Come back. Leastways come back and visit us.' Into the silence that followed, 'But don't say a word that I asked 'ee to,' she added cunningly. 'She'm that contrary she'll do the opposite and not see 'ee, and I'll get the blame. But Tregaran shouldn't go out of the family like that. 'Tis wicked. Think of your father, think of your Uncle Nigel, think what they died for.'

I'd never seen her cry before as now she did, tears rolling down her cheeks and dripping on the lace collar, her hands clasping and unclasping the handle of her bag. I knelt beside her and tried to soothe her. All that she said beat against me, guilt and yearning contending for place. I couldn't promise her anything, but I couldn't resist either. And that was the other reason why I went back to Tregaran again, to make my peace and see my grand-mother for one last time.

But there was one third reason, equally compelling, why I went. It was something I had put aside since Phil's return. Now it rose to the surface of my thoughts and wouldn't go away. Before Em went I asked her a question of my own. It was the one I had asked Vicar Towshed in the church, and the effect on her was the same as on him. She seized her hat and jammed it on so that the brim was tilted at an angle, and the hatpins stuck out like straws. 'Get on with 'ee,' she cried. 'Whatever be 'ee thinking of. Non-sense, what put such ideas in your head?' Her agitation seemed familiar, was such that she could not even find her way to the door. It made me sad. It reminded me of old times when I had distressed her; it reminded me of that far-off day when Phil and I had first met and she had given herself away. I thought, as I had then, she knows more than she lets on, and I was grieved that even now, after all these years, she still couldn't confide in me.

'Em,' I said, 'we've known each other a quarter century. You've lied and cheated to protect Evelyn Tregaran. But you owe me something too. Don't forget I'm more a Tregaran than she is. And so is Phil. We have a right to uncover the past. After all, we are bound by it more than you.'

Perhaps that touched some nerve for she stood still and turned round. I can't say if she had changed since the days of my childhood; I've explained that since my tenth year I never quite trusted her again. I'd had good reason to distrust her since. But she was still the closest person that I'd had belonging to me, as part of my family. She said slowly, almost majestically, as if she were standing in the Chapel before her God, 'Miss Joycelyn Tregaran, you've no call to say that of me. What's been done, been done for duty's sake, that's all. And what you ask bain't mine to tell. Ask her yourself. But be careful. She bain't always in her right mind these days, not all she tells should be told.'

She left then without a further word, no goodbye as there had been no hullo. I watched her go down the hill, stumbling in her haste to catch her bus, an old country woman too far from home, and lost. I wondered if I should ever see her again. But her non-answer had also put me on guard. And so just as when I was a child a desire to know the truth had clawed at me, so now it began again, like a gorse burr beneath the skin.

I didn't tell Phil where I was going. (Not from deceit, but from the wish, perhaps misplaced, to spare him alarm.) I waited until a convenient time when I knew he would be gone all day. I knew he was preoccupied. Business meetings, attempts to raise cash, attempts to discover when a mine would be sold, not always easy to find out in this secretive mining world, these were the practical problems he was dealing with; my difficulties were much less tangible. I planned to take the local bus that Em had used, first to the market town, then to walk as I used to do. But first I'd phone to make sure George was out. I'd see my grandmother, but that was all. I'd no wish to speak to George.

The bus stop was in the village square, and I came down the hill in good time. The village was unusual in several ways, mainly because of its square, an open green in front of the church where villagers were allowed to graze sheep, sometimes goats. I suppose in ancient times these village rights would have been important. Nowadays it was used for a recreation field; there were swings and slides, and that day several children were playing noisily while their mothers waited at the bus stop. The houses which surrounded the green were made of stone; some were thatched, some slate roofed, all looked prosperous. The war had been kinder to farmers than most, although labourers still had a hard life, and like miners, relied on their small-holdings to supplement their wages. The village shop was crowded too; this was a day for gossiping. But as I approached the talking stopped. No one exactly turned to stare but I sensed eyes watching me. One woman called her children and pushed them inside; another left; one by one they all drifted away until only the passengers remained. And when at last the bus drew up and we climbed inside I couldn't help contrasting the frosty silence with that friendly chattering. And again the whys and wherefores of their reaction puzzled me.

I approached Tregaran on foot as I usually did, along the familiar narrow road, which I'd seen choked with army vehicles for so many years. It had returned to its pre-war calm, yet I sensed it never would be the same, even when all traces of that army were gone. The drive was still torn up and a rim of frost had congealed the largest ruts.

231

The bushes had not been replaced and many more trees were missing. As for the house, although the sandbags had been removed the wooden hoardings were still in place, making it look like a seaside shanty. It occurred to me that Tregaran had reverted to the way it had been all through my childhood and I was surprised. I'd always assumed George was proud of it and at least would have made a good country squire. Hadn't that always been his ambition?

There was no one about, a discreet telephone call had verified that, and the front door was unlocked. It felt odd, returning like a stranger to a house which I had known inside out, and which itself now seemed foreign and remote. Halfway up the stairs I stopped. The hall was littered with beams and lathes; desks had been piled against the wall, most of Sir Edward's restoration work was lost beyond recall. Except that the room was larger, its chaos reminded me of our cottage. I thought, if Sir Edward could see it now what would he think. Or perhaps he has seen and has given up. But my grandfather whom I never knew, he must be turning in his grave. For the first time I was glad that my grandmother kept to her room. She would have been heartbroken.

Overhead a tattered map reminded me how every morning the duty clerk used to stick in pins. Some of them were still rusting away along the Italian coast. I remembered how he used to joke as he drove them in. 'Another nail in Hitler's coffin,' he used to say. How long ago it seemed when I had sat there listening to him, hiding my real feelings.

The corridor in front of my grandmother's room was unchanged, except the crate of wine was gone. I suppose George supplied her openly. When she heard my knock she did not mistake me for Em this time. She was seated in her usual place before the window, the curtains half drawn, for the day was dark and a storm was threatening.

The semi-shadow gave a softness to her face that was misleading. I looked at her. She was still large but her vast weight had caved in upon itself, like an over-ripe apple. Her eyes were closed but she made vague gestures for me to approach as if she wanted me in front of her before she made the effort to open them. I thought, you tried to destroy me as a child; you ruined my girlhood; you thought you could control my life. But your power is gone. You have nothing left to hurt me with.

'Always said you would come back. Knew you wouldn't keep away for long. Always thought you'd come begging.'

It was the same harsh voice, pitiless in its condemnation. And the eyes when they opened were the same too, their pupils opaque with age perhaps, but the venom glittering, like a snake with a broken back. 'I knew there'd be things you'd want from me.

'You could have had it all,' she went on. 'You and George. Oh yes, I grant he is a fool in some ways, but that was part of the bargain. I paid more in my turn. All you had to do was give in. But you couldn't agree to that, could you? Wanted your cake and eat it too. Hope it chokes you.'

After a while she roused herself. 'How dare Tregarn come back,' she said, 'how dare you flaunt your affair with him. Best hide your head for shame. I warned you when you were a child, I'd have nothing disgraceful harm our name. I warned you to leave him alone. I told you before that there's not much I don't hear of, and my reach is long.'

I almost said, 'You didn't recognize him two years ago; neither you nor George. You didn't think of him as a gentleman so, for you, he couldn't be one. Your class snobbery blinded you.' Instead I said, 'Does that include altering facts?'

She folded her hands across her chest, gripping it tightly as if holding a secret. 'What do you mean?' she asked, just like Em, but her voice and expression gave her away. And when I reiterated the question that had been haunting me, although in truth I had meant to lead up to it more gently, 'You're smart,' she said, 'smarter than I thought. Michael Towshed was right about you. He always said I underestimated you. But I never let that worry me. "Let her find out how far my tolerance goes," I told him, "let her work to find out who she is."'

She suddenly threw off the rug that covered her, and stretched her arms in the air, a parody of her younger self when she was posturing for a lover with her gnarled fingers now resembling claws. 'So what do you think now,' she said. 'What do you suspect, Miss Know It All? That your mother was a whore? That your father never married her? That you were born out of wedlock? Of course he never married her. I wouldn't have let him anyhow. And when it came to the point he never would have had the nerve to resist me. So you see,' she added almost nonchalantly, as if what she was saying was well known, as if she were confirming a previous conversation, 'I didn't have to take you in.'

'Then why did you?'

She smiled. I can't tell you the effect that smile had on me, as unexpected as a knife stab, as obscene as a gush of blood. 'I needed someone, that's all. I thought a girl child would be more malleable. Besides,' she stretched again, 'I'd always wanted a girl myself.'

Her reply was bleak but in a way I preferred it to subterfuge. I made myself keep talking in the cold, collected way she preferred. 'But why me?' I insisted. 'There was another child, after all; what about Nigel's son?'

She considered. Her health might have been gone but not her mind. I could see her searching for words that would wound, twisting the knife. 'Ah yes,' she said, 'Nigel's son.' And after a long pause, 'Yes, I grant you him. But the Tregarns already had got hold of him. I'd never have had a Tregarn in the house. Besides . . .'

'But he was a boy,' I broke in, 'the eldest son's son. Your favourite's son. If we were both illegitimate, how could you shut him out?'

She went on as if I hadn't interrupted her, 'How they all resented Nigel's hold on me; how they hated him. But he always was the happy child, the giving one. Your father was tight as a tick, never a joyful word from him. Nigel and I were the ones who were close.'

I had a vision of those two sons of hers, one beloved, doted on, brimming with confidence, secure of himself; the other, like myself, awkward, retreating into silence and reserve. I suddenly saw my own unhappiness projected back into my father's life. I saw him recreated in me.

She was watching me curiously. 'They all disliked my older son,' she said, 'until he felt it in himself. But why should he be blamed for being what he was? Why should he be blamed for anything?'

She stared at me with her hard dark eyes. 'Think,' she said. 'Would he be likely to do what he knew I would abhor? Which of my two sons spent most time with the Tregarns? Who made a friend of that idiot Tom, who went with him everywhere although it broke my heart? Who killed himself and Nigel so a Tregarn could live? And who encouraged that sister to run after him, to throw herself upon him, the master's son? Oh, I agree Nigel Tregaran would have made the better catch but failing him, didn't John Tregaran do?'

I heard what she said but it made no sense. I grasped at straws, trying to turn her voice off. 'Nigel never would have betrayed me,' she was saying. 'Not with the sister of a man who hated me. Blood is stronger than water. Nigel was the son I loved; why should he have dishonoured me? He died without heirs, the heir who should have succeeded me; he had no sons to disgrace me. But your father did.'

Nigel had no sons.

'What are you saying,' I cried. But I knew. I knew because when I thought about it, really thought, it was the only thing that made sense, that made a pattern from that old entangled relationship: Tom, Alice, John, the three inseparables. But on a deeper level it made sense too, explaining that kinship I had always felt, that oneness of being home when I was with Phil, of belonging.

And now, with one stroke, she had turned all that harmony to revulsion.

'Ah yes,' she said, and there was a triumph in her voice. 'Now it sinks in. Didn't you wonder why you looked alike? Didn't you ever think of that? Nigel died without issue; your father sired two. I chose the girl. It's that simple.'

Chapter 12

Into the silence that followed, 'Well, well,' said George. He must have come into the room without my noticing him, perhaps he had been listening at the keyhole. 'That's a pretty story now, that makes a pretty picture.' He banged the door shut. 'I can see the headlines can't you, "Incest besets old Cornish family." Or is it even more complicated than that, are we just scratching the surface?'

He leaned forward towards my grandmother and shouted loudly, the loudness somehow shocking after that awful silence, 'Come on now, confess, whose son was Nigel anyhow?'

And as her face crumpled like wet tissue, 'Alright, alright, Ma, I'm not raking up more muck than I have to. Nigel was a saint, we all know that, and Brother John was the devil incarnate. But where does that leave us? I'm married to a bastard anyhow, and she's sleeping with her own half-brother.'

He laughed. 'Always told my father he was a fool to settle in this God-forsaken hole. Always told him country folk were peculiar. "Being a country gentleman means sacrificing things," I said. "Civilized things we take for granted, like food and wine and social life." But I never thought 'twould sink to this, living in a Gothic novel.'

He suddenly shouted again, 'Damn you both for making a fool of us. And damn you most, Evelyn Tregaran, for cheating me.'

She blinked her eyes. 'Now George,' she whined, 'you're being unkind. Haven't you got all you wanted? Why don't you two make up and be nice together and let things be as we always planned? Don't break your promise. Give me a drink. You've made my head ache.'

She spoke petulantly, like a child, or like a woman to her lover. And George, suddenly laughing again, brought out the bottle he had been hiding behind his back and came close to her chair. 'Of course you need a drink,' he said. 'Here's a glass.' He picked one up from a side stand. 'Be my guest, have several, my dear, since I paid for them. Let's drink the lot to ease your conscience. But tell us first,' he held the glass just out of reach, 'was he Jack Tregarn's get?'

The question came out like a dart. She cringed. 'That's not true,' she cried, her face mottled blue and white. 'Never was unfaithful to my husband. The Tregarns spread those rumours to do me harm. Zack led me on, just so he could laugh behind my back. Don't believe a word he says. Hate has twisted him.'

'And it hasn't you?' He gave her the glass contemptuously, watched as she drank, watched as she lay back again wiping her mouth. 'True or not,' he muttered, 'you wished it were. You wished he were Jack's son; that would have made him perfect. That's why you made a pet of him, loved him so, thinking of your lover. And that's why you hated little John; because by then Jack'd gone out of your life, and poor little John had to take the blame for that too.'

Her eyes had closed; her hands were folded across her breast; she might have drifted into the easy sleep of old age. In any case she had gone a long way from us, perhaps back to happier times when a man had loved and wanted her, when her sons had needed her. I thought, and just like old times, here I am, listening to them without joining in, a girl again, trapped between them at the table, letting them carve up my life. But what they are saying has no impact on me; what they hint at is monstrously false. But I believed it.

238

'She'll sleep a while,' George said, turning his back. 'Poor old creature, what a life, believing that the world dances to her tune and constantly surprised when it doesn't. Half the people have forgotten her, the rest think she's already dead. But she won't change her will, I'll make sure of that. So if you or Tregarn think to profit at my expense you'd better think again. My God tho', this leaves you in a mess. I wonder,' and for a moment he sounded genuinely concerned, 'why didn't she say something when you were a child? Saved you a heap of trouble. And what about him? Did he guess? Perhaps a little incest means nothing to him, perhaps he's used to it.' He smirked, as if the idea pleased him. 'And what a bastard your father was,' he went on, 'certainly gave you something in common. Other than being bastards yourselves, that is . . .'

'Leave us alone,' I cried, goaded into speech. 'Just leave us alone. I only want to know one thing. How did you find out? Was it you or your father who tore the church page out?'

'Don't know why you're so upset,' he said, 'but you catch on fast. If you mean Vicar Towshed's books, why no, your grandma took care of that years ago; easy for her then, and afterwards she'd got the poor man in her pocket.' He grinned. 'No, I got a bit inquisitive myself, suspicious like when she began to talk too much. Prised part of the info out of her, easy to do with a brandy sniffer. Set me back a bit, I don't mind admitting that, put a damper on that bargain she harps on about, to find my heiress wasn't an heiress after all, only an illegitimate orphan. But the last twist, you and Tregarn, that's news to me. And I don't like it.'

He paused, took a long sip from the bottle. Like my grandmother he shared the ability to make the unspeakable sound normal, as if he were discussing a normal event, without a scrap of real feeling. 'Speaking of Tregarn,' he said, 'puts a new complexion on things, doesn't it? For me, for you. You'd be better off with me.'

As I violently shook my head, 'What the hell, Tregarn's taken advantage of me twice. Once when I mistook him for a Canadian, once when I talked with him in Italy. I'll discount Italy. We were both wounded then, and he was in a worse state than I was; he may have misunderstood, mistaking pity for generosity. But he cheated on me in my own house, and that's something I don't forgive. You tell him that. Tell him I'll be damned if he'll take advantage of me a third time.'

'He already has,' I said, 'you've forgotten our time on the moors.'

He drank again. 'Perhaps so,' he said. 'But speaking of the moors reminds me of another thing. Tell Tregarn to get the hell away from them. They're my father's territory.'

He suddenly gave his braying laugh without amusement. 'Evelyn Tregaran thinks she controls things,' he said, 'but that's been finished with. My father's still the one who counts. A few discreet hints dropped here, dropped there, Major Tregarn'll have his come-uppance. He's got a police record anyhow, wouldn't want to bring that up, would we? To say nothing of cuckolding the chief magistrate's son. Tell him my father's interested in those mining rights. And I'm still interested in you.'

'You're mad,' I said, 'the whole thing's mad. Phil's got as much right here as anyone. This is a free land, after all. And I've chosen him, not you.'

'Right or not, just let him try.' George took another drink, each one fuelling his anger. His eyes bulged, his face grew red, he began to breathe heavily through his mouth as if he had been running. I could smell the whisky on his breath, and when he moved I noticed that he favoured one leg as if it still hurt him. Before I could stop him he had grabbed my arm in a grip so tight I felt the bruises start. 'Tell him if he knows what's good for him he'll clear off while the going's easy. And take that cretin uncle with him. The divorce's not final yet and damned if I'll let it continue.'

He felt with his free hand for the bottle. 'She's right you know,' he said. 'Together we'd have it made. War hero and his heiress wife making a go of things. Turning Tregaran into a postwar modern hotel, that wouldn't be difficult. You've had experience billeting men, take on my father's workers instead. My father's factories'll love this place, they'll flock here in their thousands.' He winked at me. 'We're sitting on a little gold mine,' he said, 'the sort of mine I understand. So you see I need you still, Mrs Gatering.'

He emphasized the word. 'Always thought you were a bitch,' he said. 'Knew you were a first-class whore but that prim manner was deceiving. Now I know you for what you are, damned if it hasn't rewhetted my appetite. But don't try my patience too far. We've unfinished business of our own, remember. And in the eyes of the law, and God, you're still my wife.'

For an awful moment I thought he was going to try and kiss me. Then he let me go so abruptly I almost fell, raising the bottle in mock salute. 'Think it over, there's a good girl,' he said. 'You've got no future with him. But don't count on anything. I'm not afraid of scandal as she is,' he jerked with his thumb, 'and I can take care of Tregarn. But if you and that old fool,' again the thumb jerk, 'think I'll pay to tart up this place a second time to keep you quiet, you're in for a big surprise.'

We looked at each other then, two enemies sizing up the situation; two combatants levelling off, waiting for the right moment. Then he stepped aside to let me pass, I ran to the door and opened it. And on the chair behind us, Evelyn Tregaran reared up her head, her eyes bright with intelligence.

I don't remember how I got away from the house, or

how I found my way back along the road. I don't even remember much about the bus ride back, lost in my own bewilderment. I do recall rain, lashing first in spurts against the windows of the bus, then sluicing down in cruel waves, so that the driver had to lean out and use a towel to wipe the windscreen clear. It was his chirpy goodwill that drew me out of myself, how despite the dreadful weather he remained cheerful, goodnaturedly helping passengers on board, greeting people by name, and willingly making small detours to bring them closer to their homes. I began to notice how everyone was in a good mood that night, as if the Christmas spirit was in the air. Women sat with their baskets full, their grey wartime coats smelling like sheep wool, their round faces polished pink with cold. They chatted amicably among themselves while small children squirmed upon their knees, or leaned back with their feet stuck out and sucked on sweets. Once as we passed a row of council houses, a woman darted from the door with a covered plate. When she thrust it in at the driver's side, the smell of hot gravy and meat filled the bus as he took a hearty bite, and the regulars grinned and nodded approval. 'Makes a good pasty, his missus does.' The whisper went from seat to seat. 'But he'm too mean to spare naught for us.' He pushed the plate beneath the dashboard, grinning himself, while everyone laughed. I thought, they can't be so bad after all, nor is my grandmother. She's getting old, that's all. She's inventing things. But still the marks of her venom burned. And I couldn't get the thought of George out of my mind. For the first time ever I was scared of him. Not that I felt for a moment he believed my grandmother either, but he was capable of using her. I sensed a determination, a will, that had nothing to do with drunkenness, a menace, the more frightening because it was unexpected.

In another village square a stall of fruit glistened in the rain, apples, pears, yellow and red, beside which a crate of oranges gleamed in their tinfoil wraps, like rows of Christmas lights. Suddenly the war seemed far away and unimportant. I hadn't seen fruit arranged like that for years; I didn't remember when I'd last seen oranges, and like the children I almost clapped my hands. It seemed fitting somehow to display them like that, in the rain, putting on a show. I thought, no matter what happens, let it happen right, that's what counts, so that after all if it is the end we go out bravely, without regrets. And when we reached our village (I could almost bring myself to think of it as 'ours'), I clambered out after the other women in a haze of goodwill, as if the dark hid their earlier hostility, as if in the dark we could be friends.

There were no street lights and the little shop had shut its doors. People scurried away without lingering. When I turned and began to climb the hill, tiredness came down upon me like a weight, as if all the trauma of the day was resting upon my back. I remember thinking that my feet were strangely heavy; I plodded, like one of those cart horses I used to watch as a child. When I reached our little cottage its black window panes seemed as threatening as the first night, although I had begun to feel safe inside. I didn't even stop to take off my wet clothes but began to light all the oil lamps until the house was bathed in their golden glow. I lit the fire and set the table for a meal. I wanted desperately for this to be our home, to seem like home, for its light and warmth to be seen and felt. I didn't want to think of Phil out in the storm. I wanted him to hurry back, so we could talk. But there were so many things to talk about I didn't know which to present to him first. They began to crowd upon me then, my grand-mother's revelation, George Gatering's threats, like so many tangible presences. I felt them circling just within reach, waiting to pounce. And when in a panic I brought out more candles, pushing the shadows back into their place, the sparkling cleanness of the rooms, the freshly

243

painted walls made such a contrast with their former ugliness, a fury seized me that anyone should want to destroy it. And a fear that they had found the means.

It was now that the next event in a series occurred, each one at random but inextricably entwined, so that each seemed to be an integral part of some whole. And that whole itself not yet fully grasped, only sensed, like the light at a tunnel's end before the end itself appears. There was a knock at the cottage door, a rat-tat-tat, determined and insistent. The noise of the rain was so loud it would have drowned any normal approach, but sure that it was Phil I ran to unlock the bolt. When I drew it back it was a woman who stood there, no one I knew and yet, instinctively, I knew her sort. A farmer's wife, solid as oak, sure of her worth, dressed for market day in her best, she planted her feet in their old boots across the threshold as if expecting to be invited in. And when the invitation didn't materialize, in she came anyway, setting her packages down by the door, shaking her coat like a dog, and thrusting the pins in her old felt hat as if to show she could take if off and settle down if she wanted to.

She came to the issue at once. 'Seed 'ee on the bus,' she said. 'Had heard talk, but never believed a bit of it until then. Well now, I says to myself, that's never Miss Tregaran from the Big House – Mrs Gatering, I should say. But if 'tis, I'll just step in to have a word like, on me way back.'

She never took her eyes off me as she spoke; she had round blue eyes herself, and round red cheeks, and her mouth was pursed up as if she had bitten down on a piece of fruit. 'Won't know me,' she went on, 'but before the war, I comed from down your way. My father were a fisherman, and my ma, and her ma afore her, worked for Tregaran in the old days.'

Her glance was keen. 'Bit afore my time,' she said, 'but

if things hadn't gone wrong suppose I'd 'ave worked there meself.

'The others swore 'twere 'ee,' she said. 'Well, what else could a body think, seeing as how Sir Edward's bailiff spread some tale afore 'ee ever set foot in the place. Comed into the pub 'ee did, great girt man with great girt beard, full of this and that, enough gossip to fill a tub of ale with froth. Didn't set much store by it myself, but my man did. He be farmer up the way,' she added unnecessarily. 'Leasehold, part of Gatering land, leastways it belonged once to the Carnaze estate so I s'pose Sir Edward thinks 'tis his. My husband and his dad work the same farm that've been in the family for generations. Quiet men, the pair of them, scared to death things might go wrong. And stubborn. Put their feet down, 'tis like them stuck in some bog up on the moors they sets their heart on. Didn't like the sound of what Gatering's bailiff told, no more than did the other men.'

She said, 'Always did say that Phil Tregarn would cause trouble, as soon expect a shark to blunt its teeth. Well, what he wants to come here for, thinking to set up a mine again, spoiling all the land thereabouts, buying up our grazing rights? What he wants to bring 'ee here, cause some fuss that did. "My missus'll not work for 'em," they said. Made 'em down tools on the spot. Left 'ee in a sorry mess. But that's the way it was. And now today, the same man comed back, same beard, same tale, certain sure Tregarn be angling after Greytor Mine, up yonder as 'ee knows, abutting on my husband's fields. And there today, there'ee be, bold as brass, living proof that it be 'ee. So I says to meself, I'll up and ask her meself, for old times' sake, no harm to that; and for old times' she'll tell me the truth of it. And so I does.'

Made breathless by this spate of words she leaned across the table top. 'What's Phil Tregarn up to then, setting hisself up with a mine of his own, as if he were a lord

245

hisself? Don't he know the trouble 'twill cause, Sir Edward Gatering not a man to make an enemy of? And don't he know how village folk is, ornery as mules when they'm crossed?'

It was useless to try to explain that Phil meant no harm to their land, equally useless to argue that Sir Edward wanted the mine too and since his mining practices were a disgrace, he was more likely to cause the damage. But old prejudices die hard. Like Em, she didn't think a man could rise above himself; she didn't want him to.

I didn't have the heart to say anything, but I didn't resent her speaking. Had I been in her place I might have done the same.

She suddenly sighed, the sigh of a woman who knows the world, to whom sex and love are matter-of-fact, as common as a stable yard. 'But there,' she said. 'I'm a girt great fool myself, and the past can't be forgot. I knew Phil Tregarn well once. Oh, not me myself, you understand, he be younger than me, but my sisters did. Took out both of them in turn, led them some dance, but my, 'ee were a handsome lad, 'twere worth it.'

She eyed me openly again. I thought of all those village girls that Phil had told me about. True, that was long ago, but whereas once they hadn't troubled me, now I didn't like to think of them. Yet I sensed she hadn't mentioned them to be unkind, merely to state a fact.

'So do 'ee warn 'im while there's time,' she said. 'True or not, pub be full of angry men, quiet men who don't talk much but who bain't likely to take things lying down. And to my mind, that's not fair. The Good Book says we all've got a right to defend ourselves. And old ties ain't easily forgot.'

She gave her hat one more firm shove, picked her parcels up, turned and stumped deliberately to the door without waiting for a reply, and certainly not expecting to be thanked. I thought, that's the loyalty my grandmother always was talking about, but not offered in a way she'd understand. I suddenly liked the woman very much. And if her message had been other than it was I'd have felt I'd found a friend.

As it was she had not been gone five minutes, too short a time for me to take in all she'd said, when I heard the sound of Phil's bike spluttering noisily up the hill. But when he came in dripping wet, he was not alone. Tom came with him. And that was the second event.

I've explained that Tom had been helping Phil, and in the normal way I'd have been glad to see him. Usually Phil took him back to his own home or left him within walking distance, with a paper tucked in his pocket to tell Zack when and where the next place to meet. On a night like this that was obviously impossible. Now as I hastily laid another place and put more potatoes and eggs to cook, brought blankets and rugs to make a bed, I felt constrained. I hadn't expected another visitor, one I couldn't turn out. My face must have given me away. 'What's wrong?' Phil asked, when Tom was in the scullery washing himself. I shook my head. 'Later,' I said. But whereas before I had wanted to talk, now I didn't, not with another person in the house. And yet of all the people I knew, Tom was perhaps the closest to us, and the one who might have known the truth. If only he could unlock it, from wherever his injuries had hidden it.

Truth's some slippery, he'd once said. Now it writhed and twisted in my brain, just out of grasp, like the fish he'd likened it to.

Yet the evening was not an unhappy one. For one thing Phil was in a jubilant mood, despite the wetting he'd had. 'I've something to tell you too, later,' he teased. His excitement was infectious, and just having him there soothed my mind. Then for another, Tom was more coherent than I'd ever seen him. Once he had been fed, and he had a prodigious appetite, he eased himself back in his chair and broke out into song. He had a strong melodious voice and like many Cornishmen knew music. I'd never heard him sing before although Phil had. Phil'd hum or whistle a bar to start Tom off, and then stop and let him take over. Once the tune had caught hold, the words did too, effortlessly, all those old songs Tom must have learned forty years ago, before 'his' war had destroyed his memory. I remember one of them still, about a seagull floating over the sea, free as the wind. 'I'd like that,' Tom said, with his sudden beaming smile. ''Twould be some nice, flying like that.' He scratched his head and sang the verse again. Afterwards, we were to remember that too. Then, looking at them both, watching them beating time in unison, sharing a tankard of beer, I thought, there's nothing wrong here, nothing that the outside should touch. A rush of wind and rain beat on the windows like hail. I remember how Tom wrinkled his nose. 'A good sou'wester,' he said, 'keep a body at home, that will.'

It was close to eleven o'clock before we settled for the night, turning out the lamps and leaving Tom in front of the fire, stretched out in an easy chair with a fresh pint of ale. We lit our candles, climbed the stairs, closed the door at the top, drew the curtains in our room. 'Now then,' said Phil. He was sitting on the edge of the bed unlacing his boots. 'Out with it.' And I told him first what my grandmother had said.

His reaction was immediate and furious, completely masculine. 'You don't believe that stuff,' he cried. He finished unlacing his boot and let it drop with a resounding thud. 'That's old bitch's tricks. She's up to her former games, trying to scare you back into the fold. Think girl, think. There're other ways of finding out. Isn't there a central clearing place for births, marriages and deaths? It used to be in Somerset House although God knows where it is now during the war. All we've got to do is ask. So what does she hope to hide?'

'I don't understand,' I said.

He looked at me and drew me down. 'What a worried frown,' he said. 'The end of the world. Of course 'tis lies.' He suddenly smiled at me. 'There were two Tregaran sons,' he said. 'Strange, I've got to thinking about them a lot, especially when I was in France. Perhaps being in a war myself made them seem real. One's my father, one's yours; and that old woman claims they're the same man. But I've been thinking of the one I suppose was my dad; remember, I told you he visited us once. He was too tall to see his face, well, he would be tall to a child, but I'm sure he was kind. Gentle like. I've a good feeling, remembering him. Not the sort of man, I'd say, to leave a woman and child in the lurch. Otherwise why come to see us at all? No, what she's said's not true, although she wants to make you think it is.'

'Then what?' I said.

He smiled again and smoothed my cheek. 'One thing I've learned in the army,' he said, 'people don't hide things that don't exist.' And as I stared at him, 'There isn't time. People don't cut out pages to conceal what's not there; it's what's there that's important.'

He said, 'Let's wait and see. I've a hunch, that's all. And stranger things than this have occurred, when lands and estates are involved. There was a famous court case years ago, brother claimed his mother had married an English lord, sister claimed she hadn't. Nothing to do with family honour you understand. If brother was right, he would inherit; if sister was right, then sister would, since she'd married the old lord's nearest kin.'

'But Tregaran isn't that big,' I cried. 'You used to say yourself it was falling to bits.' And stopped, biting my lip, remembering what George had said. If it was important to him, then it was important.

'Perhaps,' he said, 'but you see, brothers and sisters can fall out, and go to law, and hate each other. I don't mean to fall out with you. And I assure you the feelings I'm feeling now have nothing to do with sibling love.'

He blew out the candle, reached for me, and God help me, I couldn't stop myself from reaching back. And then the third event occurred.

There was a thud, a crack of glass, a sound like a bursting bomb that made the whole house shake, rattling the window frames and causing a great updraught of air. It was followed by a scream. I'd never heard a scream like that before, of terror, anguish, pain, like an animal's bellowing. It didn't stop, not even when the other noises died away, leaving only that great volume of human sound which deafened the ears and made the senses reel.

Phil was down the stairs in a couple of strides, cursing loudly as he fumbled for the lamps, I behind him, although he tried to push me back. There was no light except from the fire, but it was sufficient to show Tom, reared back against a wall, covered with glass that clung to his thick jersey like stardust. Behind his back, the shattered casement swung to and fro as the wind caught and pulled it.

Phil knelt on one side of Tom, I the other, holding his hands between our own, trying to bring him back from whatever hell terror had pushed him into. Above our heads the rain blew in and the window banged, slow and monotonous like the screams. 'Never seen him like this before,' Phil said, his expression grim. 'Sudden noises always set him going, but not this bad. Just have to wait and bear with it. Nothing to do until the fit wears off.'

We looked at each other across a gap, where time had reverted to another war, where a bomb had fallen and blown away all that a man was, all that he could be, all that he had cared for. I've never seen a face so contorted as Tom's was now. I don't mean the physical disfigurement; I was used to that. It was as if he were confronting what had been and reliving it. It was as if the shock of physical pain that had tempered the real event had reoccurred but left him with his mental capacity intact, so that he could feel what he felt then and understand the cause and effect. My heart bled for him. As for my lover, friend, whatever name I should put on him, kneeling beside that ruined hulk, trying to breathe courage back into him, trying to soothe him into forgetfulness, I felt a rush of sympathy, that this was another burden on him.

Gradually Tom's anguish subsided. His screams died to a moaning, to a gasping, as if he were short of air. He stretched himself, gazed round with vacant look as if to ask, 'Who made that noise?' and after drinking a great mug of tea promptly fell asleep, curled up upon the pile of rugs we'd wrapped him in, like a beached whale. I'd already warmed the bed; Phil had found a piece of wood to block the open window frame and had hammered it in place without going outside. We'd swept up the shards of glass, mopped the rain off the floor, tended the fire, picked up the huge piece of stone that we found under a chair, and without comment set it aside. There was nothing else to do except keep watch and try to figure out why someone had thrown it. But when I now told Phil what I hadn't come to yet, about my encounter with George, about the farm woman's warning, 'Makes sense,' he said, suddenly angry himself, 'all part of a piece. But I don't give in easily.'

It was nice of him I thought not to blame me for giving in to Em. I suddenly remembered him as a boy, the day of my tenth birthday, that thin love-starved boy who still had time for a small sad child. I thought, he's still like that underneath.

We didn't sleep at all that night, sitting side by side across the fire from Tom, on guard I suppose, although there was no further disturbance. It was the sort of thing a drunk villager might do as he left the pub, and having vented his righteous anger, feel justified in staggering home. I preferred to believe that anyway. The thought of someone else's keeping watch on us out there in the dark, was not a pleasant one.

We did not sleep, but we talked. I can't remember all we said, sometimes I think we just said words to help the time to pass. It was Phil's turn to explain what he had meant to tell me 'later', what he had been so jubilant about and what had brought the Gatering bailiff round again. Greytor Mine was to be sold, the auction was to be next day, and Phil had been alerted in time to be there to make a bid.

'Can't outmatch Gatering pound for pound,' he said, 'but I'll give him a good run for his money. The thing is, I know Greytor's worth; he doesn't. I've done my homework, see. Not a shaft but Tom and I've been down 'un. Not a vein but we've explored it. There's clay there alright, no end to it; it's sitting pretty. And the present owner wants to sell. Thanks to the contacts I've made, I've had time to get our cash out and waiting. If, after this, you agree I should.'

He poked at the fire with the piece of wood he had been twirling between his fingers. I thought, it shan't be spoiled for him, not now, when he's worked so hard. They shan't drive him away, I won't permit it. So when we had settled that point to our satisfaction, 'It'll make things tight for a while,' he said. 'But I know that mine inside out. I know how to make it pay, how to work the clay and where, and when to start the drilling. Gatering doesn't. And I'll bet my last penny that when it comes to nip and tuck, he'll remember that. He's too shrewd a businessman not to. And for the same reason he won't chuck his money about just to gratify Son George's ambition.'

The old nickname didn't sound funny.

'That doesn't mean,' Phil went on, 'we're home and dry. But we've got a chance. And Gatering can't shut me out indefinitely. If I don't succeed this time, there will be other ones. Although I admit I'm keen for this. This has the best possibilities. No, Sir Edward's not the one to trouble us, for all his bailiff's little games. It's Son George I'm worried about.'

He said, 'Son George has changed his mind once; he may again. No knowing what he's up to. Like you I think he's dangerous. I don't want you to see him with or without witnesses. Stay away from him. Tomorrow when I leave, be sure to keep the door locked. I'm sorry I've got to go, but thank God Tom's here. He'll make a good watch dog.'

He looked so anxious now himself I hadn't the heart to say, 'Tom couldn't stop George.' But I thought it. Suddenly George had become an unknown factor. And no matter what Phil said, what my grandmother'd told me couldn't be put out of mind; I couldn't be so certain it was an invention. But I also thought again, this is Phil's chance, I'm not going to let anything spoil it. I said, only half-joking, 'You'll be the one out there in the open; an easy target. Just don't let anyone take pot shots at you. If anyone turns up that is. This rain'll finish by drowning all of us.'

I was wrong on both counts. Phil didn't need watching over as much as I did. And when morning came the storm had blown out into the prettiest day ever.

Chapter 13

That morning revealed one of the mysteries of Cornwall, how after a night of storm the dawning could be as mild and sweet as an April day. When I unbolted the door, I could smell the earth steaming in the sun as it does in spring; the sky was blue without a cloud. Except for the pile of broken glass, the empty window frame, nothing had changed, all was tranquil, calm. Tom remained hidden beneath the rugs, only the top of his head showing, snuggled down like a child, lost in a deep and gentle sleep. 'God,' Phil said, stepping to the door, 'it makes one feel grand. Good to be alive.' He stretched himself. 'Courage, Miss Prim,' he said. 'They won't be back. Today's a new day, full of promise.'

I didn't want him to leave, although I didn't tell him so. But I knew today was special for him, a chance not to be missed. And I wanted nothing to diminish that.

He left early by himself. 'Let Tom be. When he wakes he'll be his old self. And stay close indoors until I'm back. I won't be long, I'll be as quick as I can.' Neither of us said anything more about his hopes for this mine upon which his whole future depended, but he knew I was thinking of them. I did wonder which old self Tom would be, the confused and incoherent self or the placid contented one. And I wondered too how long was long, an hour, a day, a lifetime. I didn't want to remain alone in a place where hatred had come. I was done with hating anyone.

I watched Phil leave, a jaunty wave, the motor bike gunned up the hill, towards Greytor Mine, a modern Sir

Galahad searching for his own particular Grail. I thought again, we could have been happy here. But I can't stay.

I hadn't meant to think that thought. It came into my mind unexpectedly, like an enemy creeping up. But once there, there it remained, as if God had put it in place and challenged me. Suddenly all those confused thoughts concentrated on that one main one, distilling out a draught that was biting sharp. You can't stay here, not like this, not with him. Oh you can pretend it isn't happening. Yet it has. You can try to convince yourself that it's a nightmare. You are awake. You are responsible for your father's guilt; didn't Em tell you the fathers' sins are visited upon their children? You can't remain with Phil without carnal love, but love between you and him's not possible if Grandmother Tregaran has told the truth. I thought, almost sadly, that's what I always wanted wasn't it, what I asked Tom Tregarn those years ago, what I asked Em. They all warned me I wouldn't like what I found. And yet I persisted. You want your cake and eat it too, Evelyn Tregaran said. The eating makes a bitter feast.

All those fears I'd tried to block now came pouring out, so strong they seemed to fill the little house like a tidal wave, driving me outside, gasping for air like Tom. Too restless to stay still, I took to walking down the garden, first to the gate and back, then out on the road to the hill top, each time drawn back to the house and out again, as if on a see-saw. One part of me seemed to be pulled further and further away, so that the cottage itself appeared to recede, like looking at it from the wrong end of a telescope. And each time I returned Tom still slept, like a baby without a care in the world.

I can't say now whether I meant all the time to go up to the mine, or whether I went there instinctively, driven there by this conflict within me, or whether, despite myself, I still wanted to find Phil, my refuge, my loadstone. Eventually I found that I was walking along a familiar track that paralleled the main road, as if I had a mission of my own. The turf was soggy after so much rain, a vivid green, and on every bush and shrub spider webs were etched with startling clarity, hundreds of them, each strung with a line of pearly drops.

Once started I walked quickly, not turning back, not even when I came to the wider road which had been built to serve the army camp. The camp was gone, but where the tents had been pitched you could still see the pale squares of yellowed grass and, underneath the gorse, discarded beer cans reflected the sun like bits of tarnished silver. And always on my left, like giant building blocks, the tumbled rocks of Greytor stood against the horizon.

I've said I knew of Greytor by reputation, and had never been there myself. It lay off the main road, which petered out perhaps a mile or two before its base. Several other smaller paths wound around its foot, but only one climbed to the top. I knew the entrance to the old mine lay on the further, eastern side, where the cliff ended in a giant scree, but I had never been that far. From this western approach the track slanted gently uphill, with moorland fields underneath. Flocks of sheep dotted the landscape, trotting aside as I went past. In the distance cattle wandered, black and brown shapes against the green, proof if I had needed proof how close grazing land extended towards the mine shaft. The heather was still in purple flower, and the dead bracken stalks were head high, so that I had come right to the bottom of the rocks before I realized how close they were. I began to scramble up. The air freshened as I neared the peak; the wind blew sharply with a keen smell, part plant, part animal, and far off I could see the glint of water on either side, like a glint of an eye beneath a lid, the distant sea from which no place in Cornwall is long distant. Suddenly the landscape appeared to me as from a farmer's view: that clear profile of rocks obscured by waste, those moorland fields covered with spreading sand tips, the quiet jarred apart by lorries, machinery, workmen. I was sure that Phil wouldn't let it be like that. But the image lingered.

On an impulse I went round the rocks to the other side. I hadn't expected the eastern escarpment to be so steep, as if someone had used a huge shovel to scoop it out. I knew from Phil that the mine workings were under this eastern ridge and far below, in the natural bowl or yard that lay in front of them, I could clearly see cars parked, a van or two, a big black limousine. And there, against a picket fence, was Phil's bike. Men were walking about, presumably waiting for the auction to begin; some dressed in workmen's clothes were obviously miners; others in business suits looked more like prospective bidders.

The 'gentlemen' conferred importantly, or bustled in and out of the mine buildings where I supposed the auction would take place. For some reason I was reminded of that meeting on the moors when Phil had addressed the clay-workers. I didn't suppose he would have much to say today, only come up with sufficient cash to cover his bid, but I didn't like the way those other men stood in groups, arms about one another's shoulders. I didn't like that they slapped their friends on the back and laughed, chums, part of a closed fraternity. I thought, they'll never let Phil in, no matter how much money he has, and I felt constriction catch around my heart, at the narrowness of their vision.

There was no sight of Phil, but somehow the thought that he was close made me feel better. And so I stayed for a while, back to a rock, with my eyes closed, letting the wind sweep over me. And for that moment I felt at peace with the world.

Then, I can only say that as once I had sensed his presence like a warmth, a light, so now I felt a coldness come towards me, as if a cloud had gone across the sun, as if something malevolent were watching me. Yet when I opened my eyes I was still alone, and I must have slept, for the mine grounds were deserted except for one man I took to be a chauffeur. The doors to the grey mine shed had been opened and there were signs of great activity inside. I could see people passing to and fro in front of the windows and from time to time catch the sound of applause. I shivered. Suddenly Greytor felt very isolated, and I wanted to be off it, down there on level ground. Instead then of returning the way I'd come, I started along the eastern ridge, planning to wait for Phil in what I called the 'courtyard'.

The hike down was harder than I'd expected although the bottom looked so close. For one thing parts of the eastern slope were made of sheer granite, impossible to cross. I had to climb up or down to avoid these high rocks, seeking out little patches of green hollowed out in between. Although they looked less dangerous, they were deceptively full of water, bog patches sinking deep below the surface of the land, so that I waded, rather than walked from one to the next, as if moving from oasis to oasis. Progress was slow. I knew the proceedings were scheduled to begin at noon and it must be well into afternoon. For the first time I began to worry about leaving Tom. I actually wondered if I'd arrive home before dusk; suppose the way was blocked and I had to climb up again. I started to hurry, not looking back, not looking ahead, concentrating on what was in front. When I rounded a large boulder and saw that I had come out just above the mine shaft, with the rest of the path clearly marked, running along a high drop between large blocks of stone, for a moment I shut my eyes in relief. But when I opened them relief vanished.

A man was sitting on one of the rocks, smoking. When I came in sight he turned and threw the cigarette away. 'Hullo Joycelyn,' said George. 'I thought it was you. Now who could that be, I said to myself, hanging about on a mountaintop, like a Goddamn gypsy? Only my wife, I thought, my dear, beloved, deluded wife, making her way back to me, waiting to throw herself at me.'

I tried to ignore the tone in his voice. 'And what are you doing here anyway?' I asked. 'Rather off the beaten track for you.'

'Communing with nature, enjoying the view. Waiting for daddy to buy me a mine.' His tone was sarcastic, anger just below the surface. 'Watching him spend his money which he'd be better off spending on me. Watching him fence with Phil Tregarn for a bloody handful of rocks that're no good to anyone.'

I didn't know what to say. In that mood everything would offend him. I tried to edge my way past but he held out his hand to hinder me. 'Daddy's tired of ideas that don't pay off,' he said. 'Daddy likes instant success. Won't put money into a hotel that doesn't belong to me, will put money underground. But damn it, if you'll stay, between us we could talk him round.'

I thought, inconsequently, the open air doesn't agree with George. The wind had made his eyes water and he kept rubbing them, and his lips were chapped. He held some car keys in his hand and kept playing with them, and when he lit another cigarette I saw how his fingers were trembling. He must have been the man I'd mistaken for a chauffeur. But none of these things mattered. It had been what he'd said last, that last thing, that was important.

I said carefully, 'What do you mean, doesn't belong to you. I thought grandma had written a will.'

'Think what you like,' he broke in savagely, 'but wills can be contested, right. Hers is full of holes. First, I learn you're not legitimate, so where's your claim that'll stand up better in the courts than Tregarn's? Of course he'll challenge any will your grandma makes. He'd be a fool not to. His claim's as good as yours, better, because he's older and a man. And second, if you're not married to me, what's my stake worth? I ask you that, not the bloody paper it's written on. So you see, my darling, I can't let you go, not even if I wanted to.'

I didn't know if he were joking or not, these were legal matters beyond my scope, but that wasn't the point. He thought he was right. And that explained his change of heart, that explained why he was dangerous.

'Come on, George,' was all I said, 'let me pass. It's getting cold. Phil's waiting for me.'

'No he isn't.' The denial was terse. 'He's inside, bidding his life-savings away on a piece of granite. Of course he's thinking how to make a lien on his grandmother; he'll need to. Thinks he's won a victory either way. He hasn't tangled with me yet.

'That leaves you and me alone,' he went on. 'On a mountainside. How romantic, how divine, how fitting, isn't this how we met?'

Once again I tried to get round him. He stood up now, threw his second cigarette away and began to limp up the path, not exactly hurrying, with a deliberate sort of stride. It was his walk that made me uneasy. I was used to George's way of speaking, but I didn't like the way he stalked perhaps was the best description, as if he were some jungle cat after its prey. 'I don't find it cold,' he said. 'Perhaps the cold's in you. In fact I think the air's distinctly warm. If Tregarn gets his mine,' he added, 'surely that should keep him preoccupied. Doesn't seem fair he should get everything. And if he's no time for you, I do.'

He burst out, 'Nothing works with you gone. I could try to act as squire a hundred years, you bloody Cornish'll never let me belong. Unless my name begins with Tre or Pol or Pen, I might as well not exist. My bloody father's given up on me, like one of his factories that hasn't made a profit. So you're all I've got left, my last card.'

I was weary of his whining. 'Listen George,' I said. 'Do you know what your trouble is? You had everything your heart could desire: family, schooling, money, fast cars, women, all handed to you on a plate, without your lifting a little finger. You had everything you wanted, too much, too soon. You don't even know how to work for things. You don't know what work is.'

I suppose I let my contempt show. His expression changed, grew dark. 'Into Socialism now, are we?' he said. 'My, aren't we the one to preach. Kettle calling the pot black. Adulteress, bitch, pervert.'

With each insult he took another step until I was backed around the corner, out of sight of the mine, trapped in one of those little muddy patches of grass, an outcrop of cliff behind my back, an open drop in front of me. 'I saw you coming down,' he was hissing at me, 'so up I came. Thought you could do with a welcome. Thought it would be friendly to make you feel at home. Always did fancy a piece out in the open.'

'Don't touch me.' The thought that he might was sickening. I tried to keep calm, tried to think of things to say. He continued to smile, advancing upon me, savouring every moment's fear, anticipating every movement, until he was standing right in front of me, so close I could see the veins in his eyes and along his nose, drinker's veins they call them. I thought, if he puts his hands on me, I shall scream. But when he leapt at me, his leg must have crumbled under him, and we rolled together in the mud, until the cliff edge stopped us. I was on the outside, looking down the scree at a hundred feet or more of void. And there was nothing between me and it except the tufts of bog grass along the lip.

I clawed at him, trying to break his hold, trying to force him off. 'Nice,' he said, holding both my hands easily, 'nice, you've livened up. Better than that lump of dead meat I remember. Come on now, fight a bit, let's see you express yourself. I like my women active.'

He had me pinned beneath his weight, his heavy body

261

spread on mine, his heavy head leaning on my shoulders. I could smell his sweat. The more I struggled the more he grinned, seeming to enjoy showing off, until in desperation I tried to bite. Then he scowled, took a handkerchief and thrust it in my mouth. 'There,' he said. 'Let's see how you talk through that. And now we'll get down to our unfinished business.'

I could feel him fumbling with his clothes, fumbling with mine, trying to strip my jacket off. I tried to heave him away, but however hard I tried I was unable to shift that weight. It stifled me. I felt I couldn't breathe; the gag choked me until everything began to blur, turn grey, as if the colours had been drained out. And then just as the pressure became intolerable, I suddenly felt it lifted off, as if a hand had come down from the sky and prised me free.

Perhaps I did lose consciousness at this point. Then gradually breath came back. Light returned, colours snapped back, the sky overhead still pale blue, the grass still its vivid green. I was propped up against the cliff; George was lying full length along the edge. And Tom was standing between us, his foot planted on George's chest.

My first thought was a stupid one, how had Tom got there. Then I realized he must have been following me. One look at the old fisherman's jersey he always wore showed how ripped it was as if he had come sliding down the rocks, and his trousers were grass stained, wet to the knees from floundering through the bogs. But it wasn't these things I noticed first. It was the piece of stone he held in his good hand, a stone large enough to brain a man. That, and what he said.

'I told 'ee to leave Alice be,' his voice low, his mouth tight. 'Told 'ee she weren't for 'ee. Don't 'ee come round no more, sneaking up to her like some randy dog. Or 'twill be my teeth you'll find instead.'

'Call the old idiot off.' George's face had gone red, his fair hair was plastered to his head as he attempted to pry

Tom's foot away. 'By God, I'll have him shut up so fast he won't know what hit him.'

I tore the cloth out of my mouth, with hands that seemed too large for me. I whispered through parched lips, 'Tom, what "he"? Who was the "he" that came after Alice?'

'Why, Nigel Tregaran, of course,' he said, not looking at me, not turning round, standing there with that raised rock as if made of rock himself. 'Always wanted what John had as if 'e hadn't enough himself. Always wanted to spoil things for us. We was happy once, wasn't us, me, Alice, John. Didn't John love Alice like 'e ought; didn't she love 'im, the two of them together until the older brother came along and stirred things up.'

Tears fell from his good eye in slow sad drops, glistening on his grizzled cheeks. He gripped the stone more fiercely. 'And didn't I catch Nigel out; didn't I make him swear to do right by her even tho' it broke my heart; even tho' it destroyed John? Even tho' it killed her, poor soul, like a butterfly caught in a trap.'

He wept unashamedly, not paying the slightest attention to George who writhed and twisted under him, like an insect on a pin. 'What else could I do?' he said simply. 'What should I have done, unless what I do now, too late, too soon?'

Those were the last words I heard him speak. What happened next passed in slow motion like a film that unwinds itself; each frame so distinct that even now when I think of it I feel surprised that I didn't stretch my hand out and stop the reel. George gathered himself for one great effort, lunged upwards, gripping Tom's legs about the knees, trying to unbalance him. Tom, his face distorted with strain, tried in turn to rear back, flailing with his outspread hands as he used to do. As he wavered, the stone dropped from his grasp. It fell full force on George's head, sent George sprawling backwards over the lip, sent

Tom stumbling on the rebound after him. A thousand times in dreams I see them go, first George, a limp rag doll, his head a red mass, his blue eyes glazed; then Tom, spread-eagled, face first, as if he were flying. I shall never forget the look he had, eyes closed, mouth closed but smiling, a calm face at last, at rest. Then both had disappeared, bouncing down the open scree, out of sight, lost into space, nothing left but the wind and the bog grass, and a high-pitched screaming. And it was not for a long time, not until others had come to find me, that I realized neither would come back and that the screams were of my making.

I shall have to move forward quickly over the next part, I remember so little of it. An inquest, I know there was an inquest, with myself as only witness. I know there was a funeral for Tom, a Tregarn wake as he would have enjoyed; a Tregarn funeral in the village church close to the sea. I know there was a quieter one for George, the details hushed up, his father stern-eyed, his family dressed in black, the women veiled and silent. We never went back to the cottage after all; we left it and the village, and went away, I don't remember where or for how long. Funny, time that had once haunted me now had no meaning. Phil gave up the mine he had bought; at least he held it in abeyance. There is only one last thing to record here before we took up life somewhere else, my final meeting with Em just after my grandmother's death.

Phil brought her into the room where I was sitting. 'Oh Miss Joycelyn,' she said. 'Oh Miss Joycelyn, 'ee look some peaked, 'ee do look proper washed out, no mistake,' as if all the effects of that day were in my face.

'I've comed to see 'ee on me own account,' she said, her voice cracked, her cheeks reddened with crying. 'Nay don't 'ee budge,' as Phil made to move, ''ee owes it to yourself to listen.'

She wouldn't sit down, stood in her mourning dress, the

only time I saw her hair unplaited. 'I never meant to do 'ee harm,' she said. Once begun she spoke in a sing-song, as if she were keening. 'Some of it were done without my knowing. I brought the book out from the church when she asked me to; but she did the ripping. That were afore Vicar Towshed's time, but he noticed it. Don't know what he said to she, but afterwards the church got a new belfry tower to pay for his silence. At the time I thought 'twere for the best, to hide a thing so unbecoming.'

''Twas always so from the start,' she said, 'Nigel and John, Nigel and John, one against the other. She pitted them like two fighting bulls, tho' neither had it in them. Never a moment's peace with 'em, a thorn in her side, she'd not even have them christened. "Neither be God's children," she used to say, "I bore Nigel for the love that should have been; John was ripped out of me."'

She sighed, wiping her eyes with a small lace handkerchief. 'No matter what the world says, Nigel had no real malice. Free and easy with everyone, charm enough to talk you out of living. 'Twere no more his fault than John's. And John so quiet, he'd hide hisself from his own feelings.'

She sighed again, in her black dress and long grey hair like a Celtic witch who foresees the future. 'And no more Alice's fault, blithe as a bird, floating without a care in her head, a child in woman's body. When Nigel came home from abroad he took one look, couldn't leave well alone, dazzled her, poor little thing, until she were blinded. And then, when 'twas too late, what to do, three lives blighted.

'Tom it was who forced the wedding. Frightened Nigel to agree, frightened Alice into accepting. Kept it secret like, just the three of 'em to name the child and give its mother blessing. Zack never knew, of course. He'd 'ave shot the pair of 'em, mad with grief as it were at his sister's shaming. Bad enough that there was a child, but better an illegitimate child than have his sister married to a Tregaran.

'As for my mistress, it killed her, to have her son betray her. She tore the pages out, no way the old vicar could stop her; threatened him with disgrace if he breathed a word. How she worked to annul the match, beggared herself with the effort, ready to force her son to renounce his word, and make his son a bastard. Nobody knowed, that I swear, all done in secret. 'Twas during the war, and weren't that a help. Drove both sons off to the front, glad to be rid of 'em. Once they'd gone from home, Alice were an easier target. Alice already had gone away to have the baby in private; simple to tell her the marriage was false, and that her baby was fatherless. Oh, 'twas cruel to that poor creature. "I gave her money, what more could she want." That's what my mistress harped on. Alice took the money to live on, but that couldn't pay for the damage.'

She sighed a third time. 'My mistress were punished. When the war ended, she were the loser. In a panic then, she looked round to salvage what were the end of the matter. I found 'ee Miss in the home where your mother dropped 'ee. So 'twas true you comed out of the gutter. But your father would never have done what 'e did, had not his brother taken Alice.'

She put her handkerchief away, her part of the story ended. 'I did 'ee both wrong,' she said simply. 'Tho' the sum of it never were clear afore. I did 'ee wrong to hide what 'ee were, and wrong to hide the past. And now, like all God's works, 'tis come home to roost. I'll never be free of it no more, just as she was.'

'Wait.' Phil and I spoke together. He looked at me, and I at him, an unspoken question between us suddenly answered. He said, 'Now if I understand you right, Miss Em, and if it's true what the lawyers have just finished explaining, since our grandmother died intestate, Tregaran House belongs to me. I find that amazing. Of all the things I could have dreamed of when a child, this would have been the least expected.'

He reached over and took my hand. 'But since my wife and I have decided to go abroad, at her request I ask you to stay on as long as you care to.'

At her first shake of denial – "Tis all right, Em,' I told her, speaking for the first time. 'Grandmother's will wasn't valid. Phil inherits everything. I didn't want it anyhow, and George is dead.'

Speaking his name like that made him seem so. I hadn't been able to talk of him or Tom before. I held out my arms to her. 'Tregaran needs you, Em,' I said, 'you always were its best keeper.'

In the end, she agreed, of course. We shut up most of the house, left her where she had lived so long, in that old kitchen full of the past. Zack stayed on also. He wouldn't come with us although we invited him. 'Better off where I belong,' he told us. 'Besides, don't fancy leaving Tom. You two go your ways, find your own place of happiness.'

We looked at each other, looked away. No need to say what we both thought, where each is the other is content. But Cornwall wasn't that place yet for us, too many memories to hinder us. So we did go abroad, part of the postwar exodus, lived in mining towns all over the world, found new fulfilment in new lands. But if sometimes in my dreams I am a child again and wake with a start, if I hear above the screams of tropical birds the cooing of the wood pigeons, a longing takes hold of me to feel the wind and rain, to run along the beach and taste the cold salt spray, to watch the waves come creaming in across the sand. 'Homesick love?' Phil asks me then. I only smile at him, and say, 'Where you are is home.'

Conclusion

So that is why Tregaran House remains empty since Em's death, and why its lands are fenced about, and why the trees are beginning to overshadow its parklands so that the sea is almost hidden from the terrace. I myself have never been back again, although Phil goes sometimes when he is on business trips, and our sons both speak of returning there to live as Cornish farmers. Tregarn is empty too, Zack dying soon after Evelyn. Divided all their lives, in love and hate, they could not exist long without the other. And if Em had left unanswered some of the questions about Phil's birth and mine, perhaps for us that was best. There are some mysteries in life that should remain unresolved, at least for us. Let others solve them.

Both houses are empty now, yet both are so strongly built only fire or earthquake could level them. And even then, the foundations would stand, those Celtic stones laid down before Domesday. Our past is buried in those stones; we shall never be free of them.

Sometimes they say strangers from the holiday camp down the road go to Tregarn, picking their way among the bleached boat ribs, pointing at the bullet holes. Or casual passers-by, driving along in the white clay dust, turn in at Tregaran to explore its empty grounds. Curiously they come up to the blank windows and peer in. They stare at the wooden floorboards, the peeling wallpaper, the shrouded furniture, and wonder who its owners are, and why they abandoned it. 'Where have they gone?' they ask.

In the village they tell another story. They say on summer nights when the stars are out, or at dusk, between the turning of the tides, three figures pass among the trees. They are always inseparable, arm in arm, laughing, singing together. One is older, stolid, dependable, the one that binds them; the second is young, with thin long face and thick black hair and sad eager eyes; the third is a girl, light as a feather, dancing on her toes, swirling her skirts like moonbeams.

Hearing of them, whose happiness still runs free, I am strangely comforted. They soothe my longings. And it seems to me that in those dreams I have, when my tenth birthday has not yet come, and Tregaran House lies waiting, I put my touch upon a future time when those three will be joined by others.

I see a boy in too big a suit and a girl in a dirty party dress. 'What are you doing, boy, on my land?' she'll ask. And he, laughing down at her from a tree branch, will reply, ''Tain't your land, any more than mine. We belongs to it. And when it wants us back, it'll come looking for us.'